THE WO...

# THE LOST...

JOHN MEADE FALKNE... ...shire, the son of an Anglic... moved to Dorset, he attended local schools ... and Weymouth, but in 1873 entered Marlborough College. He went up to Oxford in 1878, graduating in History in 1882. After a period of tutoring the children of Andrew Noble, of the engineering, armaments, and shipbuilding firm of Armstrong Mitchell (later Armstrong Whitworth), he became Noble's private secretary, and then entered the firm, rising from Secretary to, in 1915, Chairman. Though he travelled widely abroad in the service of the Company, he lived in Durham from the 1890s until his death.

He is best known as the author of three novels: *The Lost Stradivarius* (1895), *Moonfleet* (1898), now regarded as a children's classic, and *The Nebuly Coat* (1903). A collection of his poems was privately published shortly before his death (and reprinted shortly after it). He also wrote guides to Oxfordshire, Berkshire, and Bath.

Sir Henry Newbolt wrote of him in his Memoirs: 'On many things of art he was a learned though unrecognised authority—on old violins, old forms of spiritual wickedness, old dances and old wines' (*The Lost Stradivarius* displays all but the last). But the novels also reveal an interest in unusual states of mind, including in *The Lost Stradivarius* the psychic and the occult; in all his fiction there is the inevitability of a final reckoning that will atone for all wrongs.

EDWARD WILSON is Fellow in Medieval English Language and Literature at Worcester College, Oxford. He is the author of books and articles on medieval English literature and medieval manuscripts, as well as articles on Wordsworth, John Meade Falkner, and John Betjeman.

THE WORLD'S CLASSICS

JOHN MEADE FALKNER

# *The Lost Stradivarius*

*Edited with an Introduction by*
EDWARD WILSON

Oxford   New York
OXFORD UNIVERSITY PRESS
1991

Oxford University Press, Walton Street, Oxford OX2 6DP

Oxford New York Toronto
Delhi Bombay Calcutta Madras Karachi
Petaling Jaya Singapore Hong Kong Tokyo
Nairobi Dar es Salaam Cape Town
Melbourne Auckland

and associated companies in
Berlin Ibadan

Oxford is a trade mark of Oxford University Press

Introduction, Note on the Text, Select Bibliography, Chronology, and
Explanatory Notes © Edward Wilson 1991

First published 1895
First published by Oxford University Press 1954
First issued as a World's Classics paperback 1991

British Library Cataloguing in Publication Data
Data available

Library of Congress Cataloging in Publication Data
Falkner, John Meade, 1858–1932.
The lost stradivarius/John Meade Falkner; edited with an
introduction by Edward Wilson.
p.   cm.—(The World's classics)
Includes bibliographical references.
I. Wilson, Edward, 1940–   .   II. Title.   III. Series.
PR4699.F147L6  1991    813'.4—dc20      90-29068
ISBN 0–19–282848–7

Printed in Great Britain by
BPCC Hazell Books, Aylesbury, Bucks.

# ACKNOWLEDGEMENTS

EVERY editor should always hear at his back the ironic lines from James Bramston's *The Man of Taste* (1733):

> Huge commentators grace my learned shelves,
> Notes upon books out-do the books themselves.
> Criticks indeed are valuable men,
> But hyper-criticks are as good agen.

The detailed apparatus to this edition has been demanded not only by Time, which has altered not just the senses of words but a whole cultural hinterland beyond a modern reader's recognition, but by Falkner himself, who delighted in sowing his novel with literary and antiquarian allusions. Indeed, a character, Mr Gaskell, in *The Lost Stradivarius* itself, when reading an eighteenth-century diary in pursuit of highly sensational matter cannot resist telling us that 'the minute details given were often of high antiquarian interest'.

It should be remembered, however, that the antiquarian for Falkner was accomplished, in Johnson's phrase, 'without anxious exactness'. Though he undoubtedly altered some facts deliberately for the purposes of his fiction, other 'errors' are the result of an indifference to accuracy; likewise, he evidently quoted poetry, unchecked, from memory, often inaccurately but, which is impressive, never unmetrically. More importantly, the antiquarian for Falkner had the force of poetry. Just as his antiquarian works on Oxfordshire, Berkshire, and Bath gleam with poetic quotation from Anglo-Saxon to Tennyson, so his fiction, and his poetry, have an antiqueness which in itself the romantic sensibility finds enchanted ground.

In the Explanatory Notes I have tried to identify all overt quotations and allusions, as well as the unacknowledged

## ACKNOWLEDGEMENTS

sources and springs of his imagination; to explain words (and senses of words) no longer current; and to place the novel in the cultural context of its time.

The help which I have received on particular points is acknowledged in the Notes. However, it is also a pleasure to thank the Dean and Chapter of Durham Cathedral for permission to quote from Hensley Henson's unpublished Diary (their Librarian, Mr Roger C. Norris, gave much valuable help); the Yale Center for British Art, New Haven (Paul Mellon Collection) for permission to reproduce the Batoni portrait on the cover of this edition; Mr Gareth Fitzpatrick for great assistance on my visit to Boughton House, Northamptonshire; Mr D. R. C. West, the Honorary Archivist of Marlborough College, for his offices over an article in *The Marlburian*; Dr David Bradshaw, Fellow of Worcester College, Oxford, for his readiness to answer a variety of questions; and Dr Andrew Lintott, Fellow of Worcester College, Oxford, without whose historical and literary references I could not have properly annotated Falkner's allusions to the ancient history of the Naples region. Mrs Judith Luna, of Oxford University Press, lent strength by her interest and enthusiasm. Finally, I am indeed deeply indebted to Dr Kenneth Warren, Fellow of Jesus College, Oxford, for the generosity with which he has placed his great knowledge of things Falknerian at my disposal and for discussing them with me.

*Worcester College, Oxford*                    E. W.
*23 October 1990*

# CONTENTS

# INTRODUCTION

*As the following pages contain information which is
withheld for much of the novel, readers may prefer to read
the story first and to treat the Introduction as a Postscript.*

*The Lost Stradivarius*, first published in 1895, was
Falkner's first novel. Set in Oxford and Naples in the
1840s it is a story of visitation from the dead and of occult
possession by a violin and by a piece of seventeenth-
century music, a *Gagliarda*. True to its genre, the ghost
story, it first and foremost arouses a pleasurable terror. It
is, however, constructed within a neo-Platonic metaphysical framework by which is examined on the one hand
the nature and significance of psychical and occult
experience, and on the other the relationship between
beauty and morality—all preoccupations of the decade of
its publication. The narration is divided between the story
as told by Sophia Maltravers, sister of the 'hero', John
Maltravers, and an appended 'Note' contributed by John's
friend from Oxford days, Mr Gaskell. This division
permits a dual perspective: a more straightforward narrative by Sophia in which sound sense and evangelical piety
govern her (and thus our) responses, and a more learned
and intellectual account from Mr Gaskell.

In the remarks which follow, the novel is first placed in
the context of the ghost story of its time. *The Lost
Stradivarius*'s concern with the psychical, the occult, and
the aesthetic is then seen to have its origins in the cultural
situation of the Oxford of Falkner's own undergraduate
days. Through the dual structure of the narrative, the
accounts of Sophia and Mr Gaskell, Falkner is able to
leave unresolved the novel's tensions and conflicts.

Falkner's contemporary, Vernon Lee (whose real name
was Violet Paget), in the preface to her collection of tales

entitled *Hauntings. Fantastic Stories* (1890), put the view that the past and its ghosts are suggestive, poetic, and mysterious:

That is the thing—the Past, the more or less remote Past, of which the prose is clean obliterated by distance—that is the place to get our ghosts from. Indeed we live ourselves, we educated folk of modern times, on the borderland of the Past, in houses looking down on its troubadours' orchards and Greek folks' pillared courtyards; and a legion of ghosts, very vague and changeful, are perpetually to and fro, fetching and carrying for us between it and the Present.

This understanding led Vernon Lee in a direction quite other than the scientific investigations of the Society for Psychical Research which had been founded in 1882:

Hence, my four little tales are of no genuine ghosts in the scientific sense; they tell of no hauntings such as could be contributed by the Society for Psychical Research, of no spectres that can be caught in definite places and made to dictate judicial evidence.

So, too, had Henry James in his prefatory discussion of *The Turn of the Screw* (1898) dismissed the 'new type' of ghost story:

. . . the mere modern 'psychical' case, washed clean of all queerness as by exposure to a flowing laboratory tap, and equipped with credentials vouching for this—the new type clearly promised little, for the more it was respectably certified the less it seemed of a nature to rouse the dear old sacred terror.

Yet an interest in the investigation of supernatural phenomena was active in the Oxford of Falkner's undergraduate days (1878–82). In 1880 the Phasmatological Society had been founded, and a list of members of March 1880 (Bodleian Library, GA Oxon. b. 147 (81) ) defined its aims:

The Objects of the Society are the investigation, and, where possible, the explanation of authenticated instances of so-called Supernatural Occurrences.

The membership list of June 1881 added further guidance:

Members and Corresponding Members are reminded that stories communicated to the Society would gain in value in so far as they comply with the following suggestions:—

I. That it should be stated whether the occurrence came under the notice of more than one person: if so, as many independent accounts as possible should be given.

II. That the place, time, and duration of the phenomenon should be accurately recorded.

III. That information should be given of legends, tales or rumours which existed prior to the occurrence.

As one of its members, Sir (as he became) Charles Oman, recalled:

The Phas was narrower in its aims than the Society for Psychical Research, as it did not meddle with telepathy, 'veridical hallucinations', thought-reading, the averages of coincidence, and such-like topics, but (as its name showed) specialized on ghosts and apparitions.[1]

None of the surviving membership lists (March 1880, June 1881, and March 1882) gives Falkner as a member, and the only one from his college, Hertford, was T. S. Lea (March 1880), who was one of six Fellows of the Society (of 26 members and 18 corresponding members) at that time. Like Falkner, the son of a clergyman and a Scholar of Hertford, he took a Second in Greats in Trinity Term 1880. Though he was reading a different subject, History, Falkner could have come into contact with the interests and methods of the Society during the two years that he and Lea were both at Hertford.

Whether or not Falkner came into contact with 'the Phas', its suggestions for the communication of stories do indicate the criteria, commonsensical enough, by which Sophia Maltravers and Mr Gaskell attempt to determine if

---

[1] Sir Charles Oman, *Memories of Victorian Oxford* (London, 1941), p. 81; see also pp. 220–31. I owe this reference to Mr Alan Bell, Librarian of Rhodes House Library, Oxford.

the phenomena observed by John Maltravers are psycho-logical in origin, in some way interior to the perceiver, or if they are indeed objective spiritual realities. These alternatives exist in tension both within Sophia and more particularly within Mr Gaskell, and also between them. They also correspond in literary terms to two kinds of ghost story: the psychological and the occult.[2]

At first, Sophia struggles to be sceptical: 'Whether the image which he saw was subjective or objective, I cannot pretend to say.' She acknowledges that 'our limited experience would lead us to believe that it was a phantom conjured up by some unusual condition of his own brain', but also admits that there are phenomena which 'baffle human reason', and that in this case the likeliest explana-tion is that her brother saw 'the actual bodily form of one long deceased'. Though later she is able to provide a non-supernatural explanation for the coat of arms in the 'phantasmal dancing-room' of Mr Gaskell's imagination, she affirms to her brother her belief in the spirit world: 'If there be evil spirits, as we are taught there are . . .'.

Mr Gaskell's response is, as might be expected from his superior education (he gained First Class Honours at Oxford), more carefully argued and intellectual than Sophia's, but, unlike her, with the passage of time he becomes dismissive of a supernatural explanation. In Sophia's narrative of the time when he was an under-graduate he quickly rejects the explanation that what John has seen 'is merely the phantasm of an excited imagination', not least because he himself has sensed the presence of a supernatural visitant. From the first he was 'convinced that causes other than those which we usually call natural were at work'; he believed that John's romantic feelings for Constance Temple, combined with the music of the *Gagliarda*, had endowed him with a 'sixth sense' which

[2] See J. Briggs, *Night Visitors: The Rise and Fall of the English Ghost Story* (London, 1977), pp. 76–97, 111–64.

permitted him to see what is normally invisible. He speaks, anachronistically of course, with the optimism which was felt by many in the last decade of the nineteenth century, that the existence of psychic and spiritual phenomena was a provable way-out of the materialistic and mechanistic world-view which many thought was the legacy of Darwinism:[3]

We are at present only on the threshold of such a knowledge of that art [music] as will enable us to use it eventually as the greatest of all humanising and educational agents. Music will prove a ladder to the loftier regions of thought. (pp. 25–6)

In the past Mr Gaskell had 'often' come close to full psychic experiences, but 'though a hand has been stretched forward as it were to rend the veil, yet it has never been vouchsafed me to see behind it'. In fact, it emerges later that the eighteenth-century scene which he had pictured to himself was just such a vision of what was beyond the veil, and for which, as we have seen, only the detail of the coat of arms can be explained by conventional criteria. For such an experience as John's he has a real awe: 'It is not for us to attempt to pierce the mystery which veils from our eyes the secrets of an after-death existence' (p. 28).

Mr Gaskell's talk of 'causes other than those which we usually call natural', a 'sixth sense', communication with what is 'behind the veil', is the language used by those of Falkner's contemporaries who either believed in, or at least investigated, supernatural phenomena. Possible contact with 'the Phas' at Oxford was not the only available source for such a vocabulary. In 1883 Falkner had become a tutor to the children of Andrew Noble, of the firm of Armstrong Mitchell & Co.; he later entered the firm itself,

[3] See S. Hynes, *The Edwardian Turn of Mind* (Princeton, NJ, and London, 1968), pp. 132–47. There was then nothing crankish about membership of the Society for Psychical Research: it included eminent politicians, bishops, writers, and scientists, as well as members of high society.

and for the rest of his life remained an intimate of the Noble family, and of his former pupil, John, in particular. Though Falkner was not himself a member of the Society for Psychical Research, Mrs Saxton Noble, who had married Andrew Noble's second son, Saxton, in 1891, appears in its *Proceedings* in listings of its Members from March 1907 until November 1910. Falkner was certainly on friendly terms with Saxton, not only because both worked for the same firm, but also socially. He dedicated a poem, 'The New House', to him when Saxton bought his London home, and after the First World War Saxton's wife purchased the manor of Fleet, the village of Falkner's novel *Moonfleet* (1898), possibly having been introduced to it by Falkner.[4] Through Mrs Saxton Noble a serious interest in what lies 'behind the veil' may have existed in the Noble circle by the time *The Lost Stradivarius* was written.

It is remarkable, therefore, that after the clear acceptance of the supernatural by Mr Gaskell as reported in Sophia's narrative, in his own Note which is appended to it, and presented as written a quarter of a century after his undergraduate days, there is a clear disbelief in the objective existence of evil spirits. Though he rules out insanity on John's part, he speaks now not of John's being 'allowed in a measure' to see behind the veil but doubtingly of the 'vision which he [John] thought he saw'; for the 'singular phenomena' he has 'no explanation'. Now the talk is of 'hallucination', and though he himself again has 'fantastic visions' they involve no inexplicable knowledge. The move is away from the supernatural: 'if I were superstitious I should say that some evil spirit . . .'. He imagines that 'the mind may in a state of extreme tension conjure up to itself some forms of moral evil', and

---

[4] B. Cooley, 'John Meade Falkner: A Critical Study of his Life and Writings', unpublished Liverpool University MA thesis (1962), pp. 129–30.

'possible appearances of the supernatural' are the mere result of 'fancy and legend'; only a mind weakened by terror believes in apparitions. Though only 'fools or braggarts' wish to sleep in haunted houses, 'no sane mind believes in foolish apparitions'.

Where Sophia retains her belief in occult spirits, Mr Gaskell, though still 'a sincere Christian', does not. This may simply be an inconsistency of which Falkner was unaware (as Sophia says that she knew no Latin and Mr Gaskell presents her as able to translate it). However, there are more generous and interesting explanations which may be truer. First, Mr Gaskell's Note is psychologically more protective to himself, to his friend John, and to John's son, Edward (to whom both Sophia's narrative and the Note are addressed): to assert that John was in an unusual mental state is less horrifying than to believe that he trafficked with evil spirits; moral degradation was bad enough without adding the possibility of real diabolic possession to his errors. Secondly, in Sophia's narrative we have in her response the 'old sacred terror', as James put it, and in Mr Gaskell's more intellectually structured reaction an analysis which is closer to the 'flowing laboratory tap', though still giving credence and respect to the spirit world. Yet when Mr Gaskell in his Note adopts a dismissive scepticism the effect is to enhance the terror. For the tap does not wash all clean: the verification in Naples of the eighteenth-century scene which he imagined at Oxford, and the exact correspondence between John's Oxford 'vision' and the Royston portrait, remain un-explained by natural causes. When doubt and dismissal have had their say, the mysterious remains thereby the more suggestive, poetic, and powerful.

In terms of literary genre Falkner can create a fruitful and enhancing relation between the occult and the psychological ghost story, as Henry James was to do in *The Turn of the Screw*. Tales of the occult, magic, and diabolism are, as Julia Briggs observed, part of 'the mood of the Nineties', and an association between music and the Devil was traditional.[5] The story of the violinist Tartini's dream in 1713 in which he 'made a Compact with his Satanic Majesty' where the Devil played him a violin sonata of which his own in G Minor was a poor reflection was well known—it was told in George Hart's *The Violin* (1875), a work used by Falkner in the novel (see pp. 41, 66 nn.), and alluded to in Vernon Lee's 'A Wicked Voice' (*Hauntings*), a story in which a ghostly voice is called a 'violin of flesh and blood made by the Evil One's hand'. To counterpoise these traditional elements with the more modern psychological 'case' was a felicitous stroke, and one which does indeed give the Devil his due.

Not only does *The Lost Stradivarius* have a carefully presented psychical concern, but it has, too, a serious metaphysical one. It was based on Falkner's firsthand acquaintance with the classical sources of neo-Platonism and Alexandrine philosophy (see pp. 6, 51, 143, 146–7 nn). Neo-Platonism was one of the tributaries which in the 1880s and 1890s fed the widespread interest in the occult, magic, and secret wisdom, and which permeated the arcana of Rosicrucianism, Theosophy, and the Order of the Golden Dawn.[6] The most distinguished follower of these movements was Yeats, but Falkner was drawn to Rosicrucianism.[7] The poet Sir Henry Newbolt, who met Falkner at the Nobles' residence at Chillingham between 1901 and 1906, relates that 'he loved the Rosicrucians, and would flatter his friends by including them with himself as "We of the *Illuminati*" '.[8] Something of the

---

[5] Briggs, *Night Visitors*, pp. 76 ff., 120.

[6] See most recently F. Kinahan, *Yeats, Folklore, and Occultism* (Boston and London, 1988).

[7] For a contemporary account of the Rosicrucians see A. E. Waite, *The Real History of the Rosicrucians* (London, 1887); Kinahan, p. 32 n. 25, represents Waite as more credulous and less dispassionate than is actually the case.

[8] *My World as in my Time* (London, 1932), p. 265.

appeal the movement would have for Falkner can be seen in Edward Bulwer Lytton's Rosicrucian novel *Zanoni* (1842, and regularly reprinted throughout the nineteenth century): set in the late eighteenth century and for its first two-thirds in the Bay of Naples area (cf. *The Lost Stradivarius*) it is a distinctive blend of mystery, literary learning, and romance. There may well be an autobiographical note in Mr Gaskell's observation that the study of neo-Platonism 'if carried to any extent, is probably dangerous to the English character, and certainly was to a man of Maltravers's romantic sympathies'. The understanding of its attractions seems to come from the inside:

Its passionate longing for the vague and undefined good, its tolerance of aesthetic impressions, the pleasant superstitions of its dynamic pantheism, all touched responsive chords in his nature. (p. 147)

Rigid orthodoxy and 'romantic sympathies' seem to have co-existed in Falkner, and it may be this which accounts for the elusive quality which Hensley Henson, who first as Dean of Durham Cathedral (1912–18) and then as Bishop (1920–39) had got to know Falkner (who lived in Durham from the 1890s to his death), several times observed in his diary:[9]

He is a very strange man, and makes his conversation a shrouding veil for his thoughts more successfully than most men whom I know [19 October 1915] . . . He is a curiously evasive creature. What his real convictions, if there be any, actually are not his most intimate friends can discover [10 July 1926] . . . He was one of the most elusive, versatile, and 'intriguing' persons of my acquaintance [23 July 1932].

On the one hand, Henson noted, Falkner 'takes up a purely medieval attitude. What the Church orders or does must not be criticized or resented!' (19 October 1915).

---

[9] The unpublished diaries are in the Dean and Chapter Library, Durham Cathedral.

Yet though a devoted and learned admirer of Anglican church music and a regular attender at church services he never, to Henson's knowledge, received Holy Communion:

I once challenged him on the subject of his absence from Communion, and asked him whether, in his heart, he was a Papist. He explained the first by confessing opinions which were rather pantheistic than orthodox, and the last he flatly denied. . . . I was divided in mind as to whether he could most fitly be described as a pagan or as an Erasmian medievalist [23 July 1932].

The division was probably in Falkner's mind, too, but it was one which enabled him to understand John Maltravers's aesthetic pantheism from within.

A division and debate over aestheticism, over the relationship between art and morality, is central to *The Lost Stradivarius*, and is another point at which the novel touches one of the most sensitive issues of the late nineteenth century. In Chapter 4 Mr Gaskell quotes 'some beautiful verses by Mr. Keble'; the verses are mis-attributed and, as is not uncommon in Falkner's citations (evidently from memory), misquoted. The stanzas are from a poem first published, anonymously, in *The British Magazine, and Monthly Register of Religious and Ecclesiastical Information . . .*, ix, 271, 1 March 1836. Under the general heading 'Lyra Apostolica', and with an epigraph from Homer ('the much-enduring God-like Odysseus') the text of the full poem reads:

> Cease, Stranger, cease those piercing notes,
>    The craft of Siren choirs;
> Hush the seductive voice, that floats
>    Upon the languid wires.
>
> Music's etherial fire was given,
>    Not to dissolve our clay,
> But draw Promethean beams from heaven,
>    And purge the dross away.

> Weak self! with thee the mischief lies,
> Those throbs a tale disclose;
> Nor age nor trial have made wise
> The Man of many woes.

In 1836 also, this and other poems which had appeared in *The British Magazine* under the title 'Lyra Apostolica' were published in book form with the same general title; the poem from which Mr Gaskell had quoted was now under the sub-section 'Ancient Scenes', without its Greek epigraph, but with a Greek title (= 'Islands of the Sirens'; in the Contents the title is given only in English as 'Siren Isles'). Both titles, 'Ancient Scenes', and 'Siren Isles', should be borne in mind at the end of the novel when the location moves to the area of the Siren Isles off southern Italy, and Mr Gaskell refers to ancient scenes of Roman wickedness around the Bay of Naples. The volume was edited anonymously by John Newman, and the poems, by six authors, including and chiefly Newman and Keble, retained the anonymity they had in *The British Magazine*, though the different authors were now severally distinguished by the 'signing' of the poems with a lower-case Greek letter. It was only in the 1879 edition of *Lyra Apostolica*, after the date of both the Oxford scene (1842) and Sophia's narrative (1867), when neither Mr Gaskell nor Sophia could have known the author, that Newman, in a 'Postscript' to the original 'Advertisement', provided a key to the authorship of the poems: 'Siren Isles', now substituted for the Greek title of the book form, was not by Keble but Newman. Newman's Tractarian poetics, in which aesthetic pleasure has its beginning and end in religion and ethics, are at the heart of Mr Gaskell's argument.[10]

---

[10] For an excellent discussion of *Lyra Apostolica* see G. B. Tennyson, *Victorian Devotional Poetry: The Tractarian Mode* (Cambridge, Mass., and London, 1981), pp. 114–37.

As with the psychical and the metaphysical, the intellectual opposition to John Maltravers's growing possession by the music of the *Gagliarda* and by the Stradivarius itself is given by Mr Gaskell. When he speaks in his Note of neo-Platonism's 'tolerance of aesthetic impressions' he is using (and attacking) the language of Walter Pater, a Fellow of Brasenose throughout Falkner's time as an undergraduate at Oxford. Again, as with 'the Phas', one should bear in mind the Oxford background to Falkner's concerns. In 1877, the year before Falkner went up to Oxford, the *Oxford and Cambridge Undergraduate's Journal* had attacked the Aesthetic Movement for seeking 'insidiously' to obtain *'implicit* sanction' for 'Pagan worship of bodily form and beauty' and for rejecting 'all exterior systems of morals or religion'.[11]

In *The Nebuly Coat* (1903) Falkner felt able to imagine a young aesthete in terms which, though satiric, were without anxiety:

Was not the young man conscious that, though his rooms might be small, there was about them a delicate touch which made up for much, that everything breathed of refinement, from the photographs and silver toddy-spoon upon the mantelpiece to Rossetti's poems and *Marius the Epicurean* [by Pater, 1885] which covered negligently a stain on the green tablecloth? (ch. 15)

In *The Lost Stradivarius* the debt is not to the grave, even sombre, *Marius the Epicurean* but to the more sensationally charged (and received) *Studies in the History of the Renaissance* (1873). Mr Gaskell's 'aesthetic impressions' distinctively recalls Pater's doctrine in the 'Conclusion' of *The Renaissance*, where the word 'impressions' is used nine times in four pages, that life is a perpetual flux in which 'each object is loosed into a group of impressions—

---

[11] Quoted in R. Ellmann, *Oscar Wilde* (London, 1987), p. 85.

colour, odour, texture—in the mind of the observer'. For Pater this solipsistic theory meant that:

While all melts under our feet, we may well grasp at any exquisite passion, or any contribution to knowledge that seems by a lifted horizon to set the spirit free for a moment, or any stirring of the senses, strange dyes, strange colours, and curious odours, or work of the artist's hands, or the face of one's friend. . . . What we have to do is to be for ever curiously testing new opinions, and courting new impressions, never acquiescing in a facile orthodoxy . . . (World's Classics edn., p. 152)

It is Pater's doctrine of 'the love of art for its own sake' that Mr Gaskell has in mind when he later says that for burning the Stradivarius 'I shall probably be blamed by those who would exalt art at the expense of everything else'.

Echoes from throughout Pater's *The Renaissance* are found in *The Lost Stradivarius*. Besides the marked contribution of the 'Conclusion', the essay on Pico della Mirandola probably furnishes an important narrative feature. As Adrian Temple and John Maltravers come under malefic influences they are marked by a strikingly white complexion. In the essay on Pico, Pater quotes from Sir Thomas More's translation of a Latin biography: ' "his colour white, intermingled with comely reds" '. However, it is not the reds but the whiteness which is alluded to in a later passage on his appearance which refers to 'that over-brightness which in the popular imagination always betokens an early death', and which led to the prophecy that he 'would depart in the time of lilies—prematurely, that is, like the field-flowers which are withered by the scorching sun almost as soon as they are sprung up'. Pico must have been one of the 'Renaissancists' read by John Maltravers, and Pico's own studies as reported by Pater, 'the astrologers, the Cabala, and Homer, and Scripture, and Dionysius the Areopagite', have some striking identities with those pursued by Adrian Temple and John

Maltravers (see pp. 6, 141 and nn.). The lily-white complexion is the outward and visible indication of this brotherhood, and the lilies in the Domacavalli coat of arms, whatever their origins in a papal blazon, have also an echo closer to home in Pater's 'the time of lilies'. Of course, Pater has turned Pico into an Aesthete of his own time: 'his [Pico's] own brief existence flamed itself away' just as Pater asserted that 'To burn always with this hard, gem-like flame, to maintain this ecstasy, is success in life' ('Conclusion'). The lily, made notorious by Oscar Wilde, and a pale complexion, were the well-known public attributes of the Aesthetic Men of the 1880s and '90s.[12] It is thus in the light of these close echoes of *The Renaissance* that *The Lost Stradivarius* can be seen in a wider context as paralleled by the attack on the aestheticism of the same work made by Henry James in his fiction, especially *Roderick Hudson* (1875).[13]

*The Renaissance* also helps in the interpretation of the delicately ambiguous relationship in the novel between Maltravers and the 'Italian boy' Raffaelle Carotenuto. Pater, reflecting his own homosexual propensity, made much of male beauty and male friendship. In 'Two Early French Stories' he speaks of the relationship between Amis and Amile as 'a great friendship, a friendship pure and generous, pushed to a sort of passionate exaltation, and more than faithful unto death'; in 'Pico' he writes of 'a conversation, deeper and more intimate than men usually fall into at first sight'; in 'Leonardo da Vinci' we see Leonardo 'in his boyhood fascinating all men by his beauty', and Andréa Salaino, 'beloved of Leonardo for his curled and waving hair'; in 'Winckelmann' we hear of 'his romantic, fervent friendships with young men . . . more beautiful than Guido's archangel'.

[12] See Ellmann, *Oscar Wilde*, pp. 84, 129–30.
[13] See R. Ellmann, 'Henry James Among the Aesthetes', in his *a long the riverrun* (London, 1988), pp. 132–49.

When Sophia first arrives at the Villa de Angelis she hears 'an Italian youth', Raffaelle Carotenuto, in 'a rich alto voice singing very sweetly to a mandoline some soothing or religious melody'. However, Sophia's knowledge of Italian is 'so slight' that she is unable to converse with, or understand, Dr Baravelli, and she talks later of 'my own ignorance of the Italian tongue'. In truth, she can have no idea of what Raffaelle is singing, and, in view of John's reprobate life at the Villa, it is highly improbable that John is being soothed by hymns. She speaks of Raffaelle's 'evident affection to his master', and when she and her brother are to return to England her offer of a few pounds to 'the boy' as a 'token of my esteem' provokes a dramatic response as he refuses the money and:

shed tears when he learnt that he was to be left in Italy, and begged with many protestations of devotion that he might be allowed to accompany us to England. My heart was not proof against his entreaties, supported by so many signs of attachment, and it was agreed, therefore, that he should at least attend us as far as Worth Maltravers. John showed no surprise at the boy being with us. (pp. 124–5)

Even allowing for the fact that relations were strained between John Maltravers and Mr Gaskell at the end of their Oxford days, this scene is pointedly different from the leave-taking between the two undergraduates when Mr Gaskell:

held out his hand frankly, and his voice trembled a little as he spoke—partly perhaps from real emotion, but more probably from the feeling of reluctance which I have noticed men always exhibit to discovering any sentiment deeper than those usually deemed conventional in correct society. (p. 75)

The relationship between John and Raffaelle is masterly in its irresolution. Because it is seen through Sophia's eyes, we can but speculate that the boy sang to John of earthly, not divine love, and we still cannot know whether he sang a song of conventional love or of his own love for

John, like one of Winckelmann's 'fiery friendships' in Pater's hectic phrase. Similarly, the contrast between Raffaelle and Mr Gaskell may just be one of national characteristics, but on the other hand Naples and England are elsewhere in the novel contrasted in terms of moral wholesomeness. It was an identical contrast which Henry James observed in a letter to his sister, Alice, 25 April 1880, when, after seeing his artist friend Paul Zhukovski in Posilipo, Naples, he had visited an English friend, Somerset Beaumont, at his villa at Frascati, near Rome:

This day, which was in itself most charming, derived an extra merit from the contrast of Beaumont's admirable, honest, reasonable, wholesome English nature with the fantastic immoralities and aesthetics of the circle I had left at Naples.[14]

One may also note that after his release from prison Oscar Wilde, and Lord Douglas, took a villa for a time at Posilipo.

Such ambiguity over the nature of the relationship between John and Raffaelle may also reflect Falkner's own uncertainty over his friendship with John Noble (1865–1938), some seven years younger than himself. Even after Falkner's marriage, at the age of forty-one, to Evelyn Adye four years after the publication of the novel, the friendship was to remain the most significant relationship of his life. The suggestion is not at all that it was homosexual in nature, but that its intensity may in 1895 have prompted an unease over 'any sentiment deeper than those usually deemed conventional in correct society'. It is another instance of unresolvedness which may account for that elusive quality in Falkner which so struck Hensley Henson.

Mr Gaskell's Note, and his discussion with John reported in Sophia's narrative, are the focus of the intellectual and aesthetic issues which John's occult and

[14] Henry James: Letters, ed. L. Edel, British edn. (London, 1978), ii. 288; Edel calls the 'circle' a 'veritable nest of homosexuals'.

psychic experiences provoke. He is himself a 'sincere Christian . . . though no Catholic', and despite his disavowal of theology in favour of 'practical religion', his account of the Beatific and Malefic Visions shows a knowledge of 'medieval philosophers and theologians'.

Sophia presents a complementary response: where Mr Gaskell, even as an undergraduate, had been to Rome and been much impressed by the music in the Roman churches, Sophia is shocked by what she finds the paganism of Catholic Naples. She self-deprecatingly refers to herself as 'a plain English girl' and to her ideas as 'rustic and insular'. Her religious tradition is evangelical: her reading is in that tradition (cf. pp. 85, 132 nn.); she lays stress on individual duty; and she dislikes liturgical innovation (such as early morning Communion) but is prepared to be flexible. The tombs and heraldry of her ancestors arouse a sense of obligation to continue their acts of piety. If she is without Mr Gaskell's intellectual power, she has sound sense and can see a moral issue with clarity, as in the juxtaposition of the alabaster Cupid and the crucifix, the same warring opposites which we heard earlier between 'Hark the herald angels' and the *Gagliarda*.

It is a happy touch of Falkner's to bring together in the last paragraph of the novel Mr Gaskell and Sophia, Christian intellect and evangelical piety, in the Maltravers chapel. Mr Gaskell envies the Maltravers Crusader ancestors their 'full and unwavering faith', in such contrast to the intellectual dilettantism of his own time. That simple and firm Crusader faith still shines forth in Sophia. The passage modulates beautifully the literal and the metaphorical: the 'bright sunlight' in the chapel and the 'dark shadow of John Maltravers' ruined life'. The neo-Platonic paradoxes of the divine darkness yield to Sophia's robust assertion that for some the light of this world is indeed darkness.

# NOTE ON THE TEXT

No manuscript of the novel survives, and the only
authority is the edition published by William Blackwood
and Sons (Edinburgh and London) in 1895; this was
reprinted without textual change by the same firm in
1896. There are copies of both the 1895 edition and the
1896 reprint in the Bodleian Library, Oxford, which I
have used.

This edition is reproduced from The World's Classics
edition of 1954, and it has been collated with that of 1895.
The divergences in the 1954 edition are owing not only to
simple carelessness but also to what was evidently seen as
deliberate 'correction': for example, p. 22, l. 7, 1954
inserts 'from' after 'different', presumably to avoid the
implied 'different . . . to', an idiom to which some
mistakenly object, and Falkner was in any case capable of
'None of us were' (p. 78, ll. 15–16); p. 63, l. 9, 1954
prints 'fancy-dress balls' for 'fancy balls', though the latter
is an attested earlier expression.

I have ignored differences in house style (for example,
1895 has no period after 'Mr.', 'Mrs.', etc., uses double
quotation marks for speech, and Roman numerals for
chapter numbers, etc.) and followed the 1954 edition.
1895 is itself inconsistent as between 'Maltravers' '  and
'Maltravers's', and I have followed 1954's regular
'Maltravers' '. The 1895 edition has 'THE LOST STRADI-
VARIUS' as the running headline of all pages, but the 1954
edition alternates this with 'SOPHIA MALTRAVERS' STORY' or
'MR. GASKELL'S NOTE', and I have retained the 1954
practice.

In two instances I have retained the 1954 reading where
1895 cannot represent Falkner's intentions:

p. 16, l. 10: 'on' (1895 'in')
p. 38, l. 6: 'effected' (1895 'affected')

After hesitation, I have restored 1895's 'painting' (p. 112, l. 17) for 'paintings' since the singular may be in the sense 'pictorial decoration' in allusion to mural art as at Pompeii and not to the plural 'framed pictures'.

Otherwise, I have in all substantive cases (bar the two noted above) where possible silently restored the 1895 readings. The following is a list of those it was not possible to incorporate into the printed text (the 1954 reading is followed by that of 1895):

p. 11, l. 22: this/this first
p. 55, l. 26: time/minutes
p. 56, l. 23: grown/grown gradually
p. 63, l. 7: black leather/black
      l. 9: fancy-dress/fancy
p. 67, l. 9: she/she had
p. 76, l. 12: was/was quite
p. 88, l. 23: was/*delete*
p. 90, l. 9: for/for any
p. 97, l. 30: him/him again
p. 111, l. 14: an/another
p. 119, l. 4: you/you may

Though not a substantive point, I have none the less restored the second medial 'e' in 'Westmoreland' (pp. 29, 130), a good old spelling for a good old county.

# SELECT BIBLIOGRAPHY

BIOGRAPHY

A. Cochrane, in *The Dictionary of National Biography 1931–1940*.

Sir Edmund Craster, 'Personal Note on John Meade Falkner' in the old World's Classics edn. of *The Nebuly Coat and The Lost Stradivarius* (1954).

C. Hawtree, edn. of *The Nebuly Coat* (World's Classics, 1988), Introduction.

B. Jones, *John Meade Falkner 1858–1932*, no. 18 (1984) in the 'Dorset Worthies' series pub. by the Dorset County Museum, Dorchester.

K. Warren, *John Meade Falkner in Durham (1899–1932): A Perspective on a Small Cathedral City*, the Durham Cathedral Lecture for 1989 (Durham, 1989).

K. Warren, *Armstrongs of Elswick* (Basingstoke and London, 1989); a history of the firm which Falkner served for almost all his working life.

WORKS

Falkner's principal literary works are his three novels, *The Lost Stradivarius* (1895), *Moonfleet* (1898), and *The Nebuly Coat* (1903), and the selection of his *Poems* (c.1930, with another edition posthumously in 1933). For his other works see the following 'Chronology'; see also for full bibliographical details G. Pollard, 'John Meade Falkner, 1858–1932' (Some Uncollected Authors XXV), *Book Collector*, 9 (1960), 318–25.

CRITICISM

B. Cooley, 'John Meade Falkner: A Critical Study of his Life and Writings', unpublished Liverpool University MA thesis (1962); includes a chapter on the life.

Sir William Haley, 'John Meade Falkner', *Essays by Divers Hands* (Transactions of the Royal Society of Literature), NS 30 (1960), 55–67.

# SELECT BIBLIOGRAPHY

V. S. Pritchett, 'An Amateur' [JMF], *The Living Novel* (London, 1946), pp. 159–65.

E. Wilson, 'Literary and Antiquarian Allusions in John Meade Falkner's *The Nebuly Coat*', *Notes and Queries*, NS 37 (1990), 59–65.


BACKGROUND

(a) *The Ghost Story*

J. Briggs, *Night Visitors: The Rise and Fall of the English Ghost Story* (London, 1977).

*The Oxford Book of English Ghost Stories*, chosen by M. Cox and R. A. Gilbert (1986); includes Vernon Lee's 'A Wicked Voice', quoted in the Introduction.

(b) *Intellectual Context: The Psychic, the Occult, the Aesthetic, Travel*

W. E. Buckler, *Walter Pater: The Critic as Artist of Ideas* (New York and London, 1987).

D. J. DeLaura, *Hebrew and Hellene in Victorian England: Newman, Arnold, and Pater* (Austin, Tx., and London, 1969).

R. Ellmann, *Oscar Wilde* (London, 1987).

R. Ellmann, *a long the riverrun: Selected Essays* (London, 1988), pp. 132–49.

H. Fraser, *Beauty and Belief: Aesthetics and Religion in Victorian Literature* (Cambridge, 1986).

C. Hibbert, *The Grand Tour* (London, 1987).

G. Hough, *The Last Romantics* (London, 1949).

S. Hynes, *The Edwardian Turn of Mind* (Princeton, NJ, and London, 1968).

F. Kinahan, *Yeats, Folklore, and Occultism: Contexts of the Early Work and Thought* (Boston and London, 1988).

J. Oppenheim, *The Other World: Spiritualism and Psychical Research in England, 1850–1914* (Cambridge, 1985).

J. Pemble, *The Mediterranean Passion: Victorians and Edwardians in the South* (Oxford, 1987).

# A CHRONOLOGY OF
# JOHN MEADE FALKNER

1858    John Meade Falkner [JMF] born 8 May at Manningford Bruce, Wiltshire, son of the Revd Thomas Alexander Falkner [TAF], an Anglican curate, and Elizabeth Grace Falkner (née Mead)

1859    TAF becomes Assistant Curate at Holy Trinity Church, Dorchester, Dorset

1869    JMF attends Hardye's School, Dorchester, under the Headmastership of the Revd Thomas Ratsey Maskew whose names were to be used in the characters of sexton Ratsey and Thomas Maskew in *Moonfleet* (1898)

1871    TAF becomes Assistant Curate at St Mary's, Weymouth; JMF attends Weymouth College; his mother dies of typhoid

1873    January, JMF enters Marlborough College; a Foundation Scholar; leaves Marlborough at Easter, 1877

1878    October, enters Hertford College, Oxford, as a Commoner, but a year later is elected to the Lusby Scholarship at the College

1881    TAF becomes Curate in Charge at Buckland Ripers, near Weymouth and Fleet, the village of *Moonfleet*

1882    Trinity (Summer) Term: JMF obtains Third Class Honours in Modern (i.e. post-classical) History (there were 2 Firsts, 13 Seconds, 17 Thirds, and 19 Fourths)

1883    Spring, JMF becomes private tutor to the children of Andrew (later Sir Andrew) Noble, of the engineering, armaments, and shipbuilding firm of Armstrong Mitchell & Co. of Elswick and Walker on Tyne; later becomes Andrew Noble's private secretary

1887    Death of his father; JMF's brothers and sisters

return to Weymouth in poverty, and receive financial help from JMF

1888-9    JMF becomes Secretary of Armstrong Mitchell & Co.

1894    *Handbook for Travellers in Oxfordshire* published

1895    *The Lost Stradivarius* published

1896    *A Midsummer Night's Marriage* published in the *National Review* (August)

1898    *Moonfleet* published

1899    18 October, marries Evelyn Violet Adye, younger daughter of General Sir John Adye; there were to be no children. *A History of Oxfordshire* published

1901    JMF becomes a Director of Armstrong Whitworth & Co. (as the firm had become)

1902    *Handbook for Berkshire* published

1903    *The Nebuly Coat* published

1913    Becomes Vice-Chairman of Armstrong Whitworth & Co.

1915    Becomes Chairman of Armstrong Whitworth & Co. on the death of Sir Andrew Noble

1916    *Charalampia* (a story) published in the *Cornhill Magazine* (December)

1918    *Bath in History and Social Tradition by An Appreciative Visitor* [JMF] published

1920    Retires as Chairman of Armstrong Whitworth & Co.

1921    Becomes Honorary Librarian to the Dean and Chapter of Durham Cathedral

1924    Becomes Honorary Reader in Palaeography at Durham University

1925    H. D. Hughes, *A History of Durham Cathedral Library*, to which JMF contributed the Introduction and ch. xiv ('Some Later Durham Bibliophiles'), published

1926    Resigns as a Director of Armstrong Whitworth & Co.

1927    Becomes an Honorary Fellow of Hertford College, Oxford

1929    Publication of *The Statutes of the Cathedral Church of Durham* . . ., ed. A. Hamilton Thompson 'from the Latin text prepared by Mr J. Meade Falkner', Surtees Society 143; 'to Mr Falkner indeed no tribute is too high, as the editor has merely watered what he planted' (p. xviii)

c.1930    *Poems* (a selection) privately printed

1932    22 July, John Meade Falkner dies at his home in Durham; after cremation at Darlington his ashes were interred at Burford, Oxfordshire

1933    Another edition of *Poems* printed by JMF's widow, who died in 1940

# THE LOST
# STRADIVARIUS

◄◄◄◄◄ ◐ ►►►►►

*A tale out of season is as music in mourning*
ECCLESIASTICUS xxii. 6*

Letter from MISS SOPHIA MALTRAVERS to her
Nephew, SIR EDWARD MALTRAVERS, then a Student*
at Christ Church, Oxford

*13 Pauncefort Buildings, Bath,*
*Oct. 21, 1867.*

*MY DEAR EDWARD,*

*It was your late father's dying request that certain events
which occurred in his last years should be communicated to you
on your coming of age. I have reduced them to writing, partly
from my own recollection, which is, alas! still too vivid, and
partly with the aid of notes taken at the time of my brother's
death. As you are now of full age, I submit the narrative to
you. Much of it has necessarily been exceedingly painful to me
to write, but at the same time I feel it is better that you should
hear the truth from me than garbled stories from others who
did not love your father as I did.*

*Your loving Aunt,*

*SOPHIA MALTRAVERS*

*To Sir Edward Maltravers, Bart.*

# MISS SOPHIA MALTRAVERS'
# STORY

◄◄◄◄◄◄ ☾ ►►►►►►

## Chapter 1

YOUR father, John Maltravers, was born in 1820 at
Worth,* and succeeded his father and mine, who
died when we were still young children. John was
sent to Eton in due course, and in 1839, when he
was nineteen years of age, it was determined that
he should go to Oxford. It was intended at first to
enter him at Christ Church; but Dr. Sarsdell, who
visited us at Worth in the summer of 1839, persuaded Mr. Thoresby, our guardian, to send him
instead to Magdalen Hall.* Dr. Sarsdell*was himself
Principal of that institution, and represented that
John, who then exhibited some symptoms of delicacy, would meet with more personal attention
under his care than he could hope to do in so large
a college as Christ Church. Mr. Thoresby, ever
solicitous for his ward's welfare, readily waived
other considerations in favour of an arrangement
which he considered conducive to John's health,
and he was accordingly matriculated at Magdalen
Hall in the autumn of 1839.

Dr. Sarsdell had not been unmindful of his
promise to look after my brother, and had secured
him an excellent first-floor sitting-room, with a bedroom adjoining, having an aspect towards New
College Lane.

I shall pass over the first two years of my brother's residence at Oxford, because they have nothing to do with the present story. They were spent, no doubt, in the ordinary routine of work and recreation common in Oxford at that period.

From his earliest boyhood he had been passionately devoted to music, and had attained a considerable proficiency on the violin. In the autumn term of 1841 he made the acquaintance of Mr. William Gaskell, a very talented student at New College, and also a more than tolerable musician. The practice of music was then very much less common at Oxford than it has since become, and there were none of those societies existing which now do so much to promote its study among undergraduates. It was therefore a cause of much gratification to the two young men, and it afterwards became a strong bond of friendship, to discover that one was as devoted to the pianoforte as was the other to the violin. Mr. Gaskell, though in easy circumstances, had not a pianoforte in his rooms, and was pleased to use a fine instrument by D'Almaine* that John had that term received as a birthday present from his guardian.

From that time the two students were thrown much together, and in the autumn term of 1841 and Easter term of 1842 practised a variety of music in John's rooms, he taking the violin part and Mr. Gaskell that for the pianoforte.

It was, I think, in March 1842 that John purchased for his rooms a piece of furniture which was destined afterwards to play no unimportant part in the story I am narrating. This was a very large and low wicker chair of a form then coming into fashion in Oxford, and since, I am told, become a familiar

4

object of most college rooms. It was cushioned with a gaudy pattern of chintz, and bought for new of an upholsterer at the bottom of the High Street.

Mr. Gaskell was taken by his uncle to spend Easter in Rome, and obtaining special leave from his college to prolong his travels, did not return to Oxford till three weeks of the summer term were passed and May was well advanced. So impatient was he to see his friend that he would not let even the first evening of his return pass without coming round to John's rooms. The two young men sat without lights until the night was late; and Mr. Gaskell had much to narrate of his travels, and spoke specially of the beautiful music which he had heard at Easter in the Roman churches. He had also had lessons on the piano from a celebrated professor of the Italian style, but seemed to have been particularly delighted with the music of the seventeenth-century composers, of whose works he had brought back some specimens set for piano and violin.

It was past eleven o'clock when Mr. Gaskell left to return to New College; but the night was unusually warm, with a moon near the full, and John sat for some time in a cushioned window-seat before the open sash thinking over what he had heard about the music of Italy. Feeling still disinclined for sleep, he lit a single candle and began to turn over some of the musical works which Mr. Gaskell had left on the table. His attention was especially attracted to an oblong book, bound in soiled vellum, with a coat of arms stamped in gilt upon the side. It was a manuscript copy of some early suites by Graziani* for violin and harpsichord, and was apparently written at Naples in the year 1744,

5

many years after the death of that composer. Though the ink was yellow and faded, the transcript had been accurately made, and could be read with tolerable comfort by an advanced musician in spite of the antiquated notation.

Perhaps by accident, or perhaps by some mysterious direction which our minds are incapable of appreciating, his eye was arrested by a suite of four movements with a *basso continuo*, or figured bass, for the harpsichord. The other suites in the book were only distinguished by numbers, but this one the composer had dignified with the name of 'l'Areopagita.'* Almost mechanically John put the book on his music-stand, took his violin from its case, and after a moment's tuning stood up and played the first movement, a lively *Coranto*.* The light of the single candle burning on the table was scarcely sufficient to illumine the page; the shadows hung in the creases of the leaves, which had grown into those wavy folds sometimes observable in books made of thick paper and remaining long shut; and it was with difficulty that he could read what he was playing. But he felt the strange impulse of the old-world music urging him forward, and did not even pause to light the candles which stood ready in their sconces on either side of the desk. The *Coranto* was followed by a *Sarabanda*,* and the *Sarabanda* by a *Gagliarda*.* My brother stood playing, with his face turned to the window, with the room and the large wicker chair of which I have spoken behind him. The *Gagliarda* began with a bold and lively air, and as he played the opening bars, he heard behind him a creaking of the wicker chair. The sound was a perfectly familiar one—as of some person placing a hand on either arm of the

6

chair preparatory to lowering himself into it, followed by another as of the same person being
leisurely seated. But for the tones of the violin,
all was silent, and the creaking of the chair was
strangely distinct. The illusion was so complete that
my brother stopped playing suddenly, and turned
round expecting that some late friend of his had
slipped in unawares, being attracted by the sound
of the violin, or that Mr. Gaskell himself had returned. With the cessation of the music an absolute
stillness fell upon all; the light of the single candle
scarcely reached the darker corners of the room, but
fell directly on the wicker chair and showed it to
be perfectly empty. Half amused, half vexed with
himself at having without reason interrupted his
music, my brother returned to the *Gagliarda*; but
some impulse induced him to light the candles in the
sconces, which gave an illumination more adequate
to the occasion. The *Gagliarda* and the last movement, a *Minuetto*, were finished, and John closed
the book, intending, as it was now late, to seek his
bed. As he shut the pages a creaking of the wicker
chair again attracted his attention, and he heard
distinctly sounds such as would be made by a person raising himself from a sitting posture. This time,
being less surprised, he could more aptly consider
the probable causes of such a circumstance, and
easily arrived at the conclusion that there must be
in the wicker chair osiers responsive to certain notes
of the violin, as panes of glass in church windows
are observed to vibrate in sympathy with certain
tones of the organ. But while this argument ap-
proved itself to his reason, his imagination was but
half convinced; and he could not but be impressed
with the fact that the second creaking of the chair

7

had been coincident with his shutting the music-book; and, unconsciously, pictured to himself some strange visitor waiting until the termination of the music, and then taking his departure.

His conjectures did not, however, either rob him of sleep or even disturb it with dreams, and he woke the next morning with a cooler mind and one less inclined to fantastic imagination. If the strange episode of the previous evening had not entirely vanished from his mind, it seemed at least fully accounted for by the acoustic explanation to which I have alluded above. Although he saw Mr. Gaskell in the course of the morning, he did not think it necessary to mention to him so trivial a circumstance, but made with him an appointment to sup together in his own rooms that evening, and to amuse themselves afterwards by essaying some of the Italian music.

It was shortly after nine that night when, supper being finished, Mr. Gaskell seated himself at the piano and John tuned his violin. The evening was closing in; there had been heavy thunder-rain in the afternoon, and the moist air hung now heavy and steaming, while across it there throbbed the distant vibrations of the tenor bell at Christ Church. It was tolling the customary 101 strokes, which are rung every night in term-time as a signal for closing the college gates.* The two young men enjoyed themselves for some while, playing first a suite by Cesti, and then two early sonatas by Buononcini.* Both of them were sufficiently expert musicians to make reading at sight a pleasure rather than an effort; and Mr. Gaskell especially was well versed in the theory of music, and in the correct rendering of the *basso continuo*.* After the Buononcini Mr.

Gaskell took up the oblong copy of Graziani, and turning over its leaves, proposed that they should play the same suite which John had performed by himself the previous evening. His selection was apparently perfectly fortuitous, as my brother had purposely refrained from directing his attention in any way to that piece of music. They played the *Coranto* and the *Sarabanda*, and in the singular fascination of the music John had entirely forgotten the episode of the previous evening, when, as the bold air of the *Gagliarda* commenced, he suddenly became aware of the same strange creaking of the wicker chair that he had noticed on the first occasion. The sound was identical, and so exact was its resemblance to that of a person sitting down that he stared at the chair, almost wondering that it still appeared empty. Beyond turning his head sharply for a moment to look round, Mr. Gaskell took no notice of the sound; and my brother, ashamed to betray any foolish interest or excitement, continued the *Gagliarda*, with its repeat. At its conclusion Mr. Gaskell stopped before proceeding to the minuet, and turning the stool on which he was sitting round towards the room, observed, 'How very strange, Johnnie,'—for these young men were on terms of sufficient intimacy to address each other in a familiar style,—'How very strange! I thought I heard some one sit down in that chair when we began the *Gagliarda*. I looked round quite expecting to see some one had come in. Did you hear nothing?'

'It was only the chair creaking,' my brother answered, feigning an indifference which he scarcely felt. 'Certain parts of the wicker-work seem to be in accord with musical notes and respond to them; let us continue with the *Minuetto*.'

Thus they finished the suite, Mr. Gaskell demanding a repetition of the *Gagliarda*, with the air of which he was much pleased. As the clocks had already struck eleven, they determined not to play more that night; and Mr. Gaskell rose, blew out the sconces, shut the piano, and put the music aside. My brother has often assured me that he was quite prepared for what followed, and had been almost expecting it; for as the books were put away, a creaking of the wicker chair was audible, exactly similar to that which he had heard when he stopped playing on the previous night. There was a moment's silence; the young men looked involuntarily at one another, and then Mr. Gaskell said, 'I cannot understand the creaking of that chair; it has never done so before, with all the music we have played. I am perhaps imaginative and excited with the fine airs we have heard to-night, but I have an impression that I cannot dispel that something has been sitting listening to us all this time, and that now when the concert is ended it has got up and gone.' There was a spirit of raillery in his words, but his tone was not so light as it would ordinarily have been, and he was evidently ill at ease.

'Let us try the *Gagliarda* again,' said my brother; 'it is the vibration of the opening notes which affects the wicker-work, and we shall see if the noise is repeated.' But Mr. Gaskell excused himself from trying the experiment, and after some desultory conversation, to which it was evident that neither was giving any serious attention, he took his leave and returned to New College.

## Chapter 2

I SHALL not weary you, my dear Edward, by
recounting similar experiences which occurred on
nearly every occasion that the young men met
in the evenings for music. The repetition of the
phenomenon had accustomed them to expect it.
Both professed to be quite satisfied that it was to be
attributed to acoustical affinities of vibration between the wicker-work and certain of the piano
wires, and indeed this seemed the only explanation
possible. But, at the same time, the resemblance of
the noises to those caused by a person sitting down
in or rising from a chair was so marked, that even
their frequent recurrence never failed to make a
strange impression on them. They felt a reluctance
to mention the matter to their friends, partly from a
fear of being themselves laughed at, and partly to
spare from ridicule a circumstance to which each
perhaps, in spite of himself, attached some degree
of importance. Experience soon convinced them
that the first noise as of one sitting down never
occurred unless the *Gagliarda* of the 'Areopagita'
was played, and that this noise being once heard,
the second only followed it when they ceased playing for the evening. They met every night, sitting
later with the lengthening summer evenings, and
every night, as by some tacit understanding, played
the 'Areopagita' suite before parting. At the opening bars of the *Gagliarda* the creaking of the chair
occurred spontaneously with the utmost regularity.
They seldom spoke even to one another of the

11

subject; but one night, when John was putting away his violin after a long evening's music without having played the 'Areopagita,' Mr. Gaskell, who had risen from the pianoforte, sat down again as by a sudden impulse and said—

'Johnnie, do not put away your violin yet. It is near twelve o'clock and I shall get shut out, but I cannot stop to-night without playing the *Gagliarda*. Suppose that all our theories of vibration and affinity are wrong, suppose that there really comes here night by night some strange visitant to hear us, some poor creature whose heart is bound up in that tune; would it not be unkind to send him away without the hearing of that piece which he seems most to relish? Let us not be ill-mannered, but humour his whim; let us play the *Gagliarda*.'

They played it with more vigour and precision than usual, and the now customary sound of one taking his seat at once ensued. It was that night that my brother, looking steadfastly at the chair, saw, or thought he saw, there some slight obscuration, some penumbra, mist, or subtle vapour which, as he gazed, seemed to struggle to take human form. He ceased playing for a moment and rubbed his eyes, but as he did so all dimness vanished and he saw the chair perfectly empty. The pianist stopped also at the cessation of the violin, and asked what ailed him.

'It is only that my eyes were dim,' he answered.

'We have had enough for to-night,' said Mr. Gaskell; 'let us stop. I shall be locked out.' He shut the piano, and as he did so the clock in New College tower struck twelve. He left the room running, but was late enough at his college door to be reported, admonished with a fine against such late hours, and

12

confined for a week to college; for being out after midnight was considered, at that time at least, a somewhat serious offence.

Thus for some days the musical practice was compulsorily intermitted, but resumed on the first evening after Mr. Gaskell's term of confinement was expired. After they had performed several suites of Graziani, and finished as usual with the 'Areopagita,' Mr. Gaskell sat for a time silent at the instrument, as though thinking with himself, and then said—

'I cannot say how deeply this old-fashioned music affects me. Some would try to persuade us that these suites, of which the airs bear the names of different dances, were always written rather as a musical essay and for purposes of performance than for persons to dance to, as their names would more naturally imply. But I think these critics are wrong at least in some instances. It is to me impossible to believe that such a melody, for instance, as the *Giga** of Corelli*which we have played, was not written for actual purposes of dancing. One can almost hear the beat of feet upon the floor, and I imagine that in the time of Corelli the practice of dancing, while not a whit inferior in grace, had more of the tripudistic* or beating character than is now esteemed consistent with a correct ball-room performance. The *Gagliarda* too, which we play now so constantly, possesses a singular power of assisting the imagination to picture or reproduce such scenes as those which it no doubt formerly enlivened. I know not why, but it is constantly identified in my mind with some revel which I have perhaps seen in a picture, where several couples are dancing a licentious measure in a long room lit by a number of

13

silver sconces of the debased model common at the end of the seventeenth century. It is probably a reminiscence of my late excursion that gives to these dancers in my fancy the olive skin, dark hair, and bright eyes of the Italian type; and they wear dresses of exceedingly rich fabric and elaborate design. Imagination is whimsical enough to paint for me the character of the room itself, as having an arcade of arches running down one side alone, of the fantastic and paganised Gothic of the Renaissance.* At the end is a gallery or balcony for the musicians, which on its coved* front has a florid coat of arms of foreign heraldry. The shield bears, on a field *or*, a cherub's head blowing on three lilies—a blazon I have no doubt seen somewhere in my travels, though I cannot recollect where.* This scene, I say, is so nearly connected in my brain with the *Gagliarda*, that scarcely are its first notes sounded ere it presents itself to my eyes with a vividness which increases every day. The couples advance, set,* and recede, using free and licentious gestures which my imagination should be ashamed to recall. Amongst so many foreigners, fancy pictures, I know not in the least why, the presence of a young man of an English type of face, whose features, however, always elude my mind's attempt to fix them. I think that the opening subject of this *Gagliarda* is a superior composition to the rest of it, for it is only during the first sixteen bars that the vision of by-gone revelry presents itself to me. With the last note of the sixteenth bar a veil is suddenly drawn across the scene, and with a sense almost of some catastrophe it vanishes. This I attribute to the fact that the second subject must be inferior in conception to the first, and by some sense of incongruity destroys the fabric which the fascination of the preceding one built up.'

My brother, though he had listened with interest to what Mr. Gaskell had said, did not reply, and the subject was allowed to drop.

## Chapter 3

IT was in the same summer of 1842, and near the middle of June, that my brother John wrote inviting me to come to Oxford for the Commemoration festivities.* I had been spending some weeks with Mrs. Temple, a distant cousin of ours, at their house of Royston*in Derbyshire, and John was desirous that Mrs. Temple should come up to Oxford and chaperone her daughter Constance and myself at the balls and various other entertainments which take place at the close of the summer term. Owing to Royston being some two hundred miles from Worth Maltravers, our families had hitherto seen little of one another, but during my present visit I had learned to love Mrs. Temple, a lady of singular sweetness of disposition, and had contracted a devoted attachment to her daughter Constance. Constance Temple was then eighteen years of age, and to great beauty united such mental graces and excellent traits of character as must ever appear to reasoning persons more enduringly valuable than even the highest personal attractions. She was well read and witty, and had been trained in those principles of true religion which she afterwards followed with devoted consistency in the self-sacrifice and resigned piety of her too short life. In person, I may remind you, my dear Edward, since death removed her ere you were of years to appreciate

15

either her appearance or her qualities, she was tall, with a somewhat long and oval face, with brown hair and eyes.

Mrs. Temple readily accepted Sir John Maltravers' invitation. She had never seen Oxford herself, and was pleased to afford us the pleasure of so delightful an excursion. John had secured convenient rooms for us above the shop of a well-known printseller in High Street, and we arrived in Oxford on Friday evening, June 18, 1842.* I shall not dilate to you on the various Commemoration festivities, which have probably altered little since those days, and with which you are familiar. Suffice it to say that my brother had secured us admission to every entertainment, and that we enjoyed our visit as only youth with its keen sensibilities and uncloyed pleasures can. I could not help observing that John was very much struck by the attractions of Miss Constance Temple, and that she for her part, while exhibiting no unbecoming forwardness, certainly betrayed no aversion to him. I was greatly pleased both with my own powers of observation which had enabled me to discover so important a fact, and also with the circumstance itself. To a romantic girl of nineteen it appeared high time that a brother of twenty-two should be at least preparing some matrimonial project; and my friend was so good and beautiful that it seemed impossible that I should ever obtain a more lovable sister or my brother a better wife. Mrs. Temple could not refuse her sanction to such a scheme; for while their mental qualities seemed eminently compatible, John was in his own right master of Worth Maltravers, and her daughter sole heiress of the Royston estates.

SOPHIA MALTRAVERS' STORY

The Commemoration festivities terminated on Wednesday night with a grand ball at the Music-Room in Holywell Street. This was given by a Lodge of University Freemasons, and John was there with Mr. Gaskell—whose acquaintance we had made with much gratification—both wearing blue silk scarves and small white aprons.* They introduced us to many other of their friends similarly adorned, and these important and mysterious insignia sat not amiss with their youthful figures and boyish faces. After a long and pleasurable programme, it was decided that we should prolong our visit till the next evening, leaving Oxford at half-past ten o'clock at night and driving to Didcot, there to join the mail for the west.* We rose late the next morning and spent the day rambling among the old colleges and gardens of the most beautiful of English cities. At seven o'clock we dined together for the last time at our lodgings in High Street, and my brother proposed that before parting we should enjoy the fine evening in the gardens of St. John's College. This was at once agreed to, and we proceeded thither, John walking on in front with Constance and Mrs. Temple, and I following with Mr. Gaskell. My companion explained that these gardens were esteemed the most beautiful in the University, but that under ordinary circumstances it was not permitted to strangers to walk there of an evening. Here he quoted some Latin about 'aurum per medios ire satellites,'*which I smilingly made as if I understood, and did indeed gather from it that John had bribed the porter to admit us. It was a warm and very still night, without a moon, but with enough of fading light to show the outlines of the garden front. This long low line of buildings built in Charles I's reign looked so exquisitely beautiful that I shall never forget it, though I have not since seen its oriel windows and creeper-covered walls. There was a very heavy dew on the broad lawn, and we walked at first only on the paths. No one spoke, for we were oppressed by the very beauty of the scene, and by the sadness which an imminent parting from friends and from so sweet a place combined to cause. John had been silent and depressed the whole day, nor did Mr. Gaskell himself seem inclined to conversation. Constance and my brother fell a little way behind, and Mr. Gaskell asked me to cross the lawn if I was not afraid of the dew, that I might see the garden front to better advantage from the corner. Mrs. Temple waited for us on the path, not wishing to wet her feet. Mr. Gaskell pointed out the beauties of the perspective as seen from his vantage-point, and we were fortunate in hearing the sweet descant of nightingales for which this garden has ever been famous. As we stood silent and listening, a candle was lit in a small oriel at the end, and the light showing the tracery of the window added to the picturesqueness of the scene.

Within an hour we were in a landau driving through the still warm lanes to Didcot. I had seen that Constance's parting with my brother had been tender, and I am not sure that she was not in tears during some part at least of our drive; but I did not observe her closely, having my thoughts elsewhere.

Though we were thus being carried every moment further from the sleeping city, where I believe that both our hearts were busy, I feel as if I had been a personal witness of the incidents I am about to narrate, so often have I heard them from my brother's lips. The two young men, after parting with us in the High Street, returned to their respective colleges. John reached his rooms shortly before eleven o'clock. He was at once sad and happy—sad at our departure, but happy in a new-found world of delight which his admiration for Constance Temple opened to him. He was, in fact, deeply in love with her, and the full flood of a hitherto unknown passion filled him with an emotion so overwhelming that his ordinary life seemed transfigured. He moved, as it were, in an ether superior to our mortal atmosphere, and a new region of high resolves and noble possibilities spread itself before his eyes. He slammed his heavy outside door (called an 'oak') to prevent anyone entering and flung himself into the window-seat. Here he sat for a long time, the sash thrown up and his head outside, for he was excited and feverish. His mental exaltation was so great and his thoughts of so absorbing an interest that he took no notice of time, and only remembered afterwards that the scent of a syringa-bush was borne up to him from a little garden-patch opposite, and that a bat had circled slowly up and down the lane, until he heard the clocks striking three. At the same time the faint light of dawn made itself felt almost imperceptibly; the classic statues on the roof of the schools* began to stand out against the white sky, and a faint glimmer to penetrate the darkened room. It glistened on the varnished top of his violin-case lying on the table, and on a jug of toast-and-water*placed there by his college servant or scout every night before he left. He drank a glass of this mixture, and was moving towards his bedroom door when a sudden thought struck him. He turned back,

19

took the violin from its case, tuned it, and began to
play the 'Areopagita' suite. He was conscious of that
mental clearness and vigour which not unfrequently
comes with the dawn to those who have sat watching or reading through the night: and his thoughts
were exalted by the effect which the first consciousness of a deep passion causes in imaginative minds.
He had never played the suite with more power;
and the airs, even without the piano part, seemed
fraught with a meaning hitherto unrealised. As he
began the *Gagliarda* he heard the wicker chair
creak; but he had his back towards it, and the sound
was now too familiar to him to cause him even to
look round. It was not till he was playing the repeat
that he became aware of a new and overpowering
sensation. At first it was a vague feeling, so often
experienced by us all, of not being alone. He did
not stop playing, and in a few seconds the impression of a presence in the room other than his own
became so strong that he was actually afraid to look
round. But in another moment he felt that at all
hazards he must see what or who this presence was.
Without stopping he partly turned and partly
looked over his shoulder. The silver light of early
morning was filling the room, making the various
objects appear of less bright colour than usual, and
giving to everything a pearl-grey neutral tint. In
this cold but clear light he saw seated in the wicker
chair the figure of a man.

In the first violent shock of so terrifying a discovery, he could not appreciate such details as
those of features, dress, or appearance. He was
merely conscious that with him, in a locked room
of which he knew himself to be the only human
inmate, there sat something which bore a human

form. He looked at it for a moment with a hope, which he felt to be vain, that it might vanish and prove a phantom of his excited imagination, but still it sat there. Then my brother put down his violin, and he used to assure me that a horror overwhelmed him of an intensity which he had previously believed impossible. Whether the image which he saw was subjective or objective, I cannot pretend to say: you will be in a position to judge for yourself when you have finished this narrative. Our limited experience would lead us to believe that it was a phantom conjured up by some unusual condition of his own brain; but we are fain to confess that there certainly do exist in nature phenomena such as baffle human reason; and it is possible that, for some hidden purposes of Providence, permission may occasionally be granted to those who have passed from this life to assume again for a time the form of their earthly tabernacle. We must, I say, be content to suspend our judgment on such matters; but in this instance the subsequent course of events is very difficult to explain, except on the supposition that there was then presented to my brother's view the actual bodily form of one long deceased. The dread which took possession of him was due, he has more than once told me when analysing his feelings long afterwards, to two predominant causes. Firstly, he felt that mental dislocation which accompanies the sudden subversion of preconceived theories, the sudden alteration of long habit, or even the occurrence of any circumstance beyond the walk of our daily experience. This I have observed myself in the perturbing effect which a sudden death, a grievous accident, or in recent years the declaration of war,* has exercised

21

upon all except the most lethargic or the most determined minds. Secondly, he experienced the profound self-abasement or mental annihilation caused by the near conception of a being of a superior order. In the presence of an existence wearing, indeed, the human form, but of attributes widely different and superior to his own, he felt the combined reverence and revulsion which even the noblest wild animals exhibit when brought for the first time face to face with man. The shock was so great that I feel persuaded it exerted an effect on him from which he never wholly recovered.

After an interval which seemed to him interminable, though it was only of a second's duration, he turned his eyes again to the occupant of the wicker chair. His faculties had so far recovered from the first shock as to enable him to see that the figure was that of a man perhaps thirty-five years of age and still youthful in appearance. The face was long and oval, the hair brown, and brushed straight off an exceptionally high forehead. His complexion was very pale or bloodless. He was clean shaven, and his finely cut mouth, with compressed lips, wore something of a sneering smile. His general expression was unpleasing, and from the first my brother felt as by intuition that there was present some malign and wicked influence. His eyes were not visible, as he kept them cast down, resting his head on his hand in the attitude of one listening. His face and even his dress were impressed so vividly upon John's mind, that he never had any difficulty in recalling them to his imagination; and he and I had afterwards an opportunity of verifying them in a remarkable manner. He wore a long cut-away coat of green cloth with an edge of gold embroidery, and a white satin waistcoat figured with rose-sprigs, a full cravat of rich lace, knee-breeches of buff silk, and stockings of the same. His shoes were of polished black leather with heavy silver buckles, and his costume in general recalled that worn a century ago. As my brother gazed at him, he got up, putting his hands on the arms of the chair to raise himself, and causing the creaking so often heard before. The hands forced themselves on my brother's notice: they were very white, with the long delicate fingers of a musician. He showed a considerable height; and still keeping his eyes on the floor, walked with an ordinary gait towards the end of the bookcase at the side of the room farthest from the window. He reached the bookcase, and then John suddenly lost sight of him. The figure did not fade gradually, but went out, as it were, like the flame of a suddenly extinguished candle.

The room was now filled with the clear light of the summer morning: the whole vision had lasted but a few seconds, but my brother knew that there was no possibility of his having been mistaken, that the mystery of the creaking chair was solved, that he had seen the man who had come evening by evening for a month past to listen to the rhythm of the *Gagliarda*. Terribly disturbed, he sat for some time half dreading and half expecting a return of the figure; but all remained unchanged: he saw nothing, nor did he dare to challenge its reappearance by playing again the *Gagliarda*, which seemed to have so strange an attraction for it. At last, in the full sunlight of a late June morning at Oxford, he heard the steps of early pedestrians on the pavement below his windows, the cry of a milkman, and other sounds which showed the world was awake.

23

It was after six o'clock, and going to his bedroom he flung himself on the outside of the bed for an hour's troubled slumber.

## *Chapter 4*

WHEN his servant called him about eight o'clock my brother sent a note to Mr. Gaskell at New College, begging him to come round to Magdalen Hall as soon as might be in the course of the morning. His summons was at once obeyed, and Mr. Gaskell was with him before he had finished breakfast. My brother was still much agitated, and at once told him what had happened the night before, detailing the various circumstances with minuteness, and not even concealing from him the sentiments which he entertained towards Miss Constance Temple. In narrating the appearance which he had seen in the chair, his agitation was still so excessive that he had difficulty in controlling his voice.

Mr. Gaskell heard him with much attention, and did not at once reply when John had finished his narration. At length he said, 'I suppose many friends would think it right to affect, even if they did not feel, an incredulity as to what you have just told me. They might consider it more prudent to attempt to allay your distress by persuading you that what you have seen has no objective reality, but is merely the phantasm of an excited imagination; that if you had not been in love, had not sat up all night, and had not thus overtaxed your physical powers, you would have seen no vision. I shall not argue thus, for I am as certainly convinced as of the fact that we sit here, that on all the nights when we have played this suite called the 'Areopagita,' there has been some one listening to us, and that you have at length been fortunate or unfortunate enough to see him.'

'Do not say fortunate,' said my brother; 'for I feel as though I shall never recover from last night's shock.'

'That is likely enough,' Mr. Gaskell answered, coolly; 'for as in the history of the race or individual, increased culture and a finer mental susceptibility necessarily impair the brute courage and powers of endurance which we note in savages, so any super-natural vision such as you have seen must be purchased at the cost of physical reaction. From the first evening that we played this music, and heard the noises mimicking so closely the sitting down and rising up of some person, I have felt convinced that causes other than those which we usually call natural were at work, and that we were very near the manifestation of some extraordinary phenomenon.'

'I do not quite apprehend your meaning.'

'I mean this,' he continued, 'that this man or spirit of a man has been sitting here night after night, and that we have not been able to see him, because our minds are dull and obtuse. Last night the elevating force of a strong passion, such as that which you have confided to me, combined with the power of fine music, so exalted your mind that you became endowed, as it were, with a sixth sense, and suddenly were enabled to see that which had pre-viously been invisible. To this sixth sense music gives, I believe, the key. We are at present only on the threshold of such a knowledge of that art as will enable us to use it eventually as the greatest of all humanising and educational agents. Music will prove a ladder to the loftier regions of thought; indeed I have long found for myself that I cannot attain to the highest range of my intellectual power except when hearing good music. All poets, and most writers of prose, will say that their thought is never so exalted, their sense of beauty and proportion never so just, as when they are listening either to the artificial music made by man, or to some of the grander tones of nature, such as the roar of a western ocean, or the sighing of wind in a clump of firs. Though I have often felt on such occasions on the very verge of some high mental discovery, and though a hand has been stretched forward as it were to rend the veil, yet it has never been vouchsafed me to see behind it. This you no doubt were allowed in a measure to do last night. You probably played the music with a deeper intuition than usual, and this, combined with the excitement under which you were already labouring, raised you for a moment to the required pitch of mental exaltation.'

'It is true,' John said, 'that I never felt the melody so deeply as when I played it last night.'

'Just so,' answered his friend; 'and there is probably some link between this air and the history of the man whom you saw last night; some fatal power in it which enables it to exert an attraction on him even after death. For we must remember that the influence of music, though always powerful, is not always for good. We can scarcely doubt that as certain forms of music tend to raise us above the sensuality of the animal, or the more degrading passion of material gain, and to transport us into the ether of higher thought, so other forms are directly calculated to awaken in us luxurious*emotions, and to whet those sensual appetites which it is the business of a philosopher not indeed to annihilate or to be ashamed of, but to keep rigidly in check. This possibility of music to effect evil as well as good I have seen recognised, and very aptly expressed in some beautiful verses by Mr. Keble*which I have just read:

> ' "Cease, stranger, cease those witching notes,
>    The art of syren choirs;
>  Hush the seductive voice that floats
>    Across the trembling wires.
>
>  Music's ethereal power was given
>    Not to dissolve our clay,
>  But draw Promethean beams from heaven
>    To purge the dross away."'

'They are fine lines,' said my brother, 'but I do not see how you apply your argument to the present instance.'

'I mean,' Mr. Gaskell answered, 'that I have little doubt that the melody of this *Gagliarda* has been connected in some manner with the life of the man you saw last night. It is not unlikely, either, that it was a favourite air of his whilst in the flesh, or even that it was played by himself or others at the moment of some crisis in his history. It is possible that such connection may be due merely to the innocent pleasure the melody gave him in life; but the nature of the music itself, and a peculiar effect it has upon my own thoughts, induce me to believe that it was associated with some occasion when he either fell into great sin or when some evil fate, perhaps even death itself, overtook him. You will remember I have told you that this air calls up to

27

my mind a certain scene of Italian revelry in which an Englishman takes part. It is true that I have never been able to fix his features in my mind, nor even to say exactly how he was dressed. Yet now some instinct tells me that it is this very man whom you saw last night. It is not for us to attempt to pierce the mystery which veils from our eyes the secrets of an after-death existence; but I can scarcely suppose that a spirit entirely at rest would feel so deeply the power of a certain melody as to be called back by it to his old haunts like a dog by his master's whistle. It is more probable that there is some evil history connected with the matter, and this, I think, we ought to consider if it be possible to unravel.'

My brother assenting, he continued, 'When this man left you, Johnnie, did he walk to the door?'

'No; he made for the side wall, and when he reached the end of the bookcase I lost sight of him.'

Mr. Gaskell went to the bookcase and looked for a moment at the titles of the books, as though expecting to see something in them to assist his inquiries; but finding apparently no clue, he said—

'This is the last time we shall meet for three months or more; let us play the *Gagliarda* and see if there be any response.'

My brother at first would not hear of this, showing a lively dread of challenging any reappearance of the figure he had seen: indeed he felt that such an event would probably fling him into a state of serious physical disorder. Mr. Gaskell, however, continued to press him, assuring him that the fact of his now being no longer alone should largely allay any fear on his part, and urging that this would be the last opportunity they would have of playing together for some months.

At last, being overborne, my brother took his violin, and Mr. Gaskell seated himself at the pianoforte. John was very agitated, and as he commenced the *Gagliarda* his hands trembled so that he could scarcely play the air. Mr. Gaskell also exhibited some nervousness, not performing with his customary correctness. But for the first time the charm failed: no noise accompanied the music, nor did anything of an unusual character occur. They repeated the whole suite, but with a similar result.

Both were surprised, but neither had any explanation to offer. My brother, who at first dreaded intensely a repetition of the vision, was now almost disappointed that nothing had occurred; so quickly does the mood of man change.

After some further conversation the young men parted for the Long Vacation—John returning to Worth Maltravers and Mr. Gaskell going to London, where he was to pass a few days before he proceeded to his home in Westmoreland.*

## Chapter 5

JOHN spent nearly the whole of this summer vacation at Worth Maltravers. He had been anxious to pay a visit to Royston; but the continued and serious illness of Mrs. Temple's sister had called her and Constance to Scotland, where they remained until the death of their relative allowed them to return to Derbyshire in the late autumn. John and I had been brought up together from childhood. When he was at Eton we had always spent the holidays at Worth, and after my dear mother's death, when we were left quite alone, the bonds of our love were

29

naturally drawn still closer. Even after my brother went to Oxford, at a time when most young men are anxious to enjoy a new-found liberty, and to travel or to visit friends in their vacation, John's ardent affection for me and for Worth Maltravers kept him at home; and he was pleased on most occasions to make me the partner of his thoughts and of his pleasures. This long vacation of 1842 was, I think, the happiest of our lives. In my case I know it was so, and I think it was happy also for him; for none could guess that the small cloud seen in the distance like a man's hand*was afterwards to rise and darken all his later days. It was a summer of brilliant and continued sunshine; many of the old people said that they could never recollect so fine a season, and both fruit and crops were alike abundant. John hired a small cutter-yacht, the *Palestine*, which he kept in our little harbour of Encombe,* and in which he and I made many excursions, visiting Weymouth, Lyme Regis, and other places of interest on the south coast.

In this summer my brother confided to me two secrets,—his love for Constance Temple, which indeed was after all no secret, and the history of the apparition which he had seen. This last filled me with inexpressible dread and distress. It seemed cruel and unnatural that any influence so dark and mysterious should thus intrude on our bright life, and from the first I had an impression which I could not entirely shake off, that any such appearance or converse of a disembodied spirit must portend misfortune, if not worse, to him who saw or heard it. It never occurred to me to combat or to doubt the reality of the vision; he believed that he had seen it, and his conviction was enough to convince me.

He had meant, he said, to tell no one, and had given
a promise to Mr. Gaskell to that effect; but I think
that he could not bear to keep such a matter in his
own breast, and within the first week of his return
he made me his confidant. I remember, my dear
Edward, the look everything wore on that sad night
when he first told me what afterwards proved so
terrible a secret. We had dined quite alone, and he
had been moody and depressed all the evening. It
was a chilly night, with some fret blowing up from
the sea. The moon showed that blunted and de-
formed appearance which she assumes a day or two
past the full, and the moisture in the air encircled
her with a stormy-looking halo. We had stepped
out of the dining-room windows on to the little
terrace looking down towards Smedmore*and Encombe. The glaucous*shrubs that grow in between
the balusters were wet and dripping with the salt
breath of the sea, and we could hear the waves
coming into the cove from the west. After standing
a minute I felt chill, and proposed that we should
go back to the billiard-room, where a fire was lit
on all except the warmest nights. 'No,' John said,
'I want to tell you something, Sophy,' and then we
walked on to the old boat summer-house. There he
told me everything. I cannot describe to you my
feelings of anguish and horror when he told me of
the appearance of the man. The interest of the tale
was so absorbing to me that I took no note of time,
nor of the cold night air, and it was only when it
was all finished that I felt how deadly chill it had
become. 'Let us go in, John' I said; 'I am cold and
feel benumbed.'

But youth is hopeful and strong, and in another
week the impression had faded from our minds,

31

and we were enjoying the full glory of midsummer weather, which I think only those know who have watched the blue sea come rippling in at the foot of the white chalk cliffs of Dorset.

I had felt a reluctance even so much as to hear the air of the *Gagliarda*, and though he had spoken to me of the subject on more than one occasion, my brother had never offered to play it to me. I knew that he had the copy of Graziani's suites with him at Worth Maltravers, because he had told me that he had brought it from Oxford; but I had never seen the book, and fancied that he kept it intentionally locked up. He did not, however, neglect the violin, and during the summer mornings, as I sat reading or working on the terrace, I often heard him playing to himself in the library. Though he had never even given me any description of the melody of the *Gagliarda*, yet I felt certain that he not infrequently played it. I cannot say how it was; but from the moment that I heard him one morning in the library performing an air set in a curiously low key, it forced itself upon my attention, and I knew, as it were by instinct, that it must be the *Gagliarda* of the 'Areopagita.' He was using a *sordino*\* and playing it very softly; but I was not mistaken. One wet afternoon in October, only a week before the time of his leaving us to return to Oxford for the autumn term, he walked into the drawing-room where I was sitting, and proposed that we should play some music together. To this I readily agreed. Though but a mediocre performer, I have always taken much pleasure in the use of the pianoforte, and esteemed it an honour whenever he asked me to play with him, since my powers as a musician were so very much inferior to his. After we had played several pieces, he took up an oblong music-book bound in white vellum, placed it upon the desk of the pianoforte, and proposed that we should play a suite by Graziani. I knew that he meant the 'Areopagita,' and begged him at once not to ask me to play it. He rallied me lightly on my fears, and said it would much please him to play it, as he had not heard the pianoforte part since he had left Oxford three months ago. I saw that he was eager to perform it, and being loath to disoblige so kind a brother during the last week of his stay at home, I at length overcame my scruples and set out to play it. But I was so alarmed at the possibility of any evil consequences ensuing, that when we commenced the *Gagliarda* I could scarcely find my notes. Nothing in any way unusual, however, occurred; and being reassured by this, and feeling an irresistible charm in the music, I finished the suite with more appearance of ease. My brother, however, was, I fear, not satisfied with my performance, and compared it, very possibly, with that of Mr. Gaskell, to which it was necessarily much inferior, both through weakness of execution and from my insufficient knowledge of the principles of the *basso continuo*. We stopped playing, and John stood looking out of the window across the sea, where the sky was clearing low down under the clouds. The sun went down behind Portland in a fiery glow which cheered us after a long day's rain. I had taken the copy of Graziani's suites off the desk, and was holding it on my lap turning over the old foxed and yellow pages. As I closed it a streak of evening sunlight fell across the room and lighted up a coat of arms stamped in gilt on the cover. It was much faded and would ordinarily have been hard to make

33

out; but the ray of strong light illumined it, and in an instant I recognised the same shield which Mr. Gaskell had pictured to himself as hanging on the musicians' gallery of his phantasmal dancing-room. My brother had often recounted to me this effort of his friend's imagination, and here I saw before me the same florid foreign blazon, a cherub's head blowing on three lilies on a gold field. This discovery was not only of interest, but afforded me much actual relief; for it accounted rationally for at least one item of the strange story. Mr. Gaskell had no doubt noticed at some time this shield stamped on the outside of the book, and bearing the impression of it unconsciously in his mind, had reproduced it in his imagined revels. I said as much to my brother, and he was greatly interested, and after examining the shield agreed that this was certainly a probable solution of that part of the mystery. On the 12th of October John returned to Oxford.

## Chapter 6

M y brother told me afterwards that more than once during the summer vacation he had seriously considered with himself the propriety of changing his rooms at Magdalen Hall. He had thought that it might thus be possible for him to get rid at once of the memory of the apparition, and of the fear of any reappearance of it. He could either have moved into another set of rooms in the Hall itself, or else gone into lodgings in the town—a usual proceeding, I am told, for gentlemen near the end of their course at Oxford. Would to God that he had indeed done so! but with the supineness which has, I fear,

my dear Edward, been too frequently a charac-
teristic of our family, he shrank from the trouble
such a course would involve, and the opening of the
autumn term found him still in his old rooms. You
will forgive me for entering here on a very brief
description of your father's sitting-room. It is, I
think, necessary for the proper understanding of
the incidents that follow. It was not a large room,
though probably the finest in the small buildings
of Magdalen Hall, and panelled from floor to ceiling with oak which successive generations had
obscured by numerous coats of paint. On one side
were two windows having an aspect on to New
College Lane, and fitted with deep cushioned seats
in the recesses. Outside these windows there were
boxes of flowers, the brightness of which formed in
the summer term a pretty contrast to the grey and
crumbling stone, and afforded pleasure at once to
the inmate and to passers-by. Along nearly the
whole length of the wall opposite to the windows,
some tenant in years long past had had mahogany
book-shelves placed, reaching to a height of perhaps five feet from the floor. They were handsomely
made in the style of the eighteenth century and
pleased my brother's taste. He had always exhibited
a partiality for books, and the fine library at Worth
Maltravers had no doubt contributed to foster his
tastes in that direction. At the time of which I write
he had formed a small collection for himself at
Oxford, paying particular attention to the bindings,
and acquiring many excellent specimens of that art,
principally, I think, from Messrs. Payne & Foss,*the
celebrated London booksellers.

Towards the end of the autumn term, having
occasion one cold day to take down a volume of

Plato from its shelf, he found to his surprise that the
book was quite warm. A closer examination easily
explained to him the reason—namely, that the flue
of a chimney, passing behind one end of the bookcase, sensibly heated* not only the wall itself, but
also the books in the shelves. Although he had been
in his rooms now near three years, he had never
before observed this fact; partly, no doubt, because
the books in these shelves were seldom handled,
being more for show as specimens of bindings than
for practical use. He was somewhat annoyed at
this discovery, fearing lest such a heat, which in
moderation is beneficial to books, might through its
excess warp the leather or otherwise injure the
bindings. Mr. Gaskell was sitting with him at the
time of the discovery, and indeed it was for his use
that my brother had taken down the volume of
Plato. He strongly advised that the bookcase should
be moved, and suggested that it would be better
to place it across that end of the room where the
pianoforte then stood. They examined it and found
that it would easily admit of removal, being, in fact,
only the frame of a bookcase, and showing at the
back the painted panelling of the wall. Mr. Gaskell
noted it as curious that all the shelves were fixed
and immovable except one at the end, which had
been fitted with the ordinary arrangement allowing
its position to be altered at will. My brother thought
that the change would improve the appearance
of his rooms, besides being advantageous for the
books, and gave instructions to the college upholsterer to have the necessary work carried out at
once.

The two young men had resumed their musical
studies, and had often played the 'Areopagita' and

other music of Graziani since their return to Oxford
in the autumn. They remarked, however, that the
chair no longer creaked during the *Gagliarda*—
and, in fact, that no unusual occurrence whatever
attended its performance. At times they were almost
tempted to doubt the accuracy of their own remem-
brances, and to consider as entirely mythical the
mystery which had so much disturbed them in the
summer term. My brother had also pointed out to
Mr. Gaskell my discovery that the coat of arms on
the outside of the music-book was identical with
that which his fancy portrayed on the musicians'
gallery. He readily admitted that he must at some
time have noticed and afterwards forgotten the
blazon on the book, and that an unconscious reminiscence of it had no doubt inspired his imagination
in this instance. He rebuked my brother for having
agitated me unnecessarily by telling me at all of so
idle a tale; and was pleased to write a few lines
to me at Worth Maltravers, felicitating me on my
shrewdness of perception, but speaking banteringly
of the whole matter.

On the evening of the 14th of November my
brother and his friend were sitting talking in the
former's room. The position of the bookcase had
been changed on the morning of that day, and Mr.
Gaskell had come round to see how the books
looked when placed at the end instead of at the side
of the room. He had applauded the new arrangement, and the young men sat long over the fire,
with a bottle of college port and a dish of medlars
which I had sent my brother from our famous tree
in the Upper Croft at Worth Maltravers. Later on
they fell to music, and played a variety of pieces,
performing also the 'Areopagita' suite. Mr. Gaskell

37

before he left complimented John on the improvement which the alteration in the place of the bookcase had made in his room, saying, 'Not only do the books in their present place very much enhance the general appearance of the room, but the change seems to me to have effected also a marked acoustical improvement. The oak panelling now exposed on the side of the room has given a resonant property to the wall which is peculiarly responsive to the tones of your violin. While you were playing the *Gagliarda* to-night, I could almost have imagined that someone in an adjacent room was playing the same air with a *sordino*, so distinct was the echo.'

Shortly after this he left.

My brother partly undressed himself in his bedroom, which adjoined, and then returning to his sitting-room, pulled the large wicker chair in front of the fire, and sat there looking at the glowing coals, and thinking perhaps of Miss Constance Temple. The night promised to be very cold, and the wind whistled down the chimney, increasing the comfortable sensation of the clear fire. He sat watching the ruddy reflection of the firelight dancing on the panelled wall, when he noticed that a picture placed where the end of the bookcase formerly stood was not truly hung, and needed adjustment. A picture hung askew was particularly offensive to his eyes, and he got up at once to alter it. He remembered as he went up to it that at this precise spot four months ago he had lost sight of the man's figure which he saw rise from the wicker chair, and at the memory felt an involuntary shudder. This reminiscence probably influenced his fancy also in another direction; for it seemed to him that very faintly, as though played far off, and with

38

the *sordino*, he could hear the air of the *Gagliarda*.
He put one hand behind the picture to steady it,
and as he did so his finger struck a very slight pro-
jection in the wall. He pulled the picture a little to
one side, and saw that what he had touched was
the back of a small hinge sunk in the wall, and
almost obliterated with many coats of paint. His
curiosity was excited, and he took a candle from the
table and examined the wall carefully. Inspection
soon showed him another hinge a little further up,
and by degrees he perceived that one of the panels
had been made at some time in the past to open,
and serve probably as the door of a cupboard. At
this point he assured me that a feverish anxiety to
re-open this cupboard door took possession of him,
and that the intense excitement filled his mind
which we experience on the eve of a discovery
which we fancy may produce important results. He
loosened the paint in the cracks with a penknife,
and attempted to press open the door; but his
instrument was not adequate to such a purpose, and
all his efforts remained ineffective. His excitement
had now reached an overmastering pitch; for he
anticipated, though he knew not why, some strange
discovery to be made in this sealed cupboard. He
looked round the room for some weapon with which
to force the door, and at length with his penknife
cut away sufficient wood at the joint to enable him
to insert the end of the poker in the hole. The clock
in the New College Tower struck one at the exact
moment when with a sharp effort he thus forced
open the door. It appeared never to have had a
fastening, but merely to have been stuck fast by the
accumulation of paint. As he bent it slowly back
upon the rusted hinges his heart beat so fast that he

could scarcely catch his breath, though he was conscious all the while of a ludicrous aspect of his position, knowing that it was most probable that the cavity within would be found empty. The cupboard was small but very deep, and in the obscure light seemed at first to contain nothing except a small heap of dust and cobwebs. His sense of disappointment was keen as he thrust his hand into it, but changed again in a moment to breathless interest on feeling something solid in what he had imagined to be only an accumulation of mould and dirt. He snatched up a candle, and holding this in one hand, with the other pulled out an object from the cupboard and put it on the table, covered as it was with the curious drapery of black and clinging cobwebs which I have seen adhering to bottles of old wine. It lay there between the dish of medlars and the decanter, veiled indeed with thick dust as with a mantle, but revealing beneath it the shape and contour of a violin.

## *Chapter* 7

JOHN was excited at his discovery, and felt his thoughts confused in a manner that I have often experienced myself on the unexpected receipt of news interesting me deeply, whether for pleasure or pain. Yet at the same time he was half amused at his own excitement, feeling that it was childish to be moved over an event so simple as the finding of a violin in an old cupboard. He soon collected himself and took up the instrument, using great care, as he feared lest age should have rendered the wood brittle or rotten. With some vigorous puffs of breath and a little dusting with a handkerchief he removed the heavy outer coating of cobwebs, and began to see more clearly the delicate curves of the body and of the scroll. A few minutes' more gentle handling left the instrument sufficiently clean to enable him to appreciate its chief points. Its seclusion from the outer world, which the heavy accumulation of dust proved to have been for many years, did not seem to have damaged it in the least; and the fact of a chimney-flue passing through the wall at no great distance had no doubt conduced to maintain the air in the cupboard at an equable temperature. So far as he was able to judge, the wood was as sound as when it left the maker's hands; but the strings were of course broken, and curled up in little tangled knots. The body was of a light-red colour, with a varnish of peculiar lustre and softness. The neck seemed rather longer than ordinary, and the scroll was remarkably bold and free.*

The violin which my brother was in the habit of using was a fine *Pressenda*,* given to him on his fifteenth birthday by Mr. Thoresby, his guardian. It was of that maker's later and best period, and a copy of the Stradivarius model.* John took this from its case and laid it side by side with his new discovery, meaning to compare them for size and form. He perceived at once that while the model of both was identical, the superiority of the older violin in every detail was so marked as to convince him that it was undoubtedly an instrument of exceptional value. The extreme beauty of its varnish impressed him vividly, and though he had never seen a genuine Stradivarius, he felt a conviction

41

gradually gaining on him that he stood in the presence of a masterpiece of that great maker. On looking into the interior he found that surprisingly little dust had penetrated into it, and by blowing through the sound-holes he soon cleared it sufficiently to enable him to discern a label. He put the candle close to him, and held the violin up so that a little patch of light fell through the sound-hole on to the label. His heart leapt with a violent pulsation as he read the characters, 'Antonius Stradiuarius Cremonensis faciebat, 1704.'*Under ordinary circumstances it would naturally be concluded that such a label was a forgery, but the conditions were entirely altered in the case of a violin found in a forgotten cupboard, with proof so evident of its having remained there for a very long period.

He was not at that time as familiar with the history of the fiddles of the great maker as he, and indeed I also, afterwards became. Thus he was unable to decide how far the exact year of its manufacture would determine its value as compared with other specimens of Stradivarius. But although the *Pressenda* he had been used to play on was always considered a very fine instrument both in make and varnish, his new discovery so far excelled it in both points as to assure him that it must be one of the Cremonese master's greatest productions.

He examined the violin minutely, scrutinising each separate feature, and finding each in turn to be of the utmost perfection, so far as his knowledge of the instrument would enable him to judge. He lit more candles that he might be able better to see it, and holding it on his knees, sat still admiring it until the dying fire and increasing cold warned him that the night was now far advanced. At last, carrying it to his bedroom, he locked it carefully into a drawer and retired for the night.

He woke next morning with that pleasurable consciousness of there being some reason for gladness, which we feel on waking in seasons of happiness, even before our reason, locating it, reminds us what the actual source of our joy may be. He was at first afraid lest his excitement, working on the imagination, should have led him on the previous night to overestimate the fineness of the instrument, and he took it from the drawer half expecting to be disappointed with its daylight appearance. But a glance sufficed to convince him of the unfounded nature of his suspicions. The various beauties which he had before observed were enhanced a hundred-fold by the light of day, and he realised more fully than ever that the instrument was one of altogether exceptional value.

And now, my dear Edward, I shall ask your forgiveness if in the history I have to relate any observation of mine should seem to reflect on the character of your late father, Sir John Maltravers. And I beg you to consider that your father was also my dear and only brother, and that it is inexpressibly painful to me to recount any actions of his which may not seem becoming to a noble gentleman, as he surely was. I only now proceed because, when very near his end, he most strictly enjoined me to narrate these circumstances to you fully when you should come of age. We must humbly remember that to God alone belongs judgment, and that it is not for poor mortals to decide what is right or wrong in certain instances for their fellows, but that each should strive most earnestly to do his own duty.

Your father entirely concealed from me the discovery he had made. It was not till long afterwards that I had it narrated to me, and I only obtained a knowledge of this and many other of the facts which I am now telling you at a date much subsequent to their actual occurrence.

He explained to his servant that he had discovered and opened an old cupboard in the panelling, without mentioning the fact of his having found anything in it, but merely asking him to give instructions for the paint to be mended and the cupboard put into a usable state. Before he had finished a very late breakfast Mr. Gaskell was with him, and it has been a source of lasting regret to me that my brother concealed also from his most intimate and trusted friend the discovery of the previous night. He did, indeed, tell him that he had found and opened an old cupboard in the panelling, but made no mention of there having been anything within. I cannot say what prompted him to this action; for the two young men had for long been on such intimate terms that the one shared almost as a matter of course with the other any pleasure or pain which might fall to his lot. Mr. Gaskell looked at the cupboard with some interest, saying afterwards, 'I know now, Johnnie, why the one shelf of the bookcase which stood there was made movable when all the others were fixed. Some former occupant used the cupboard, no doubt, as a secret receptacle for his treasures, and masked it with the book-shelves in front. Who knows what he kept in here, or who he was! I should not be surprised if he were that very man who used to come here so often to hear us play the "Areopagita," and whom you saw that night last June. He had the one shelf made, you see, to move so as to give him access to this cavity on occasion: then when he left Oxford, or perhaps died, the mystery was forgotten, and with a few times of painting the cracks closed up.'

Mr. Gaskell shortly afterwards took his leave as he had a lecture to attend, and my brother was left alone to the contemplation of his new-found treasure. After some consideration he determined that he would take the instrument to London, and obtain the opinion of an expert as to its authenticity and value. He was well acquainted with the late Mr. George Smart, the celebrated London dealer,* from whom his guardian, Mr. Thoresby, had purchased the *Pressenda* violin which John commonly used. Besides being a dealer in valuable instruments, Mr. Smart was a famous collector of Stradivarius fiddles, esteemed one of the first authorities in Europe in that domain of art, and author of a valuable work of reference in connection with it. It was to him, therefore, that my brother decided to submit the violin, and he wrote a letter to Mr. Smart saying that he should give himself the pleasure of waiting on him the next day on a matter of business. He then called on his tutor, and with some excuse obtained leave to journey to London the next morning. He spent the rest of the day in very carefully cleaning the violin, and noon of the next saw him with it, securely packed, in Mr. Smart's establishment in Bond Street.

Mr. Smart received Sir John Maltravers with deference, demanded in what way he could serve him; and on hearing that his opinion was required on the authenticity of a violin, smiled somewhat dubiously and led the way into a back parlour.

'My dear Sir John,' he said, 'I hope you have not

been led into buying any instrument by a faith in its antiquity. So many good copies of instruments by famous makers and bearing their labels are now afloat, that the chances of obtaining a genuine fiddle from an unrecognised source are quite remote; of hundreds of violins submitted to me for opinion, I find that scarce one in fifty is actually that which it represents itself to be. In fact the only safe rule,' he added as a professional commentary, 'is never to buy a violin unless you obtain it from a dealer with a reputation to lose, and are prepared to pay a reasonable price for it.'

My brother had meanwhile unpacked the violin and laid it on the table. As he took from it the last leaf of silver paper he saw Mr. Smart's smile of condescension fade, and assuming a look of interest and excitement, he stepped forward, took the violin in his hands, and scrutinised it minutely. He turned it over in silence for some moments, looking narrowly at each feature, and even applying the test of a magnifying-glass. At last he said with an altered tone, 'Sir John, I have had in my hands nearly all the finest productions of Stradivarius, and thought myself acquainted with every instrument of note that ever left his workshop; but I confess myself mistaken, and apologise to you for the doubt which I expressed as to the instrument you had brought me. This violin is of the great master's golden period,* is incontestably genuine, and finer in some respects than any Stradivarius that I have ever seen, not even excepting the famous *Dolphin** itself. You need be under no apprehension as to its authenticity: no connoisseur could hold it in his hand for a second and entertain a doubt on the point.'

My brother was greatly pleased at so favourable a verdict, and Mr. Smart continued—

'The varnish is of that rich red which Stradivarius used in his best period after he had abandoned the yellow tint copied by him at first from his master Amati.* I have never seen a varnish thicker or more lustrous, and it shows on the back that peculiar shading to imitate wear which we term "breaking up."* The purfling* also is of an unsurpassable excellence. Its execution is so fine that I should recommend you to use a magnifying-glass for its examination.'

So he ran on, finding from moment to moment some new beauties to admire.

My brother was at first anxious lest Mr. Smart should ask him whence so extraordinary an instrument came, but he saw that the expert had already jumped to a conclusion in the matter. He knew that John had recently come of age, and evidently supposed that he had found the violin among the heirlooms of Worth Maltravers. John allowed Mr. Smart to continue in this misconception, merely saying that he had discovered the instrument in an old cupboard, where he had reason to think it had remained hidden for many years.

'Are there no records attached to so splendid an instrument?' asked Mr. Smart. 'I suppose it has been with your family a number of years. Do you not know how it came into their possession?'

I believe this was the first occasion on which it had occurred to John to consider what right he had to the possession of the instrument. He had been so excited by its discovery that the question of ownership had never hitherto crossed his mind.

47

The unwelcome suggestion that it was not his after all, that the College might rightfully prefer a claim to it, presented itself to him for a moment; but he set it instantly aside, quieting his conscience with the reflection that this at least was not the moment to make such a disclosure.

He fenced with Mr. Smart's inquiry as best he could, saying that he was ignorant of the history of the instrument, but not contradicting the assumption that it had been a long time in his family's possession.

'It is indeed singular,' Mr. Smart continued, 'that so magnificent an instrument should have lain buried so long; that even those best acquainted with such matters should be in perfect ignorance of its existence. I shall have to revise the list of famous instruments in the next edition of my "History of the Violin,"*and to write,' he added smiling, 'a special paragraph on the "Worth Maltravers Stradivarius."'

After much more, which I need not narrate, Mr. Smart suggested that the violin should be left with him that he might examine it more at leisure, and that my brother should return in a week's time, when he would have the instrument opened, an operation which would be in any case advisable. 'The interior,' he added, 'appears to be in a strictly original state, and this I shall be able to ascertain when opened. The label is perfect, but if I am not mistaken I can see something higher up on the back which appears like a second label. This excites my interest, as I know of no instance of an instrument bearing two labels.'

To this proposal my brother readily assented, being anxious to enjoy alone the pleasure of so gratifying a discovery as that of the undoubted authenticity of the instrument.

As he thought over the matter more at leisure, he grew anxious as to what might be the import of the second label in the violin of which Mr. Smart had spoken. I blush to say that he feared lest it might bear some owner's name or other inscription proving that the instrument had not been so long in the Maltravers family as he had allowed Mr. Smart to suppose. So within so short a time it was possible that Sir John Maltravers of Worth should dread being detected, if not in an absolute falsehood, at least in having by his silence assented to one.

During the ensuing week John remained in an excited and anxious condition. He did little work, and neglected his friends, having his thoughts continually occupied with the strange discovery he had made. I know also that his sense of honour troubled him, and that he was not satisfied with the course he was pursuing. The evening of his return from London he went to Mr. Gaskell's rooms at New College, and spent an hour conversing with him on indifferent subjects. In the course of their talk he proposed to his friend as a moral problem the question of the course of action to be taken were one to find some article of value concealed in his room. Mr. Gaskell answered unhesitatingly that he should feel bound to disclose it to the authorities. He saw that my brother was ill at ease, and with a clearness of judgment which he always exhibited, guessed that he had actually made some discovery of this sort in the old cupboard in his rooms. He could not divine, of course, the exact nature of the object found, and thought it might probably relate to a hoard of gold; but insisted with much urgency on the obligation to at once disclose anything of this kind. My brother, however, misled, I fear, by that feeling of inalienable right which the treasure-hunter experiences over the treasure, paid no more attention to the advice of his friend than to the promptings of his own conscience, and went his way.

From that day, my dear Edward, he began to exhibit a spirit of secretiveness and reserve entirely alien to his own open and honourable disposition, and also saw less of Mr. Gaskell. His friend tried, indeed, to win his confidence and affection in every way in his power; but in spite of this the rift between them widened insensibly, and my brother lost the fellowship and counsel of a true friend at a time when he could ill afford to be without them.

He returned to London the ensuing week, and met Mr. George Smart by appointment in Bond Street. If the expert had been enthusiastic on a former occasion, he was ten times more so on this. He spoke in terms almost of rapture about the violin. He had compared it with two magnificent instruments in the collection of the late Mr. James Loding, then the finest in Europe;*and it was admittedly superior to either, both in the delicate markings of its wood and singularly fine varnish. 'Of its tone,' he said, 'we cannot, of course, yet pronounce with certainty, but I am very sure that its voice will not belie its splendid exterior. It has been carefully opened, and is in a strangely perfect condition. Several persons eminently qualified to judge unite with me in considering that it has been exceedingly little played upon, and admit that never has so intact an interior been seen. The scroll is exceptionally bold and original. Although undoubtedly from the hand of the great master, this is of a pattern entirely different and distinct from any that have ever come under my observation.'

He then pointed out to my brother that the side lines of the scroll were unusually deeply cut, and that the front of it projected far more than is common with such instruments.

'The most remarkable feature,' he concluded, 'is that the instrument bears a double label. Besides the label which you have already seen bearing "*Antonius Stradiuarius Cremonensis faciebat*," with the date of his most splendid period, 1704, so clearly that the ink seems scarcely dry, there is another smaller one higher up on the back which I will show you.'

He took the violin apart and showed him a small label with characters written in faded ink. 'That is the writing of Antonio Stradivarius himself, and is easily recognisable, though it is much firmer than a specimen which I once saw, written in extreme old age, and giving his name and the date 1736. He was then ninety-two,* and died in the following year. But this, as you will see, does not give his name, but merely the two words "*Porphyrius philosophus*."*What this may refer to I cannot say: it is beyond my experience. My friend Mr. Calvert has suggested that Stradivarius may have dedicated this violin to the pagan philosopher, or named it after him; but this seems improbable. I have, indeed, heard of two famous violins being called "Peter" and "Paul,"* but the instances of such naming are very rare; and I believe it to be altogether without precedent to find a name attached thus on a label.

'In any case, I must leave this matter to your

ingenuity to decipher. Neither the sound-post nor the bass-bar have ever been moved, and you see here a Stradivarius violin wearing exactly the same appearance as it once wore in the great master's workshop, and in exactly the same condition; yet I think the belly is sufficiently strong to stand modern stringing.* I should advise you to leave the instrument with me for some little while, that I may give it due care and attention and ensure its being properly strung.'

My brother thanked him and left the violin with him, saying that he would instruct him later by letter to what address he wished it sent.

## *Chapter 8*

WITHIN a few days after this the autumn term came to an end, and in the second week of December John returned to Worth Maltravers for the Christmas vacation. His advent was always a very great pleasure to me, and on this occasion I had looked forward to his company with anticipation keener than usual, as I had been disappointed of the visit of a friend and had spent the last month alone. After the joy of our first meeting had somewhat sobered, it was not long before I remarked a change in his manner, which puzzled me. It was not that he was less kind to me, for I think he was even more tenderly forbearing and gentle than I had ever known him, but I had an uneasy feeling that some shadow had crept in between us. It was the small cloud rising in the distance that afterwards darkened his horizon and mine. I missed the old candour and open-hearted frankness that he had always shown; and there seemed to be always something in the background which he was trying to keep from me. It was obvious that his thoughts were constantly elsewhere, so much so that on more than one occasion he returned vague and incoherent answers to my questions. At times I was content to believe that he was in love, and that his thoughts were with Miss Constance Temple; but even so, I could not persuade myself that his altered manner was to be thus entirely accounted for. At other times a dazed air, entirely foreign to his bright disposition, which I observed particularly in the morning, raised in my mind the terrible suspicion that he was in the habit of taking some secret narcotic or other deleterious drug.

We had never spent a Christmas away from Worth Maltravers, and it had always been a season of quiet joy for both of us. But under these altered circumstances it was a great relief and cause of thankfulness to me to receive a letter from Mrs. Temple inviting us both to spend Christmas and New Year at Royston. This invitation had upon my brother precisely the effect that I had hoped for. It roused him from his moody condition, and he professed much pleasure in accepting it, especially as he had never hitherto been in Derbyshire.

There was a small but very agreeable party at Royston, and we passed a most enjoyable fortnight. My brother seemed thoroughly to have shaken off his indisposition; and I saw my fondest hopes realised in the warm attachment which was evidently springing up between him and Miss Constance Temple.

Our visit drew near its close, and it was within a week of John's return to Oxford. Mrs. Temple celebrated the termination of the Christmas festivities by giving a ball on Twelfth-night, at which a large party were present, including most of the county families. Royston was admirably adapted for such entertainments, from the number and great size of its reception-rooms. Though Elizabethan in date and external appearance, succeeding generations had much modified and enlarged the house; and an ancestor in the middle of the last century had built at the back an enormous hall after the classic model, and covered it with a dome or cupola. In this room the dancing went forward. Supper was served in the older hall in the front, and it was while this was in progress that a thunderstorm began. The rarity of such a phenomenon in the depth of winter formed the subject of general remark; but though the lightning was extremely brilliant, being seen distinctly through the curtained windows, the storm appeared to be at some distance, and, except for one peal, the thunder was not loud. After supper dancing was resumed, and I was taking part in a polka (called, I remember, the *King Pippin*),* when my partner pointed out that one of the footmen wished to speak with me. I begged him to lead me to one side, and the servant then informed me that my brother was ill. Sir John, he said, had been seized with a fainting fit, but had been got to bed, and was being attended by Dr. Empson, a physician who chanced to be present among the visitors.

I at once left the hall and hurried to my brother's room. On the way I met Mrs. Temple and Constance, the latter much agitated and in tears. Mrs. Temple assured me that Dr. Empson reported favourably of my brother's condition, attributing his faintness to over-exertion in the dancing-room.

54

The medical man had got him to bed with the assistance of Sir John's valet, had given him a quieting draught, and ordered that he should not be disturbed for the present. It was better that I should not enter the room; she begged that I would kindly comfort and reassure Constance, who was much upset, while she herself returned to her guests.

I led Constance to my bedroom, where there was a bright fire burning, and calmed her as best I could. Her interest in my brother was evidently very real and unaffected, and while not admitting her partiality for him in words, she made no effort to conceal her sentiments from me. I kissed her tenderly, and bade her narrate the circumstances of John's attack.

It seemed that after supper they had gone upstairs into the music-room, and he had himself proposed that they should walk thence into the picture-gallery, where they would better be able to see the lightning, which was then particularly vivid. The picture-gallery at Royston is a very long, narrow, and rather low room, running the whole length of the south wing, and terminating in a large Tudor oriel or flat bay window looking east. In this oriel they had sat for some time watching the flashes, and the wintry landscape revealed for an instant and then plunged into outer blackness. The gallery itself was not illuminated, and the effect of the lightning was very fine.

There had been an unusually bright flash accompanied by that single reverberating peal of thunder which I had previously noticed. Constance had spoken to my brother, but he had not replied, and in a moment she saw that he had swooned. She summoned aid without delay, but it was some short time before consciousness had been restored to him.

She had concluded this narrative, and sat holding my hand in hers. We were speculating on the cause of my brother's illness, thinking it might be due to over-exertion, or to sitting in a chilly atmosphere as the picture-gallery was not warmed, when Mrs. Temple knocked at the door and said that John was now more composed and desired earnestly to see me.

On entering my brother's bedroom I found him sitting up in bed wearing a dressing-gown. Parnham, his valet, who was arranging the fire, left the room as I came in. A chair stood at the head of the bed and I sat down by him. He took my hand in his and without a word burst into tears. 'Sophy,' he said, 'I am so unhappy, and I have sent for you to tell you of my trouble, because I know you will be forbearing to me. An hour ago all seemed so bright. I was sitting in the picture-gallery with Constance, whom I love dearly. We had been watching the lightning, till the thunder had grown fainter and the storm seemed past. I was just about to ask her to become my wife when a brighter flash than all the rest burst on us, and I saw—I saw, Sophy, standing in the gallery as close to me as you are now—I saw—that man I told you about at Oxford; and then this faintness came on me.'

'Whom do you mean?' I said, not understanding what he spoke of, and thinking for a moment he referred to someone else. 'Did you see Mr. Gaskell?'

'No, it was not he; but that dead man whom I saw rising from my wicker chair the night you went away from Oxford.'

You will perhaps smile at my weakness, my dear
Edward, and indeed I had at that time no justifica-
tion for it; but I assure you that I have not yet forgotten, and never shall forget, the impression of
overwhelming horror which his words produced
upon me. It seemed as though a fear which had
hitherto stood vague and shadowy in the background, began now to advance towards me, gathering more distinctness as it approached. There was to
me something morbidly terrible about the apparition of this man at such a momentous crisis in my
brother's life, and I at once recognised that unknown
form as being the shadow which was gradually
stealing between John and myself. Though I feigned
incredulity as best I might, and employed those
arguments or platitudes which will always be used
on such occasions, urging that such a phantom
could only exist in a mind disordered by physical
weakness, my brother was not deceived by my
words, and perceived in a moment that I did not
even believe in them myself.

'Dearest Sophy,' he said, with a much calmer air,
'let us put aside all dissimulation. I *know* that what
I have to-night seen, and that what I saw last
summer at Oxford, are *not* phantoms of my brain;
and I believe that you too in your inmost soul are
convinced of this truth. Do not, therefore, endeavour to persuade me to the contrary. If I am not
to believe the evidence of my senses, it were better
at once to admit my madness—and I know that I
am not mad. Let us rather consider what such an
appearance can portend, and who the man is who
is thus presented. I cannot explain to you why this
appearance inspires me with so great a revulsion.
I can only say that in its presence I seem to be

brought face to face with some abysmal and repellent wickedness. It is not that the form he wears is hideous. Last night I saw him exactly as I saw him at Oxford—his face waxen pale, with a sneering mouth, the same lofty forehead, and hair brushed straight up so as almost to appear standing on end. He wore the same long coat of green cloth and white waistcoat. He seemed as if he had been standing listening to what we said, though we had not seen him till this bright flash of lightning made him manifest. You will remember that when I saw him at Oxford his eyes were always cast down, so that I never knew their colour. This time they were wide open; indeed he was looking full at us, and they were a light brown and very brilliant.'

I saw that my brother was exciting himself, and was still weak from his recent swoon. I knew, too, that any ordinary person of strong mind would say at once that his brain wandered, and yet I had a dreadful conviction all the while that what he told me was the truth. All I could do was to beg him to calm himself, and to reflect how vain such fancies must be. 'We must trust, dear John,' I said, 'in God. I am sure that so long as we are not living in conscious sin, we shall never be given over to any evil power; and I know my brother too well to think that he is doing anything he knows to be evil. If there be evil spirits, as we are taught there are, we are taught also that there are good spirits stronger than they, who will protect us.'

So I spoke with him a little while, until he grew calmer; and then we talked of Constance and of his love for her. He was deeply pleased to hear from me how she had shown such obvious signs of interest in his illness, and sincere affection for him.

In any case, he made me promise that I would never mention to her either what he had seen this night or last summer at Oxford.

It had grown late, and the undulating beat of the dances, which had been distinctly sensible* in his room—even though we could not hear any definite noise—had now çeased. Mrs. Temple knocked at the door as she went to bed and inquired how he did, giving him at the same time a kind message of sympathy from Constance, which afforded him much gratification. After she had left I prepared also to retire; but before going he begged me to take a prayer-book lying on the table, and to read aloud a collect which he pointed out. It was that for the second Sunday in Lent,* and evidently well known to him. As I read it the words seemed to bear a new and deeper significance, and my heart repeated with fervour the petition for protection from those 'evil thoughts which may assault and hurt the soul.' I bade him good night and went away very sorrowful. Parnham, at John's request, had arranged to sleep on a sofa in his master's bed-room.

I rose betimes the next morning and inquired at my brother's room how he was. Parnham reported that he had passed a restless night, and on entering a little later I found him in a high fever, slightly delirious, and evidently not so well as when I saw him last. Mrs. Temple, with much kindness and forethought, had begged Dr. Empson to remain at Royston for the night, and he was soon in attendance on his patient. His verdict was sufficiently grave: John was suffering from a sharp access of brain-fever; his condition afforded cause for alarm; he could not answer for any turn his sickness might take. You will easily imagine how much this intelligence*affected me; and Mrs. Temple and Constance shared my anxiety and solicitude. Constance and I talked much with one another that morning. Unaffected anxiety had largely removed her reserve, and she spoke openly of her feelings towards my brother, not concealing her partiality for him. I on my part let her understand how welcome to me would be any union between her and John, and how sincerely I should value her as a sister.

It was a wild winter's morning, with some snow falling and a high wind. The house was in the disordered condition which is generally observable on the day following a ball or other important festivity. I roamed restlessly about, and at last found my way to the picture-gallery, which had formed the scene of John's adventure on the previous night. I had never been in this part of the house before, as it contained no facilities for heating, and so often remained shut in the winter months. I found a listless pleasure in admiring the pictures which lined the walls, most of them being portraits of former members of the family, including the famous picture of Sir Ralph Temple and his family, attributed to Holbein.* I had reached the end of the gallery and sat down in the oriel watching the snow-flakes falling sparsely, and the evergreens below me waving wildly in the sudden rushes of the wind. My thoughts were busy with the events of the previous evening,—with John's illness, with the ball,—and I found myself humming the air of a waltz that had caught my fancy. At last I turned away from the garden scene towards the gallery, and as I did so my eyes fell on a remarkable picture just opposite to me.

It was a full-length portrait of a young man, life-size, and I had barely time to appreciate even its main features when I knew that I had before me the painted counterfeit*of my brother's vision. The discovery caused me a violent shock, and it was with an infinite repulsion that I recognised at once the features and dress of the man whom John had seen rising from the chair at Oxford. So accurately had my brother's imagination described him to me, that it seemed as if I had myself seen him often before. I noted each feature, comparing them with my brother's description, and finding them all familiar and corresponding exactly. He was a man still in the prime of life. His features were regular and beautifully modelled; yet there was something in his face that inspired me with a deep aversion, though his brown eyes were open and brilliant. His mouth was sharply cut, with a slight sneer on the lips, and his complexion of that extreme pallor which had impressed itself deeply on my brother's imagination and my own.

After the first intense surprise had somewhat subsided, I experienced a feeling of great relief, for here was an extraordinary explanation of my brother's vision of last night. It was certain that the flash of lightning had lit up this ill-starred picture, and that to his predisposed fancy the painted figure had stood forth as an actual embodiment. That such an incident, however startling, should have been able to fling John into a brain-fever, showed that he must already have been in a very low and reduced state, on which excitement would act much more powerfully than on a more robust condition of health. A similar state of weakness, perturbed by the excitement of his passion for Constance Temple, might surely also have conjured up the vision which

he thought he saw the night of our leaving Oxford
in the summer. These thoughts, my dear Edward,
gave me great relief; for it seemed a comparatively trivial matter that my brother should be ill,
even seriously ill, if only his physical indisposition
could explain away the supernatural dread which
had haunted us for the past six months. The clouds
were breaking up. It was evident that John had
been seriously unwell for some months; his physical
weakness had acted on his brain; and I had lent
colour to his wandering fancies by being alarmed
by them, instead of rejecting them at once or gently
laughing them away as I should have done. But
these glad thoughts took me too far, and I was
suddenly brought up by a reflection that did not
admit of so simple an explanation. If the man's form
my brother saw at Oxford were merely an effort
of disordered imagination, how was it that he had
been able to describe it exactly like that represented
in this picture? He had never in his life been to
Royston, therefore he could have no image of the
picture impressed unconsciously on or hidden away
in his mind. Yet his description had never varied.
It had been so close as to enable me to produce in
my fancy a vivid representation of the man he had
seen; and here I had before me the features and
dress exactly reproduced. In the presence of a
coincidence so extraordinary reason stood con-
founded, and I knew not what to think. I walked
nearer to the picture and scrutinised it closely.

The dress corresponded in every detail with that
which my brother had described the figure as wearing at Oxford: a long cut-away coat of green cloth
with an edge of gold embroidery, a white satin
waistcoat with sprigs of embroidered roses, gold-

lace at the pocket-holes, buff silk knee-breeches, and low down on the finely modelled neck a full cravat of rich lace. The figure was posed negligently against a fluted stone pedestal or short column on which the left elbow leant, and the right foot was crossed lightly over the left. His shoes were of polished black leather with heavy silver buckles, and the whole costume was very old-fashioned, and such as I had only seen worn at fancy-dress balls. On the foot of the pedestal was the painter's name, 'BATTONI pinxit, Romæ, 1750.'*On the top of the pedestal, and under his left elbow, was a long roll apparently of music, of which one end, unfolded, hung over the edge.

For some minutes I stood still gazing at this portrait which so much astonished me, but turned on hearing footsteps in the gallery, and saw Constance, who had come to seek for me.

'Constance,' I said, 'whose portrait is this? It is a very striking picture, is it not?'

'Yes, it is a splendid painting, though of a very bad man. His name was Adrian Temple, and he once owned Royston. I do not know much about him, but I believe he was very wicked and very clever. My mother would be able to tell you more. It is a picture we none of us like, although so finely painted; and perhaps because he was always pointed out to me from childhood as a bad man, I have myself an aversion to it. It is singular that when the very bright flash of lightning came last night while your brother John and I were sitting here, it lit this picture with a dazzling glare that made the figure stand out so strangely as to seem almost alive. It was just after that I found that John had fainted.'

The memory was not a pleasant one for either of us and we changed the subject. 'Come,' I said, 'let us leave the gallery, it is very cold here.'

Though I said nothing more at the time, her words had made a great impression on me. It was so strange that, even with the little she knew of this Adrian Temple, she should speak at once of his notoriously evil life, and of her personal dislike to the picture. Remembering what my brother had said on the previous night, that in the presence of this man he felt himself brought face to face with some indescribable wickedness, I could not but be surprised at the coincidence. The whole story seemed to me now to resemble one of those puzzle pictures or maps which I have played with as a child, where each bit fits into some other until the outline is complete. It was as if I were finding the pieces one by one of a bygone history, and fitting them to one another until some terrible whole should be gradually built up and stand out in its complete deformity.

Dr. Empson spoke gravely of John's illness, and entertained without reluctance the proposal of Mrs. Temple, that Dr. Dobie, a celebrated physician in Derby, should be summoned to a consultation. Dr. Dobie came more than once, and was at last able to report an amendment in John's condition, though both the doctors absolutely forbade anyone to visit him, and said that under the most favourable circumstances a period of some weeks must elapse before he could be moved.

Mrs. Temple invited me to remain at Royston until my brother should be sufficiently convalescent to be moved; and both she and Constance, while regretting the cause, were good enough to express

themselves pleased that accident should detain me
so long with them.

As the reports of the doctors became gradually
more favourable, and our minds were in consequence more free to turn to other subjects, I spoke
to Mrs. Temple one day about the picture, saying
that it interested me, and asking for some particu-
lars as to the life of Adrian Temple.

'My dear child,' she said, 'I had rather that you
should not exhibit any curiosity as to this man,
whom I wish that we had not to call an ancestor.
I know little of him myself, and indeed his life was
of such a nature as no woman, much less a young
girl, would desire to be well acquainted with. He
was, I believe, a man of remarkable talent, and
spent most of his time between Oxford and Italy,
though he visited Royston occasionally, and built
the large hall here, which we use as a dancing-room.
Before he was twenty wild stories were prevalent
as to his licentious life, and by thirty his name was
a by-word among sober and upright people. He had
constantly with him at Oxford and on his travels a
boon companion called Jocelyn, who aided him in
his wickednesses, until on one of their Italian tours
Jocelyn left him suddenly and became a Trappist
monk.* It was currently reported that some wild
deed of Adrian Temple had shocked even him, and
so outraged his surviving instincts of common
humanity that he was snatched as a brand from the
burning*and enabled to turn back even in the full
tide of his wickedness. However that may be,
Adrian went on in his evil course without him, and
about four years after disappeared. He was last
heard of in Naples, and it is believed that he succumbed during a violent outbreak of the plague

which took place in Italy in the autumn of 1752. That is all I shall tell you of him, and indeed I know little more myself. The only good trait that has been handed down concerning him is that he was a masterly musician, performing admirably upon the violin, which he had studied under the illustrious Tartini himself.* Yet even his art of music, if tradition speaks the truth, was put by him to the basest of uses.'

I apologised for my indiscretion in asking her about an unpleasant subject, and at the same time thanked her for what she had seen fit to tell me, professing myself much interested, as indeed I really was.

'Was he a handsome man?'

'That is a girl's question,' she answered, smiling. 'He is said to have been very handsome; and indeed his picture, painted after his first youth was past, would still lead one to suppose so. But his complexion was spoiled, it is said, and turned to deadly white by certain experiments, which it is neither possible nor seemly for us to understand. His face is of that long oval shape of which all the Temples are proud, and he had brown eyes: we sometimes tease Constance, saying she is like Adrian.'

It was indeed true, as I remembered after Mrs. Temple had pointed it out, that Constance had a peculiarly long and oval face. It gave her, I think, an air of staid and placid beauty, which formed in my eyes, and perhaps in John's also, one of her greatest attractions.

'I do not like even his picture,' Mrs. Temple continued, 'and strange tales have been narrated of it by idle servants which are not worth repeating. I have sometimes thought of destroying it; but my late husband, being a Temple, would never hear of this, or even of removing it from its present place in the gallery; and I should be loath to do anything now contrary to his wishes, once so strongly expressed. It is, besides, very perfect from an artistic point of view, being painted by Battoni, and in his happiest manner.'

I could never glean more from Mrs. Temple; but what she told me interested me deeply. It seemed another link in the chain, though I could scarcely tell why, that Adrian Temple should be so great a musician and violinist. I had, I fancy, a dim idea of that malign and outlawed spirit sitting alone in darkness for a hundred years, until he was called back by the sweet tones of the Italian music, and the lilt of the 'Areopagita' that he had loved so long ago.

## Chapter 9

JOHN's recovery, though continuous and satisfactory, was but slow; and it was not until Easter, which fell early, that his health was pronounced to be entirely re-established. The last few weeks of his convalescence had proved to all of us a time of thankful and tranquil enjoyment. If I may judge from my own experience, there are few epochs in our life more favourable to the growth of sentiments of affection and piety, or more full of pleasurable content, than is the period of gradual recovery from serious illness. The chastening effect of our recent sickness has not yet passed away, and we are at once grateful to our Creator for preserving us, and to our friends for the countless acts of watchful kindness which it is the peculiar property of illness to evoke.

No mother ever nursed a son more tenderly than did Mrs. Temple nurse my brother, and before his restoration to health was complete the attachment between him and Constance had ripened into a formal betrothal. Such an alliance was, as I have before explained, particularly suitable, and its prospect afforded the most lively pleasure to all those concerned. The month of March had been unusually mild, and Royston being situated in a valley, as is the case with most houses of that date, was well sheltered from cold winds. It had, moreover, a south aspect, and as my brother gradually gathered strength, Constance and he and I would often sit out of doors in the soft spring mornings. We put an easy-chair with many cushions for him on the gravel by the front door, where the warmth of the sun was reflected from the red brick walls, and he would at times read aloud to us while we were engaged with our crochet-work. Mr. Tennyson had just published anonymously a first volume of poems,* and the sober dignity of his verse well suited our frame of mind at that time. The memory of those pleasant spring mornings, my dear Edward, has not yet passed away, and I can still smell the sweet moist scent of the violets, and see the bright colours of the crocus-flowers in the parterres in front of us.

John's mind seemed to be gathering strength with his body. He had apparently flung off the cloud which had overshadowed him before his illness, and avoided entirely any reference to those unpleasant events which had been previously so constantly in his thoughts. I had, indeed, taken an early opportunity of telling him of my discovery of the picture of Adrian Temple, as I thought it would tend to show him that at least the last appearance of this ghostly form admitted of a rational explanation. He seemed glad to hear of this, but did not exhibit the same interest in the matter that I had expected, and allowed it at once to drop. Whether through lack of interest, or from a lingering dislike to revisit the spot where he was seized with illness, he did not, I believe, once enter the picture-gallery before he left Royston.

I cannot say as much for myself. The picture of Adrian Temple exerted a curious fascination over me, and I constantly took an opportunity of studying it. It was, indeed, a beautiful work; and perhaps because John's recovery gave a more cheerful tone to my thoughts, or perhaps from the power of custom to dull even the keenest antipathies, I gradually got to lose much of the feeling of aversion which it had at first inspired. In time the unpleasant look grew less unpleasing, and I noticed more the beautiful oval of the face, the brown eyes, and the fine chiselling of the features. Sometimes, too, I felt a deep pity for so clever a gentleman who had died young, and whose life, were it ever so wicked, must often have been also lonely and bitter. More than once I had been discovered by Mrs. Temple or Constance sitting looking at the picture, and they had gently laughed at me, saying that I had fallen in love with Adrian Temple.

One morning in early April, when the sun was streaming brightly through the oriel, and the picture received a fuller light than usual, it occurred to me to examine closely the scroll of music painted as hanging over the top of the pedestal on which the figure leant. I had hitherto thought that the signs depicted on it were merely such as painters might conventionally use to represent a piece of musical notation. This has generally been the case, I think, in such pictures as I have ever seen in which a piece of music has been introduced. I mean that while the painting gives a general representation of the musical staves, no attempt is ever made to paint any definite notes such as would enable an actual piece to be identified.* Though, as I write this, I do remember that on the monument to Handel* in Westminster Abbey there is represented a musical scroll similar to that in Adrian Temple's picture, but actually sculptured with the opening phrase of the majestic melody, 'I know that my Redeemer liveth.'

On this morning, then, at Royston I thought I perceived that there were painted on the scroll actual musical staves, bars, and notes; and my interest being excited, I stood upon a chair so as better to examine them. Though time had somewhat obscured this portion of the picture as with a veil or film, yet I made out that the painter had intended to depict some definite piece of music. In another moment I saw that the air represented consisted of the opening bars of the *Gagliarda* in the suite by Graziani with which my brother and I were so well acquainted. Though I believe that I had not seen the volume of music in which that piece was contained more than twice, yet the melody was very familiar to me, and I had no difficulty whatever in making myself sure that I had here before me the air of the *Gagliarda* and none other. It was true that it was only roughly painted, but to one who knew the tune there was no room left for doubt.

Here was a new cause, I will not say for surprise,

but for reflection. It might, of course, have been merely a coincidence that the artist should have chosen to paint in this picture this particular piece of music; but it seemed more probable that it had actually been a favourite air of Adrian Temple, and that he had chosen deliberately to have it represented with him. This discovery I kept entirely to myself, not thinking it wise to communicate it to my brother, lest by doing so I might reawaken his interest in a subject which I hoped he had finally dismissed from his thoughts.

In the second week of April the happy party at Royston was dispersed, John returning to Oxford for the summer term, Mrs. Temple making a short visit to Scotland, and Constance coming to Worth Maltravers to keep me company for a time.

It was John's last term at Oxford. He expected to take his degree in June, and his marriage with Constance Temple had been provisionally arranged for the September following. He returned to Magdalen Hall in the best of spirits, and found his rooms looking cheerful with well-filled flower-boxes in the windows. I shall not detain you with any long narration of the events of the term, as they have no relation to the present history. I will only say that I believe my brother applied himself diligently to his studies, and took his amusement mostly on horseback, riding two horses which he had had sent to him from Worth Maltravers.

About the second week after his return he received a letter from Mr. George Smart to the effect that the Stradivarius violin was now in complete order. Subsequent examination, Mr. Smart wrote, and the unanimous verdict of connoisseurs whom he had consulted, had merely confirmed the views

71

he had at first expressed—namely, that the violin was of the finest quality, and that my brother had in his possession a unique and intact example of Stradivarius's best period. He had had it properly strung; and as the bass-bar had never been moved, and was of a stronger nature than that usual at the period of its manufacture, he had considered it unnecessary to replace it. If any signs should become visible of its being inadequate to support the tension of modern stringing, another could be easily substituted for it at a later date. He had allowed a young German *virtuoso* to play on it, and though this gentleman was one of the first living performers, and had had an opportunity of handling many splendid instruments, he assured Mr. Smart that he had never performed on one that could in any way compare with this. My brother wrote in reply thanking him, and begging that the violin might be sent to Magdalen Hall.

The pleasant musical evenings, however, which John had formerly been used to spend in the company of Mr. Gaskell were now entirely pretermitted. For though there was no cause for any diminution of friendship between them, and though on Mr. Gaskell's part there was an ardent desire to maintain their former intimacy, yet the two young men saw less and less of one another, until their intercourse was confined to an accidental greeting in the street. I believe that during all this time my brother played very frequently on the Stradivarius violin, but always alone. Its very possession seemed to have engendered from the first in his mind a secretive tendency which, as I have already observed, was entirely alien to his real disposition. As he had concealed its discovery from his sister, so he had also from his friend, and Mr. Gaskell remained in complete ignorance of the existence of such an instrument.

On the evening of its arrival from London, John seems to have carefully unpacked the violin and tried it with a new bow of Tourte's make*which he had purchased of Mr. Smart. He had shut the heavy outside door of his room before beginning to play, so that no one might enter unawares; and he told me afterwards that though he had naturally expected from the instrument a very fine tone, yet its actual merits so far exceeded his anticipations as entirely to overwhelm him. The sound issued from it in a volume of such depth and purity as to give an impression of the passages being chorded, or even of another violin being played at the same time. He had had, of course, no opportunity of practising during his illness, and so expected to find his skill with the bow somewhat diminished; but he perceived, on the contrary, that his performance was greatly improved, and that he was playing with a mastery and feeling of which he had never before been conscious. While attributing this improvement very largely to the beauty of the instrument on which he was performing, yet he could not but believe that by his illness, or in some other unexplained way, he had actually acquired a greater freedom of wrist and fluency of expression, with which reflection he was not a little elated. He had had a lock fixed on the cupboard in which he had originally found the violin, and here he carefully deposited it on each occasion after playing, before he opened the outer door of his room.

So the summer term passed away. The examinations had come in their due time, and were now over. Both the young men had submitted themselves to the ordeal, and while neither would of course have admitted as much to anyone else, both felt secretly that they had no reason to be dissatisfied with their performance. The results would not be published for some weeks to come. The last night of the term had arrived, the last night too of John's Oxford career. It was near nine o'clock, but still quite light, and the rich orange glow of sunset had not yet left the sky. The air was warm and sultry, as on that eventful evening when just a year ago he had for the first time seen the figure or the illusion of the figure of Adrian Temple. Since that time he had played the 'Areopagita' many, many times; but there had never been any reappearance of that form, nor even had the once familiar creaking of the wicker chair ever made itself heard. As he sat alone in his room, thinking with a natural melancholy that he had seen the sun set for the last time on his student life, and reflecting on the possibilities of the future and perhaps on opportunities wasted in the past, the memory of that evening last June recurred strongly to his imagination, and he felt an irresistible impulse to play once more the 'Areopagita.' He unlocked the now familiar cupboard and took out the violin, and never had the exquisite gradations of colour in its varnish appeared to greater advantage than in the soft mellow light of the fading day. As he began the *Gagliarda* he looked at the wicker chair, half expecting to see a form he well knew seated in it; but nothing of the kind ensued, and he concluded the 'Areopagita' without the occurrence of any unusual phenomenon.

It was just at its close that he heard some one knocking at the outer door. He hurriedly locked away the violin and opened the 'oak.' It was Mr. Gaskell. He came in rather awkwardly, as though not sure whether he would be welcomed.

'Johnnie,' he began, and stopped.

The force of ancient habit sometimes, dear nephew, leads us unwittingly to accost those who were once our friends by a familiar or nick-name long after the intimacy that formerly justified it has vanished. But sometimes we intentionally revert to the use of such a name, not wishing to proclaim openly, as it were, by a more formal address that we are no longer the friends we once were. I think this latter was the case with Mr. Gaskell as he repeated the familiar name.

'Johnnie, I was passing down New College Lane, and heard the violin from your open windows. You were playing the "Areopagita," and it all sounded so familiar to me that I thought I must come up. I am not interrupting you, am I?'

'No, not at all,' John answered.

'It is the last night of our undergraduate life, the last night we shall meet in Oxford as students. To-morrow we make our bow to youth and become men. We have not seen much of each other this term at any rate, and I daresay that is my fault. But at least let us part as friends. Surely our friends are not so many that we can afford to fling them lightly away.'

He held out his hand frankly, and his voice trembled a little as he spoke—partly perhaps from real emotion, but more probably from the feeling of reluctance which I have noticed men always exhibit to discovering* any sentiment deeper than those usually deemed conventional in correct society. My brother was moved by his obvious wish to renew

75

their former friendship, and grasped the proffered hand.

There was a minute's pause, and then the conversation was resumed, a little stiffly at first, but more freely afterwards. They spoke on many indifferent subjects, and Mr. Gaskell congratulated John on the prospect of his marriage, of which he had heard. As he at length rose up to take his departure, he said, 'You must have practised the violin diligently of late, for I never knew anyone make so rapid progress with it as you have done. As I came along I was spellbound by your music. I never before heard you bring from the instrument so exquisite a tone: the chorded passages were so powerful that I believed there had been another person playing with you. Your Pressenda is certainly a finer instrument than I ever imagined.'

My brother was pleased with Mr. Gaskell's compliment, and the latter continued, 'Let me enjoy the pleasure of playing with you once more in Oxford; let us play the "Areopagita."'

And so saying he opened the pianoforte and sat down.

John was turning to take out the Stradivarius when he remembered that he had never even revealed its existence to Mr. Gaskell, and that if he now produced it an explanation must follow. In a moment his mood changed, and with less geniality he excused himself, somewhat awkwardly, from complying with the request, saying that he was fatigued.

Mr. Gaskell was evidently hurt at his friend's altered manner, and without renewing his petition rose at once from the pianoforte, and after a little forced conversation took his departure. On leaving he shook my brother by the hand, wished him all prosperity in his marriage and after-life, and said, 'Do not entirely forget your old comrade, and remember that if at any time you should stand in need of a true friend, you know where to find him!'

John heard his footsteps echoing down the passage and made a half-involuntary motion towards the door as if to call him back, but did not do so, though he thought over his last words then and on a subsequent occasion.

## Chapter 10

THE summer was spent by us in the company of Mrs. Temple and Constance, partly at Royston and partly at Worth Maltravers. John had again hired the cutter-yacht *Palestine*, and the whole party made several expeditions in her. Constance was entirely devoted to her lover; her life seemed wrapped up in his; she appeared to have no existence except in his presence.

I can scarcely enumerate the reasons which prompted such thoughts, but during these months I sometimes found myself wondering if John still returned her affection as ardently as I knew had once been the case. I can certainly call to mind no single circumstance which could justify me in such a suspicion. He performed punctiliously all those thousand little acts of devotion which are expected of an accepted lover; he seemed to take pleasure in perfecting any scheme of enjoyment to amuse her; and yet the impression grew in my mind that he no longer felt the same heart-whole love to her that she bore him, and that he had himself shown six months earlier. I cannot say, my dear Edward, how lively was the grief that even the suspicion of such

a fact caused me, and I continually rebuked myself
for entertaining for a moment a thought so un-
worthy, and dismissed it from my mind with reprobation. Alas! ere long it was sure again to make
itself felt. We had all seen the Stradivarius violin;
indeed it was impossible for my brother longer to
conceal it from us, and he now played continually
on it. He did not recount to us the story of its discovery, contenting himself with saying that he had
become possessed of it at Oxford. We imagined
naturally that he had purchased it; and for this I
was sorry, as I feared Mr. Thoresby, his guardian,
who had given him some years previously an excellent violin by Pressenda, might feel hurt at seeing
his present so unceremoniously laid aside. None of
us were at all intimately acquainted with the fancies
of fiddle-collectors, and were consequently quite ignorant of the enormous value that fashion attached
to so splendid an instrument. Even had we known,
I do not think that we should have been surprised
at John purchasing it; for he had recently come of
age, and was in possession of so large a fortune as
would amply justify him in such an indulgence had
he wished to gratify it. No one, however, could
remain unaware of the wonderful musical qualities
of the instrument. Its rich and melodious tones
would commend themselves even to the most un-
musical ear, and formed a subject of constant
remark. I noticed also that my brother's knowledge
of the violin had improved in a very perceptible
manner, for it was impossible to attribute the great
beauty and power of his present performance entirely to the excellence of the instrument he was
using. He appeared more than ever devoted to the
art, and would shut himself up in his room alone for

two or more hours together for the purpose of playing the violin—a habit which was a source of sorrow to Constance, for he would never allow her to sit with him on such occasions, as she naturally wished to do.

So the summer fled. I should have mentioned that in July, after going up to complete the *viva voce** part of their examination, both Mr. Gaskell and John received information that they had obtained 'first-classes.' The young men had, it appears, done excellently well, and both had secured a place in that envied division of the first-class which was called 'above the line.'* John's success proved a source of much pleasure to us all, and mutual congratulations were freely exchanged. We were pleased also at Mr. Gaskell's high place, remembering the kindness which he had shown us at Oxford in the previous year. I desired to send him my compliments and felicitations when he should next be writing to him. I did not doubt that my brother would return Mr. Gaskell's congratulations, which he had already received: he said, however, that his friend had given no address to which he could write, and so the matter dropped.

On the 1st of September John and Constance Temple were married. The wedding took place at Royston, and by John's special desire (with which Constance fully agreed) the ceremony was of a strictly private and unpretentious nature. The newly married pair had determined to spend their honeymoon in Italy, and left for the Continent in the forenoon.

Mrs. Temple invited me to remain with her for the present at Royston, which I was very glad to do, feeling deeply the loss of a favourite brother, and looking forward with dismay to six weeks of loneliness which must elapse before I should again see him and my dearest Constance.

We received news of our travellers about a fortnight afterwards, and then heard from them at frequent intervals. Constance wrote in the best of spirits, and with the keenest appreciation. She had never travelled in Switzerland or Italy before, and all was enchantingly novel to her. They had journeyed through Basle to Lucerne, spending a few days in that delightful spot, and thence proceeding by the Simplon Pass to Lugano and the Italian lakes. Then we heard that they had gone further south than had been at first contemplated; they had reached Rome, and were intending to go on to Naples.

After the first few weeks we neither of us received any more letters from John. It was always Constance who wrote, and even her letters grew very much less frequent than had at first been the case. This was perhaps natural, as the business of travel no doubt engrossed their thoughts. But ere long we both perceived that the letters of our dear girl were more constrained and formal than before. It was as if she was writing now rather to comply with a sense of duty than to give vent to the light-hearted gaiety and naïve enjoyment which breathed in every line of her earlier communications. So at least it seemed to us, and again the old suspicion presented itself to my mind, and I feared that all was not as it should be.

Naples was to be the turning-point of their travels, and we expected them to return to England by the end of October. November had arrived, however, and we still had no intimation that their return journey had commenced or was even decided on. From John there was no word, and Constance wrote less often than ever. John, she said, was enraptured with Naples and its surroundings; he devoted himself much to the violin, and though she did not say so, this meant, I knew, that she was often left alone. For her own part, she did not think that a continued residence in Italy would suit her health; the sudden changes of temperature tried her, and people said that the airs rising in the evening from the bay were unwholesome.

Then we received a letter from her which much alarmed us. It was written from Naples and dated October 25. John, she said, had been ailing of late with nervousness and insomnia. On Wednesday,* two days before the date of her letter, he had suffered all day from a strange restlessness, which increased after they had retired for the evening. He could not sleep and had dressed again, telling her he would walk a little in the night air to compose himself. He had not returned till near six in the morning, and then was so deadly pale and seemed so exhausted that she insisted on his keeping to his bed till she could get medical advice. The doctors feared that he had been attacked by some strange form of malarial fever, and said he needed much care. Our anxiety was, however, at least temporarily relieved by the receipt of later tidings which spoke of John's recovery; but November drew to a close without any definite mention of their return having reached us.

That month is always, I think, a dreary one in the country. It has neither the brilliant tints of October, nor the cosy jollity of mid-winter with its Christmas joys to alleviate it. This year it was more gloomy than usual. Incessant rain had marked its close, and the Roy, a little brook which skirted the gardens not far from the house, had swollen to unusual proportions. At last one wild night the flood rose so high as to completely cover the garden terraces, working havoc in the parterres, and covering the lawns with a thick coat of mud. Perhaps this gloominess of nature's outer face impressed itself in a sense of apprehension on our spirits, and it was with a feeling of more than ordinary pleasure and relief that early in December we received a letter dated from Laon, saying that our travellers were already well advanced on their return journey, and expected to be in England a week after the receipt by us of this advice. It was, as usual, Constance who wrote. John begged, she said, that Christmas might be spent at Worth Maltravers, and that we would at once proceed thither to see that all was in order against their return. They reached Worth about the middle of the month, and were, I need not say, received with the utmost affection by Mrs. Temple and myself.

In reply to our inquiries John professed that his health was completely restored; but though we could indeed discern no other signs of any special weakness, we were much shocked by his changed appearance. He had completely lost his old healthy and sunburnt complexion, and his face, though not thin or sunken, was strangely pale. Constance assured us that though in other respects he had apparently recovered, he had never regained his old colour from the night of his attack of fever at Naples.

I soon perceived that her own spirits were not so bright as was ordinarily the case with her; and she exhibited none of the eagerness to narrate to others the incidents of travel which is generally observable in those who have recently returned from a journey. The cause of this depression was, alas! not difficult to discover, for John's former abstraction and moodiness seemed to have returned with an increased force. It was a source of infinite pain to Mrs. Temple, and perhaps even more so to me, to observe this sad state of things. Constance never complained, and her affection towards her husband seemed only to increase in the face of difficulties. Yet the matter was one which could not be hid from the anxious eyes of loving kinswomen, and I believe that it was the consciousness that these altered circumstances could not but force themselves upon our notice that added poignancy to my poor sister's grief. While not markedly neglecting her, my brother had evidently ceased to take that pleasure in her company which might reasonably have been expected in any case under the circumstances of a recent marriage, and a thousand times more so when his wife was so loving and beautiful a creature as Constance Temple. He appeared little except at meals, and not even always at lunch, shutting himself up for the most part in his morning-room or study and playing continually on the violin. It was in vain that we attempted even by means of his music to win him back to a sweeter mood. Again and again I begged him to allow me to accompany him on the pianoforte, but he would never do so, always putting me off with some excuse. Even when he sat with us in the evening, he spoke little, devoting himself for the most part to reading. His books were almost always Greek or Latin, so that I am ignorant of the subjects of his study; but he was content that either Constance or I should play on the pianoforte, saying that the melody, so far from distracting his attention, helped him rather to appreciate what he was reading. Constance always begged me to allow her to take her place at the instrument on these occasions, and would play to him sometimes for hours without receiving a word of thanks, being eager even in this unreciprocated manner to testify her love and devotion to him.

Christmas Day, usually so happy a season, brought no alleviation of our gloom. My brother's reserve continually increased, and even his longest-established habits appeared changed. He had been always most observant of his religious duties, attending divine service with the utmost regularity whatever the weather might be, and saying that it was a duty a landed proprietor owed as much to his tenantry as himself to set a good example in such matters. Ever since our earliest years he and I had gone morning and afternoon on Sundays to the little church of Worth, and there sat together in the Maltravers chapel where so many of our name had sat before us. Here their monuments and achievements* stood about us on every side, and it had always seemed to me that with their name and property we had inherited also the obligation to continue those acts of piety, in the practice of which so many of them had lived and died. It was, therefore, a source of surprise and great grief to me when on the Sunday after his return my brother omitted all religious observances, and did not once attend the parish church. He was not present with us at breakfast, ordering coffee and a roll to be taken to his private sitting-room. At the hour at which we usually set out for church I went to his room to tell him that we were all dressed and waiting for him. I tapped at the door, but on trying to enter found it locked. In reply to my message he did not open the door, but merely begged us to go on to church, saying he would possibly follow us later. We went alone, and I sat anxiously in our seat with my eyes fixed on the door, hoping against hope that each late comer might be John, but he never came. Perhaps this will appear to you, Edward, a comparatively trivial circumstance (though I hope it may not), but I assure you that it brought tears to my eyes. When I sat in the Maltravers chapel and thought that for the first time my dear brother had preferred in an open way his convenience or his whim to his duty, and had of set purpose neglected to come to the house of God, I felt a bitter grief that seemed to rise up in my throat and choke me. I could not think of the meaning of the prayers nor join in the singing: and all the time that Mr. Butler, our clergyman, was preaching, a verse of a little piece of poetry which I learnt as a girl was running in my head:

> *How easy are the paths of ill;*
> *How steep and hard the upward ways;*
> *A child can roll the stone down hill*
> *That breaks a giant's arm to raise.*

It seemed to me that our loved one had set his foot upon the downward slope, and that not all the efforts of those who would have given their lives to save him could now hold him back.

It was even worse on Christmas Day. Ever since we had been confirmed John and I had always taken the Sacrament on that happy morning, and after service he had distributed the Maltravers dole in our chapel. There are given, as you know, on that day to each of twelve old men £5 and a green coat,* and a like sum of money with a blue cloth dress to as many old women. These articles of dress are placed on the altar-tomb of Sir Esmoun* de Maltravers, and have been thence distributed from days immemorial by the head of our house. Ever since he was twelve years old it had been my pride to watch my handsome brother doing this deed of noble charity, and to hear the kindly words he added with each gift.

Alas! alas! it was all different this Christmas. Even on this holy day my brother did not approach either the altar or the house of God. Till then Christmas had always seemed to me to be a day given us from above, that we might see even while on earth a faint glimpse of that serenity and peaceful love which will hereafter gild all days in heaven. Then covetous men lay aside their greed and enemies their rancour, then warm hearts grow warmer, and Christians feel their common brotherhood. I can scarcely imagine any man so lost or guilty as not to experience on that day some desire to turn back to the good once more, as not to recognise some far-off possibility of better things. It was thoughts free and happy such as these that had previously come into my heart in the service of Christmas Day, and been particularly associated with the familiar words that we all love so much. But that morning the harmonies were all jangled: it seemed as though some evil spirit was pouring wicked thoughts into my ear; and even while children sang 'Hark the herald angels,' I thought I could hear through it all a melody which I had learnt to loathe, the *Gagliarda* of the 'Areopagita.'

Poor Constance! Though her veil was down, I could see her tears, and knew her thoughts must be sadder even than mine: I drew her hand towards me, and held it as I would a child's. After the service was over a new trial awaited us. John had made no arrangement for the distribution of the dole. The coats and dresses were all piled ready on Sir Esmoun's tomb, and there lay the little leather pouches of money, but there was no one to give them away. Mr. Butler looked puzzled, and approaching us, said he feared Sir John was ill—had he made no provision for the distribution? Pride kept back the tears which were rising fast, and I said my brother was indeed unwell, that it would be better for Mr. Butler to give away the dole, and that Sir John would himself visit the recipients during the week. Then we hurried away, not daring to watch the distribution of the dole, lest we should no longer be able to master our feelings, and should openly betray our agitation.

From one another we no longer attempted to conceal our grief. It seemed as though we had all at once resolved to abandon the farce of pretending not to notice John's estrangement from his wife, or of explaining away his neglectful and unaccountable treatment of her.

I do not think that three poor women were ever so sad on Christmas Day before as were we on our return from church that morning. None of us had seen my brother, but about five in the afternoon Constance went to his room, and through the locked door begged piteously to see him. After a few minutes he complied with her request and opened the door. The exact circumstances of that interview she never revealed to me, but I knew from her manner when she returned that something she had seen or heard had both grieved and frightened her.

She told me only that she had flung herself in an agony of tears at his feet, and kneeling there, weary and broken-hearted, had begged him to tell her if she had done aught amiss, had prayed him to give her back his love. To all this he answered little, but her entreaties had at least such an effect as to induce him to take his dinner with us that evening. At that meal we tried to put aside our gloom, and with feigned smiles and cheerful voices, from which the tears were hardly banished, sustained a weary show of conversation and tried to wile away his evil mood. But he spoke little; and when Foster, my father's butler, put on the table the three-handled Maltravers' loving-cup that he had brought up Christmas by Christmas for thirty years, my brother merely passed it by without a taste. I saw by Foster's face that the master's malady was no longer a secret even from the servants.

I shall not harass my own feelings nor yours, my dear Edward, by entering into further details of your father's illness, for such it was obvious his indisposition had become. It was the only consolation, and that was a sorry one, that we could use with Constance, to persuade her that John's estrangement from her was merely the result or manifestation of some physical infirmity. He obviously grew worse from week to week, and his treatment of his wife became colder and more callous. We had used all efforts to persuade him to take a change of air—to go to Royston for a month, and place himself under the care of Dr. Dobie. Mrs. Temple had even gone so far as to write privately to this physician, telling him as much of the case as was prudent, and asking his advice. Not being aware of the darker sides of my brother's ailment, Dr. Dobie replied in a less serious strain than seemed to us convenient; but recommended in any case a complete change of air and scene.

It was, therefore, with no ordinary pleasure and relief that we heard my brother announce quite unexpectedly one morning in March that he had made up his mind to seek change, and was going to leave almost immediately for the Continent. He took his valet Parnham with him, and quitted Worth one morning before lunch, bidding us an unceremonious adieu, though he kissed Constance with some apparent tenderness. It was the first time for three months, she confessed to me afterwards, that he had shown her even so ordinary a mark of affection; and her wounded heart treasured up what she hoped would prove a token of returning love. He had not proposed to take her with him, and even had he done so, we should have been reluctant to assent, as signs were not wanting that it might have been imprudent for her to undertake foreign travel at that period.

For nearly a month we had no word of him. Then he wrote a short note to Constance from Naples, giving no news, and indeed, scarce speaking of himself at all, but mentioning as an address to which she might write if she wished, the Villa de Angelis at Posilipo. Though his letter was cold and empty, yet Constance was delighted to get it, and wrote henceforth herself nearly every day, pouring out her heart to him, and retailing such news as she thought would cheer him.

## Chapter 11

A MONTH later Mrs. Temple wrote to John warning him of the state in which Constance now found herself, and begging him to return at least for a few weeks in order that he might be present at the time of her confinement. Though it would have been in the last degree unkind, or even inhuman, that a request of this sort should have been refused, yet I will confess to you that my brother's recent strangeness had prepared me for behaviour on his part however wild; and it was with a feeling of extreme relief that I heard from Mrs. Temple a little later that she had received a short note from John to say that he was already on his return journey. I believe Mrs. Temple herself felt as I did in the matter, though she said nothing.

When he returned we were all at Royston, whither Mrs. Temple had taken Constance to be under Dr. Dobie's care. We found John's physical appearance changed for the worse. His pallor was as remarkable as before, but he was visibly thinner; and his strange mental abstraction and moodiness seemed little if any abated. At first, indeed, he greeted Constance kindly or even affectionately. She had been in a terrible state of anxiety as to the attitude he would assume towards her, and this mental strain affected prejudicially her very delicate bodily condition. His kindness, of an ordinary enough nature indeed, seemed to her yearning heart a miracle of condescending love, and she was transported with the idea that his affection to her, once so sincere, was indeed returning. But I grieve to say that his manner thawed only for a very short time, and ere long he relapsed into an attitude of complete indifference. It was as if his real, true, honest, and loving character had made one more vigorous effort to assert itself,—as though it had for a moment broken through the hard and selfish crust that was forming around him; but the blighting influence which was at work proved seemingly too strong for him to struggle against, and riveted its chains again upon him with a weight heavier than before. That there was some malefic influence, mental or physical, thus working on him, no one who had known him before could for a moment doubt. But while Mrs. Temple and I readily admitted this much, we were entirely unable even to form a conjecture as to its nature. It is true that Mrs. Temple's fancy suggested that Constance had some rival in his affections; but we rejected such a theory almost before it was proposed, feeling that it was inherently improbable, and that, had it been true, we could not have remained entirely unaware of the circumstances which had conduced to such a state of things. It was this inexplicable nature of my brother's affliction that added immeasurably to our grief. If we could only have ascertained its cause we might have combated it; but as it was, we were fighting in the dark, as against some enemy who was assaulting us from an obscurity so thick that we could not see his form. Of any mental trouble we thus knew nothing, nor could we say that my brother was suffering from any definite physical ailment, except that he was certainly growing thinner.

Your birth, my dear Edward, followed very shortly. Your poor mother rallied in an unusually short time, and was filled with rapture at the new treasure which was thus given as a solace to her afflictions. Your father exhibited little interest at the event, though he sat nearly half an hour with her one evening, and allowed her even to stroke his hair and caress him as in time long past. Although it was now the height of summer he seldom left the house, sitting much and sleeping in his own room, where he had a field-bed provided for him, and continually devoting himself to the violin.

One evening near the end of July we were sitting after dinner in the drawing-room at Royston, having the French windows looking on to the lawn open, as the air was still oppressively warm. Though things were proceeding as indifferently as before, we were perhaps less cast down than usual, for John had taken his dinner with us that evening. This was a circumstance now, alas! sufficiently uncommon, for he had nearly all his meals served for him in his own rooms. Constance, who was once more downstairs, sat playing at the pianoforte, performing chiefly melodies by Scarlatti or Bach, of which old-fashioned music she knew her husband to be most fond. A later fashion, as you know, has revived the cultivation of these composers, but at the time of which I write their works were much less commonly known.*Though she was more than a passable musician, he would not allow her to accompany him; indeed he never now performed at all on the violin before us, reserving his practice entirely for his own chamber. There was a pause in the music while coffee was served. My brother had been sitting in an easy-chair apart reading some classical work during his wife's performance, and taking little notice of us. But after a while he put down his book and said, 'Constance, if you will accompany me, I will get my violin and play a little while.' I cannot say how much his words astonished us. It was so simple a matter for him to say, and yet it filled us all with an unspeakable joy. We concealed our emotion till he had left the room to get his instrument, then Constance showed how deeply she was gratified by kissing first her mother and then me, squeezing my hand but saying nothing. In a minute he returned, bringing his violin and a music-book. By the soiled vellum cover and the shape I perceived instantly that it was the book containing the 'Areopagita.' I had not seen it for near two years, and was not even aware that it was in the house, but I knew at once that he intended to play that suite. I entertained an unreasoning but profound aversion to its melodies, but at that moment I would have welcomed warmly that or any other music, so that he would only choose once more to show some thought for his neglected wife. He put the book open at the 'Areopagita' on the desk of the pianoforte, and asked her to play it with him. She had never seen the music before, though I believe she was not unacquainted with the melody, as she had heard him playing it by himself, and once heard, it was not easily forgotten.

They began the 'Areopagita' suite, and at first all went well. The tone of the violin, and also, I may say with no undue partiality, my brother's performance, were so marvellously fine that though our thoughts were elsewhere when the music commenced, in a few seconds they were wholly engrossed in the melody, and we sat spellbound. It was as if the violin had become suddenly endowed with life, and was singing to us in a mystical language more deep and awful than any human words. Constance was comparatively unused to the figuring of the *basso continuo*, and found some trouble in reading it accurately, especially in manuscript; but she was able to mask any difficulty she may have had until she came to the *Gagliarda*. Here she confessed to me her thoughts seemed against her will to wander, and her attention became too deeply riveted on her husband's performance to allow her to watch her own. She made first one slight fault, and then growing nervous, another, and another. Suddenly John stopped and said brusquely, 'Let Sophy play, I cannot keep time with you.' Poor Constance! The tears came swiftly to my own eyes when I heard him speak so thoughtlessly to her, and I was almost provoked to rebuke him openly. She was still weak from her recent illness; her nerves were excited by the unusual pleasure she felt in playing once more with her husband, and this sudden shattering of her hopes of a renewed tenderness proved more than she could bear: she put her head between her hands upon the keyboard and broke into a paroxysm of tears.

We both ran to her; but while we were attempting to assuage her grief, John shut his violin into its case, took the music-book under his arm, and left the room without saying a word to any of us, not even to the weeping girl, whose sobs seemed as though they would break her heart.

We got her put to bed at once, but it was some hours before her convulsive sobbing ceased. Mrs. Temple had administered to her a soothing draught of proved efficacy, and after sitting with her till after one o'clock, I left her at last dozing off to sleep, and myself sought repose. I was quite wearied out with the weight of my anxiety, and with the crushing bitterness of seeing my dearest Constance's feelings so wounded. Yet in spite, or rather perhaps on account of my trouble, my head had scarcely touched my pillow ere I fell into a deep sleep.

A room in the south wing had been converted for the nonce into a nursery, and for the convenience of being near her infant Constance now slept in a room adjoining. As this portion of the house was somewhat isolated, Mrs. Temple had suggested that I should keep her daughter company, and occupy a room in the same passage, only removed a few doors, and this I had accordingly done. I was aroused from my sleep that night by some one knocking gently on the door of my bedroom; but it was some seconds before my thoughts became sufficiently awake to allow me to remember where I was. There was some moonlight, but I lighted a candle, and looking at my watch saw that it was two o'clock. I concluded that either Constance or her baby was unwell, and that the nurse needed my assistance. So I left my bed, and moving to the door, asked softly who was there. It was, to my surprise, the voice of Constance that replied, 'O Sophy, let me in.'

In a second I had opened the door, and found my poor sister wearing only her night-dress, and standing in the moonlight before me.

She looked frightened and unusually pale in her white dress and with the cold gleam of the moon upon her. At first I thought she was walking in her sleep, and perhaps rehearsing again in her dreams the troubles which dogged her waking footsteps. I took her gently by the arm, saying, 'Dearest Constance, come back at once to bed; you will take cold.'

She was not asleep, however, but made a motion

95

of silence, and said in a terrified whisper, 'Hush; do you hear nothing?' There was something so vague and yet so mysterious in the question and in her evident perturbation that I was infected too by her alarm. I felt myself shiver, as I strained my ear to catch if possible the slightest sound. But a complete silence pervaded everything: I could hear nothing.

'Can you hear it?' she said again. All sorts of images of ill presented themselves to my imagination: I thought the baby must be ill with croup, and that she was listening for some stertorous breath of anguish; and then the dread came over me that perhaps her sorrows had been too much for her, and that reason had left her seat. At that thought the marrow froze in my bones.

'Hush,' she said again; and just at that moment, as I strained my ears, I thought I caught upon the sleeping air a distant and very faint murmur.

'Oh, what is it, Constance?' I said. 'You will drive me mad;' and while I spoke the murmur seemed to resolve itself into the vibration, felt almost rather than heard, of some distant musical instrument. I stepped past her into the passage. All was deadly still, but I could perceive that music was being played somewhere far away; and almost at the same minute my ears recognised faintly but unmistakably the *Gagliarda* of the 'Areopagita.'

I have already mentioned that for some reason which I can scarcely explain, this melody was very repugnant to me. It seemed associated in some strange and intimate way with my brother's indisposition and moral decline. Almost at the moment that I had heard it first two years ago, peace seemed to have risen up and left our house, gathering her skirts about her, as we read that the angels left the

Temple at the siege of Jerusalem.* And now it was even more detestable to my ears, recalling as it did too vividly the cruel events of the preceding evening.

'John must be sitting up playing,' I said.

'Yes,' she answered; 'but why is he in this part of the house, and why does he always play *that* tune?'

It was as if some irresistible attraction drew us towards the music. Constance took my hand in hers and we moved together slowly down the passage. The wind had risen, and though there was a bright moon, her beams were constantly eclipsed by driving clouds. Still there was light enough to guide us, and I extinguished the candle. As we reached the end of the passage the air of the *Gagliarda* grew more and more distinct.

Our passage opened on to a broad landing with a balustrade, and from one side of it ran out the picture-gallery which you know.

I looked at Constance significantly. It was evident that John was playing in this gallery. We crossed the landing, treading carefully and making no noise with our naked feet, for both of us had been too excited even to think of putting on shoes.

We could now see the whole length of the gallery. My poor brother sat in the oriel window of which I have before spoken. He was sitting so as to face the picture of Adrian Temple, and the great windows of the oriel flung a strong light on him. At times a cloud hid the moon, and all was plunged in darkness; but in a moment the cold light fell full on him, and we could trace every feature as in a picture. He had evidently not been to bed, for he was fully dressed, exactly as he had left us in the drawing-room five hours earlier when Constance was weeping over his thoughtless words. He was playing the

97

violin, playing with a passion and reckless energy which I had never seen, and hope never to see again. Perhaps he remembered that this spot was far removed from the rest of the house, or perhaps he was careless whether any were awake and listening to him or not; but it seemed to me that he was playing with a sonorous strength greater than I had thought possible for a single violin. There came from his instrument such a volume and torrent of melody as to fill the gallery so full, as it were, of sound that it throbbed and vibrated again. He kept his eyes fixed on something at the opposite side of the gallery; we could not indeed see on what, but I have no doubt at all that it was the portrait of Adrian Temple. His gaze was eager and expectant, as though he were waiting for something to occur which did not.

I knew that he had been growing thin of late, but this was the first time I had realised how sunk were the hollows of his eyes and how haggard his features had become. It may have been some effect of moonlight which I do not well understand, but his fine-cut face, once so handsome, looked on this night worn and thin like that of an old man. He never for a moment ceased playing. It was always one same dreadful melody, the *Gagliarda* of the 'Areopagita,' and he repeated it time after time with the perseverance and apparent aimlessness of an automaton.

He did not see us, and we made no sign, standing afar off in silent horror at that nocturnal sight. Constance clutched me by the arm: she was so pale that I perceived it even in the moonlight. 'Sophy,' she said, 'he is sitting in the same place as on the first night when he told me how he loved me.' I could answer nothing, my voice was frozen in me.

I could only stare at my brother's poor withered face, realising then for the first time that he must be mad, and that it was the haunting of the *Gagliarda* that had made him so.

We stood there I believe for half an hour without speech or motion, and all the time that sad figure at the end of the gallery continued its performance. Suddenly he stopped, and an expression of frantic despair came over his face as he laid down the violin and buried his head in his hands. I could bear it no longer. 'Constance,' I said, 'come back to bed. We can do nothing.' So we turned and crept away silently as we had come. Only as we crossed the landing Constance stopped, and looked back for a minute with a heart-broken yearning at the man she loved. He had taken his hands from his head, and she saw the profile of his face clear cut and hard in the white moonlight.

It was the last time her eyes ever looked upon it.

She made for a moment as if she would turn back and go to him, but her courage failed her, and we went on. Before we reached her room we heard in the distance, faintly but distinctly, the burden* of the *Gagliarda*.

## Chapter 12

THE next morning my maid brought me a hurried note written in pencil by my brother. It contained only a few lines, saying that he found that his continued sojourn at Royston was not beneficial to his health, and had determined to return to Italy. If we wished to write, letters would reach him at the Villa de Angelis: his valet Parnham was to follow him thither with his baggage as soon as it could be got together. This was all; there was no word of adieu even to his wife.

We found that he had never gone to bed that night. But in the early morning he had himself saddled his horse *Sentinel* and ridden in to Derby, taking the early mail thence to London. His resolve to leave Royston had apparently been arrived at very suddenly, for so far as we could discover, he had carried no luggage of any kind. I could not help looking somewhat carefully round his room to see if he had taken the Stradivarius violin. No trace of it or even of its case was to be seen, though it was difficult to imagine how he could have carried it with him on horseback. There was, indeed, a locked travelling-trunk which Parnham was to bring with him later, and the instrument might, of course, have been in that; but I felt convinced that he had actually taken it with him in some way or other, and this proved afterwards to have been the case.

I shall draw a veil, my dear Edward, over the events which immediately followed your father's departure. Even at this distance of time the memory is too inexpressibly bitter to allow me to do more than briefly allude to them.

A fortnight after John's departure, we left Royston and removed to Worth, wishing to get some sea-air, and to enjoy the late summer of the south coast. Your mother seemed entirely to have recovered from her confinement, and to be enjoying as good health as could be reasonably expected under the circumstances of her husband's indisposition. But suddenly one of those insidious maladies which are incidental to women in her condition seized upon her. We had hoped and believed that all such period of danger was already happily past; but, alas! it was not so, and within a few hours of her first seizure all realised how serious was her case. Everything that human skill can do under such conditions was done, but without avail. Symptoms of blood-poisoning showed themselves, accompanied with high fever, and within a week she was in her coffin.

Though her delirium was terrible to watch, yet I thank God to this day, that if she was to die, it pleased Him to take her while in an unconscious condition. For two days before her death she recognised no one, and was thus spared at least the sadness of passing from life without one word of kindness or even of reconciliation from her unhappy husband.

The communication with a place so distant as Naples was not then to be made under fifteen or twenty days, and all was over before we could hope that the intelligence even of his wife's illness had reached John. Both Mrs. Temple and I remained at Worth in a state of complete prostration, awaiting his return. When more than a month had passed without his arrival, or even a letter to say that he was on his way, our anxiety took a new turn, as we feared that some accident had befallen him, or that the news of his wife's death, which would then be in his hands, had so seriously affected him as to render him incapable of taking any action. To repeated subsequent communications we received no answer; but at last, to a letter which I wrote to Parnham, the servant replied, stating that his master was still at the Villa de Angelis, and in a condition of health little differing from that in which he left

Royston, except that he was now slightly paler if possible and thinner. It was not till the end of November that any word came from him, and then he wrote only one page of a sheet of note-paper to me in pencil, making no reference whatever to his wife's death, but saying that he should not return for Christmas, and instructing me to draw on his bankers for any moneys that I might require for household purposes at Worth.

I need not tell you the effect that such conduct produced on Mrs. Temple and myself; you can easily imagine what would have been your own feelings in such a case. Nor will I relate any other circumstances which occurred at this period, as they would have no direct bearing upon my narrative. Though I still wrote to my brother at frequent intervals, as not wishing to neglect a duty, no word from him ever came in reply.

About the end of March, indeed, Parnham returned to Worth Maltravers, saying that his master had paid him a half-year's wages in advance, and then dispensed with his services. He had always been an excellent servant, and attached to the family, and I was glad to be able to offer him a suitable position with us at Worth until his master should return. He brought disquieting reports of John's health, saying that he was growing visibly weaker. Though I was sorely tempted to ask him many questions as to his master's habits and way of life, my pride forbade me to do so. But I heard incidentally from my maid that Parnham had told her Sir John was spending money freely in alterations at the Villa de Angelis, and had engaged Italians to attend him, with which his English valet was naturally much dissatisfied.

So the spring passed and the summer was well advanced.

On the last morning of July I found waiting for me on the breakfast-table an envelope addressed in my brother's hand. I opened it hastily. It only contained a few words, which I have before me as I write now. The ink is a little faded and yellow, but the impression it made is yet vivid as on that summer morning.

My dearest Sophy [it began]—Come to me here at once, if possible, or it may be too late. I want to see you. They say that I am ill, and too weak to travel to England.

Your loving brother,
JOHN.

There was a great change in the style, from the cold and conventional notes that he had hitherto sent at such long intervals; from the stiff 'Dear Sophia' and 'Sincerely yours' to which, I grieve to say, I had grown accustomed. Even the writing itself was altered. It was more the bold boyish hand he wrote when first he went to Oxford, than the smaller cramped and classic* character of his later years. Though it was a little matter enough, God knows, in comparison with his grievous conduct, yet it touched me much that he should use again the once familiar 'Dearest Sophy,' and sign himself 'my loving brother.' I felt my heart go out towards him; and so strong is woman's affection for her own kin, that I had already forgotten any resentment and reprobation in my great pity for the poor wanderer, lying sick perhaps unto death and alone in a foreign land.

I took his note at once to Mrs. Temple. She read

103

it twice or thrice, trying to take in the meaning of it. Then she drew me to her and, kissing me, said, 'Go to him at once, Sophy. Bring him back to Worth; try to bring him back to the right way.'

I ordered my things to be packed, determining to drive to Southampton and take train thence to London; and at the same time Mrs. Temple gave instructions that all should be prepared for her own return to Royston within a few days. I knew she did not dare to see John after her daughter's death.

I took my maid with me, and Parnham to act as courier. At London we hired a carriage for the whole journey, and from Calais posted*direct to Naples. We took the short route by Marseilles and Genoa, and travelled for seventeen days without intermission, as my brother's note made me desirous of losing no time on the way. I had never been in Italy before; but my anxiety was such that my mind was unable to appreciate either the beauty of the scenery or the incidents of travel. I can, in fact, remember nothing of our journey now, except the wearisome and interminable jolting over bad roads and the insufferable heat. It was the middle of August in an exceptionally warm summer, and after passing Genoa the heat became almost tropical. There was no relief even at night, for the warm air hung stagnant and suffocating, and the inside of my travelling coach was often like a furnace.

We were at last approaching the conclusion of our journey, and had left Rome behind us. The day that we set out from Aversa was the hottest that I have ever felt, the sun beating down with an astonishing power even in the early hours, and the road being thick with a white and blinding dust. It was soon after midnight that our carriage began rattling over the great stone blocks with which the streets of Naples are paved. The suburbs that we at first passed through were, I remember, in darkness and perfect quiet; but after traversing the heart of the city and reaching the western side, we suddenly found ourselves in the midst of an enormous and very dense crowd. There were lanterns everywhere, and interminable lanes of booths, whose proprietors were praising their wares with loud shouts; and here acrobats, jugglers, minstrels, black-vested priests, and blue-coated soldiers*mingled with a vast crowd whose numbers at once arrested the progress of the carriage. Though it was so late of a Sunday night, all seemed here awake and busy as at noonday. Oil-lamps with reeking fumes of black smoke flung a glare over the scene, and the discordant cries and chattering conversation united in so deafening a noise as to make me turn faint and giddy, wearied as I already was with long travelling. Though I felt that intense eagerness and expectation which the approaching termination of a tedious journey inspires, and was desirous of pushing forward with all imaginable despatch, yet here our course was sadly delayed. The horses could only proceed at the slowest of foot-paces, and we were constantly brought to a complete stop for some minutes before the post-boy*could force a passage through the unwilling crowd. This produced a feeling of irritation, and despair of ever reaching my destination; and the mirth and careless hilarity of the people round us chafed with bitter contrast on my depressed spirits. I inquired from the post-boy what was the origin of so great a commotion, and understood him to say in reply that it was a religious festival held annually in honour of 'Our Lady of the Grotto.'*I cannot, however, conceive of any truly religious person countenancing such a gathering, which seemed to me rather like the unclean orgies of a heathen deity than an act of faith of Christian people. This disturbance occasioned us so serious a delay, that as we were climbing the steep slope leading up to Posilipo it was already three in the morning and the dawn was at hand.

After mounting steadily for a long time we began to rapidly descend, and just as the sun came up over the sea we arrived at the Villa de Angelis. I sprang from the carriage, and passing through a trellis of vines, reached the house. A man-servant was in waiting, and held the door open for me; but he was an Italian, and did not understand me when I asked in English where Sir John Maltravers was. He had evidently, however, received instructions to take me at once to my brother, and led the way to an inner part of the house. As we proceeded I heard the sound of a rich alto voice singing very sweetly to a mandoline some soothing or religious melody. The servant pulled aside a heavy curtain and I found myself in my brother's room. An Italian youth sat on a stool near the door, and it was he who had been singing. At a few words from John, addressed to him in his own language, he set down his mandoline and left the room, pulling to the curtain and shutting a door behind it.

The room looked directly on to the sea: the villa was, in fact, built upon rocks at the foot of which the waves lapped. Through two folding windows which opened on to a balcony the early light of the summer morning streamed in with a rosy flush. My brother sat on a low couch or sofa, propped up against a heap of pillows, with a rug of brilliant colours flung across his feet and legs. He held out his arms to me, and I ran to him; but even in so brief an interval I had perceived that he was terribly weak and wasted.

All my memories of his past faults had vanished and were dead in that sad aspect of his worn features, and in the conviction which I felt, even from the first moment, that he had but little time longer to remain with us. I knelt by him on the floor, and with my arms round his neck, embraced him tenderly, not finding any place for words, but only sobbing in great anguish. Neither of us spoke, and my weariness from long travel and the strangeness of the situation caused me to feel that paralysing sensation of doubt as to the reality of the scene, and even of my own existence, which all, I believe, have experienced at times of severe mental tension. That I, a plain English girl, should be kneeling here beside my brother in the Italian dawn; that I should read, as I believed, on his young face the unmistakable image and superscription* of death; and reflect that within so few months he had married, had wrecked his home, that my poor Constance was no more;—these things seemed so unrealisable that for a minute I felt that it must all be a nightmare, that I should immediately wake with the fresh salt air of the Channel blowing through my bedroom window at Worth, and find I had been dreaming. But it was not so; the light of day grew stronger and brighter, and even in my sorrow the panorama of the most beautiful spot on earth, the Bay of Naples, with Vesuvius lying on the far side, as seen then from these windows, stamped itself for ever on my mind. It was unreal as a scene in some brilliant dramatic spectacle, but, alas! no unreality

107

was here. The flames of the candles in their silver
sconces waxed paler and paler, the lines and
shadows on my brother's face grew darker, and the
pallor of his wasted features showed more striking
in the bright rays of the morning sun.

## Chapter 13

I HAD spent near a week at the Villa de Angelis.
John's manner to me was most tender and affection-
ate; but he showed no wish to refer to the tragedy
of his wife's death and the sad events which had
preceded it, or to attempt to explain in any way his
own conduct in the past. Nor did I ever lead the
conversation to these topics; for I felt that even if
there were no other reason, his great weakness
rendered it inadvisable to introduce such subjects
at present, or even to lead him to speak at all
more than was actually necessary. I was content to
minister to him in quiet, and infinitely happy in his
restored affection. He seemed desirous of banishing
from his mind all thoughts of the last few months,
but spoke much of the years before he had gone to
Oxford, and of happy days which we had spent
together in our childhood at Worth Maltravers. His
weakness was extreme, but he complained of no
particular malady except a short cough which
troubled him at night.

I had spoken to him of his health, for I could see
that his state was such as to inspire anxiety, and
begged that he would allow me to see if there was
an English doctor at Naples who could visit him.
This he would not assent to, saying that he was
quite content with the care of an Italian doctor who

visited him almost daily, and that he hoped to be able, under my escort, to return within a very short time to England.

'I shall never be much better, dear Sophy,' he said one day. 'The doctor tells me that I am suffering from some sort of consumption, and that I must not expect to live long. Yet I yearn to see Worth once more, and to feel again the west wind blowing in the evening across from Portland, and smell the thyme on the Dorset downs. In a few days I hope perhaps to be a little stronger, and I then wish to show you a discovery which I have made in Naples. After that you may order them to harness the horses, and carry me back to Worth Maltravers.'

I endeavoured to ascertain from Signor Baravelli, the doctor, something as to the actual state of his patient; but my knowledge of Italian was so slight that I could neither make him understand what I would be at, nor comprehend in turn what he replied, so that this attempt was relinquished. From my brother himself I gathered that he had begun to feel his health much impaired as far back as the early spring, but though his strength had since then gradually failed him, he had not been confined to the house until a month past. He spent the day and often the night reclining on his sofa and speaking little. He had apparently lost that taste for the violin which had once absorbed so much of his attention; indeed I think the bodily strength necessary for its performance had probably now failed him. The Stradivarius instrument lay near his couch in its case; but I only saw the latter open on one occasion, I think, and was deeply thankful that John no longer took the same delight as heretofore in the practice of this art,—not only because the mere sound of his violin was now fraught to me with such bitter memories, but also because I felt sure that its performance had in some way which I could not explain a deleterious effect upon himself. He exhibited that absence of vitality which is so often noticeable in those who have not long to live, and on some days lay in a state of semi-lethargy from which it was difficult to rouse him. But at other times he suffered from a distressing restlessness which forbade him to sit still even for a few minutes, and which was more painful to watch than his lethargic stupor. The Italian boy, of whom I have already spoken, exhibited an untiring devotion to his master which won my heart. His name was Raffaelle Carotenuto,* and he often sang to us in the evening, accompanying himself on the mandoline. At nights, too, when John could not sleep, Raffaelle would read for hours till at last his master dozed off. He was well educated, and though I could not understand the subject he read, I often sat by and listened, being charmed with his evident attachment to my brother and with the melodious intonation of a sweet voice.

My brother was nervous apparently in some respects, and would never be left alone even for a few minutes; but in the intervals while Raffaelle was with him I had ample opportunity to examine and appreciate the beauties of the Villa de Angelis. It was built, as I have said, on some rocks jutting into the sea, just before coming to the Capo di Posilipo as you proceed from Naples. The earlier foundations were, I believe, originally Roman, and upon them a modern villa had been constructed in the eighteenth century, and to this again John had made important additions in the past two years.*

110

Looking down upon the sea from the windows of the villa, one could on calm days easily discern the remains of Roman piers and moles*lying below the surface of the transparent water; and the tufa-rock* on which the house was built was burrowed with those unintelligible excavations of a classic date so common in the neighbourhood. These subterraneous rooms and passages, while they aroused my curiosity, seemed at the same time so gloomy and repellent that I never explored them. But on one sunny morning, as I walked at the foot of the rocks by the sea, I ventured into one of the larger of these chambers,* and saw that it had at the far end an opening leading apparently to an inner room. I had walking with me an old Italian female servant who took a motherly interest in my proceedings, and who, relying principally upon a very slight knowledge of English, had constituted herself my bodyguard. Encouraged by her presence, I penetrated this inner room and found that it again opened in turn into another, and so on until we had passed through no less than four chambers.

They were all lighted after a fashion through vent-holes which somewhere or other reached the outer air, but the fourth room opened into a fifth which was unlighted. My companion, who had been showing signs of alarm and an evident reluctance to proceed further, now stopped abruptly and begged me to return. It may have been that her fear communicated itself to me also, for on attempting to cross the threshold and explore the darkness of the fifth cell, I was seized by an unreasoning panic and by the feeling of undefined horror experienced in a nightmare. I hesitated for an instant, but my fear became suddenly more intense, and springing

111

back, I followed my companion, who had set out to
run back to the outer air. We never paused until we
stood panting in the full sunlight by the sea. As
soon as the maid had found her breath, she begged
me never to go there again, explaining in broken
English that the caves were known in the neighbourhood as the 'Cells of Isis,'*and were reputed to
be haunted by demons. This episode, trifling as it
may appear, had so great an effect upon me that I
never again ventured on to the lower walk which
ran at the foot of the rocks by the sea.

In the house above, my brother had built a large
hall after the ancient Roman style, and this, with
a dining-room and many other chambers, were
decorated in the fashion of those discovered at
Pompeii.*They had been furnished with the utmost
luxury, and the beauty of the painting, furniture,
carpets, and hangings was enhanced by statues in
bronze and marble. The villa, indeed, and its fittings
were of a kind to which I was little used, and at the
same time of such beauty that I never ceased to
regard all as a creation of an enchanter's wand, or
as the drop-scene*to some drama which might suddenly be raised and disappear from my sight. The
house, in short, together with its furniture, was, I
believe, intended to be a reproduction of an ancient
Roman villa, and had something about it repellent
to my rustic and insular ideas. In the contemplation of its perfection I experienced a curious mental
sensation, which I can only compare to the physical
oppression produced on some persons by the heavy
and cloying perfume of a bouquet of gardenias or
other too highly-scented exotics.

In my brother's room was a medieval reproduction in mellow alabaster of a classic group of a

dolphin encircling a Cupid. It was, I think, the fairest work of art I ever saw, but it jarred upon my sense of propriety that close by it should hang an ivory crucifix. I would rather, I think, have seen all things material and pagan entirely, with every view of the future life shut out, than have found a medley of things sacred and profane, where the emblems of our highest hopes and aspirations were placed in insulting indifference side by side with the embodied forms of sensuality. Here, in this scene of magical beauty, it seemed to me for a moment that the years had rolled back, that Christianity had still to fight with a *living* Paganism, and that the battle was not yet won. It was the same all through the house; and there were many other matters which filled me with regret, mingled with vague and apprehensive surmises which I shall not here repeat.

At one end of the house was a small library, but it contained few works except Latin and Greek classics. I had gone thither one day to look for a book that John had asked for, when in turning out some drawers I found a number of letters written from Worth by my lost Constance to her husband. The shock of being brought suddenly face to face with a handwriting that evoked memories at once so dear and sad was in itself a sharp one; but its bitterness was immeasurably increased by the discovery that not one of these envelopes had ever been opened. While that dear heart, now at rest, was pouring forth her love and sorrow to the ears that should have been above all others ready to receive them, her letters, as they arrived, were flung uncared for, unread, even unopened, into any haphazard receptacle.

The days passed one by one at the Villa de

Angelis with but little incident, nor did my brother's health either visibly improve or decline. Though the weather was still more than usually warm, a grateful* breeze came morning and evening from the sea and tempered the heat so much as to render it always supportable. John would sometimes in the evening sit propped up with cushions on the trellised balcony looking towards Baia, and watch the fishermen setting their nets. We could hear the melody of their deep-voiced songs carried up on the night air. 'It was here, Sophy,' my brother said, as we sat one evening looking on a scene like this,—'It was here that the great epicure Pollio built himself a famous house, and called it by two Greek words meaning a "truce to care,"*from which our name of Posilipo is derived. It was his *sans-souci*,* and here he cast aside his vexations; but they were lighter than mine. Posilipo has brought no cessation of care to me. I do not think I shall find any truce this side the grave; and beyond, who knows?'

This was the first time John had spoken in this strain, and he seemed stirred to an unusual activity, as though his own words had suddenly reminded him how frail was his state. He called Raffaelle to him and despatched him on an errand to Naples. The next morning he sent for me earlier than usual, and begged that a carriage might be ready by six in the evening, as he desired to drive into the city. I tried at first to dissuade him from his project, urging him to consider his weak state of health. He replied that he felt somewhat stronger, and had something that he particularly wished me to see in Naples. This done, it would be better to return at once to England: he could, he thought, bear the journey if we travelled by very short stages.

## Chapter 14

SHORTLY after six o'clock in the evening we left
the Villa de Angelis. The day had been as usual
cloudlessly serene; but a gentle sea-breeze, of which
I have spoken, rose in the afternoon and brought
with it a refreshing coolness. We had arranged a
sort of couch in the landau with many cushions for
my brother, and he mounted into the carriage with
more ease than I had expected. I sat beside him,
with Raffaelle facing me on the opposite seat. We
drove down the hill of Posilipo through the ilex-
trees and tamarisk-bushes that then skirted the sea,
and so into the town. John spoke little except to
remark that the carriage was an easy one. As we
were passing through one of the principal streets he
bent over to me and said, 'You must not be alarmed
if I show you to-day a strange sight. Some women
might perhaps be frightened at what we are going
to see; but my poor sister has known already so much
of trouble that a light thing like this will not affect
her.' In spite of his encomiums upon my supposed
courage, I felt alarmed and agitated by his words.
There was a vagueness in them which frightened
me, and bred that indefinite apprehension which is
often infinitely more terrifying than the actual object which inspires it. To my inquiries he would
give no further response than to say that he had
whilst at Posilipo made some investigations in
Naples leading to a strange discovery, which he was
anxious to communicate to me. After traversing a
considerable distance, we had penetrated apparently into the heart of the town. The streets grew

115

narrower and more densely thronged; the houses
were more dirty and tumble-down, and the appearance of the people themselves suggested that we
had reached some of the lower quarters of the city.
Here we passed through a further network of small
streets of the name of which I took no note, and
found ourselves at last in a very dark and narrow
lane called the *Via del Giardino*. Although my
brother had, so far as I had observed, given no
orders to the coachman, the latter seemed to
have no difficulty in finding his way, driving
rapidly in the Neapolitan fashion, and proceeding
direct as to a place with which he was already
familiar.

In the Via del Giardino the houses were of great
height, and overhung the street so as nearly to touch
one another. It seemed that this quarter had been
formerly inhabited, if not by the aristocracy, at least
by a class very much superior to that which now
lived there; and many of the houses were large and
dignified, though long since parcelled out into
smaller tenements. It was before such a house that
we at last brought up. Here must have been at one
time a house or palace of some person of distinction,
having a long and fine façade adorned with delicate
pilasters, and much florid ornamentation of the
Renaissance period. The ground-floor was divided
into a series of small shops, and its upper storeys
were evidently peopled by sordid families of the
lowest class. Before one of these little shops, now
closed and having its windows carefully blocked with
boards, our carriage stopped. Raffaelle alighted, and
taking a key from his pocket unlocked the door,
and assisted John to leave the carriage. I followed,
and directly we had crossed the threshold, the boy

locked the door behind us, and I heard the carriage drive away.

We found ourselves in a narrow and dark passage, and as soon as my eyes grew accustomed to the gloom I perceived there was at the end of it a low staircase leading to some upper room, and on the right a door which opened into the closed shop. My brother moved slowly along the passage, and began to ascend the stairs. He leant with one hand on Raffaelle's arm, taking hold of the balusters with the other. But I could see that to mount the stairs cost him considerable effort, and he paused frequently to cough and get his breath again. So we reached a landing at the top, and found ourselves in a small chamber or magazine*directly over the shop. It was quite empty except for a few broken chairs, and appeared to be a small loft formed by dividing what had once been a high room into two storeys, of which the shop formed the lower. A long window, which had no doubt once formed one of several in the walls of this large room, was now divided across its width by the flooring, and with its upper part served to light the loft, while its lower panes opened into the shop. The ceiling was, in consequence of these alterations, comparatively low, but though much mutilated, retained evident traces of having been at one time richly decorated, with the raised mouldings and pendants common in the sixteenth century. At one end of the loft was a species of coved and elaborately carved dado, of which the former use was not obvious; but the large original room had without doubt been divided in length as well as in height, as the lath-and-plaster walls at either end of the loft had evidently been no part of the ancient structure.

117

My brother sat down in one of the old chairs, and seemed to be collecting his strength before speaking. My anxiety was momentarily increasing, and it was a great relief when he began, talking in a low voice as one that had much to say and wished to husband his strength.

'I do not know whether you will recollect my having told you of something Mr. Gaskell once said about the music of Graziani's "Areopagita" suite. It had always, he used to say, a curious effect upon his imagination, and the melody of the *Gagliarda* especially called up to his thoughts in some strange way a picture of a certain hall where people were dancing. He even went so far as to describe the general appearance of the room itself, and of the persons who were dancing there.'

'Yes,' I answered, 'I remember your telling me of this;' and indeed my memory had in times past so often rehearsed Mr. Gaskell's description that, although I had not recently thought of it, its chief features immediately returned to my mind.

'He described it,' my brother continued, 'as a long hall with an arcade of arches running down one side, of the fantastic Gothic of the Renaissance. At the end was a gallery or balcony for the musicians, which on its front carried a coat of arms.'

I remembered this perfectly and told John so, adding that the shield bore a cherub's head fanning* three lilies on a golden field.

'It is strange,' John went on, 'that the description of a scene which our friend thought a mere effort of his own imagination has impressed itself so deeply on both our minds. But the picture which he drew was more than a fancy, for we are at this minute in the very hall of his dream.'

I could not gather what my brother meant, and thought his reason was failing him; but he continued, 'This miserable floor on which we stand has of course been afterwards built in; but you see above you the old ceiling, and here at the end was the musicians' gallery with the shield upon its front.'

He pointed to the carved and whitewashed dado which had hitherto so puzzled me. I stepped up to it, and although the lath-and-plaster partition wall was now built around it, it was clear that its curved outline might very easily, as John said, have formed part of the front of a coved gallery. I looked closely at the relief-work which had adorned it. Though the edges were all rubbed off, and the mouldings in some cases entirely removed, I could trace without difficulty a shield in the midst; and a more narrow inspection revealed underneath the whitewash, which had partly peeled away, enough remnants of colour to show that it had certainly been once painted gold and borne a cherub's head with three lilies.

'That is the shield of the old Neapolitan house of Domacavalli,'*my brother continued; 'they bore a cherub's head fanning three lilies on a shield or. It was in the balcony behind this shield, long since blocked up as you see, that the musicians sat on that ball night of which Gaskell dreamt. From it they looked down on the hall below where dancing was going forward, and I will now take you downstairs that you may see if the description tallies.'

So saying, he raised himself, and descending the stairs with much less difficulty than he had shown in mounting them, flung open the door which I had seen in the passage and ushered us into the shop on the ground-floor. The evening light had now faded so much that we could scarcely see even in the passage, and the shop having its windows barricaded with shutters, was in complete darkness. Raffaelle, however, struck a match and lit three half-burnt candles in a tarnished sconce upon the wall.

The shop had evidently been lately in the occupation of a wine-seller, and there were still several empty wooden wine-butts, and some broken flasks on shelves. In one corner I noticed that the earth which formed the floor had been turned up with spades. There was a small heap of mould,* and a large flat stone was thus exposed below the surface. This stone had an iron ring attached to it, and seemed to cover the aperture of a well, or perhaps a vault. At the back of the shop, and furthest from the street, were two lofty arches separated by a column in the middle, from which the outside casing had been stripped.

To these arches John pointed and said, 'That is a part of the arcade which once ran down the whole length of the hall. Only these two arches are now left, and the fine marbles which doubtless coated the outside of this dividing pillar have been stripped off. On a summer's night about one hundred years ago dancing was going on in this hall. There were a dozen couples dancing a wild step such as is never seen now. The tune that the musicians were playing in the gallery above was taken from the "Areopagita" suite of Graziani. Gaskell has often told me that when he played it the music brought with it to his mind a sense of some impending catastrophe, which culminated at the end of the first movement of the *Gagliarda*. It was just at that moment, Sophy, that an Englishman who was dancing here was stabbed in the back and foully murdered.'

I had scarcely heard all that John had said, and had certainly not been able to take in its import; but without waiting to hear if I should say anything, he moved across to the uncovered stone with the ring in it. Exerting a strength which I should have believed entirely impossible in his weak condition, he applied to the stone a lever which lay ready at hand. Raffaelle at the same time seized the ring, and so they were able between them to move the covering to one side sufficiently to allow access to a small staircase which thus appeared to view. The stair was a winding one, and once led no doubt to some vaults below the ground-floor. Raffaelle descended first, taking in his hand the sconce of three candles, which he held above his head so as to fling a light down the steps. John went next, and then I followed, trying to support my brother if possible with my hand. The stairs were very dry, and on the walls there was none of the damp or mould which fancy usually associates with a subterraneous vault. I do not know what it was I expected to see, but I had an uneasy feeling that I was on the brink of some evil and distressing discovery. After we had descended about twenty steps we could see the entry to some vault or underground room, and it was just at the foot of the stairs that I saw something lying, as the light from the candles fell on it from above. At first I thought it was a heap of dust or refuse, but on looking closer it seemed rather a bundle of rags. As my eyes penetrated the gloom, I saw there was about it some tattered cloth of a faded green tint, and almost at the same minute I seemed to trace under the clothes the lines or dimensions of a human figure. For a moment I imagined it was some poor man lying

121

face downward and bent up against the wall. The idea of a man or of a dead body being there shocked me violently, and I cried to my brother, 'Tell me, what is it?' At that instant the light from Raffaelle's candles fell in a somewhat different direction. It lighted up the white bowl of a human skull, and I saw that what I had taken for a man's form was instead that of a clothed skeleton. I turned faint and sick for an instant, and should have fallen had it not been for John, who put his arm about me and sustained me with an unexpected strength.

'God help us!' I exclaimed, 'let us go. I cannot bear this; there are foul vapours here; let us get back to the outer air.'

He took me by the arm, and pointing at the huddled heap, said, 'Do you know whose bones those are? That is Adrian Temple. After it was all over, they flung his body down the steps, dressed in the clothes he wore.'

At that name, uttered in so ill-omened a place, I felt a fresh access of terror. It seemed as though the soul of that wicked man must be still hovering over his unburied remains, and boding evil to us all. A chill crept over me, the light, the walls, my brother, and Raffaelle all swam round, and I sank swooning on the stairs.

When I returned fully to my senses we were in the landau again making our way back to the Villa de Angelis.

## Chapter 15

THE next morning my health and strength were entirely restored to me, but my brother, on the contrary, seemed weak and exhausted from his efforts of the previous night. Our return journey to the Villa de Angelis had passed in complete silence. I had been too much perturbed to question him on the many points relating to the strange events as to which I was still completely in the dark, and he on his side had shown no desire to afford me any further information. When I saw him the next morning he exhibited signs of great weakness, and in response to an effort on my part to obtain some explanation of the discovery of Adrian Temple's body, avoided an immediate reply, promising to tell me all he knew after our return to Worth Maltravers.

I pondered over the last terrifying episode very frequently in my own mind, and as I thought more deeply of it all, it seemed to me that the outlines of some evil history were piece by piece developing themselves, that I had almost within my grasp the clue that would make all plain, and that had eluded me so long. In that dim story Adrian Temple, the music of the *Gagliarda*, my brother's fatal passion for the violin, all seemed to have some mysterious connection, and to have conspired in working John's mental and physical ruin. Even the Stradivarius violin bore a part in the tragedy, becoming, as it were, an actively malignant spirit, though I could not explain how, and was yet entirely unaware of the manner in which it had come into my brother's possession.

I found that John was still resolved on an immediate return to England. His weakness, it is true, led me to entertain doubts as to how he would support so long a journey; but at the same time I did not feel justified in using any strong efforts to dissuade him from his purpose. I reflected that the

123

more wholesome air and associations of England
would certainly re-invigorate both body and mind,
and that any extra strain brought about by the
journey would soon be repaired by the comforts
and watchful care with which we could surround
him at Worth Maltravers.

So the first week in October saw us once more with
our faces set towards England. A very comfortable
swinging-bed or hammock had been arranged for
John in the travelling carriage, and we determined
to avoid fatigue as much as possible by dividing our
journey into very short stages. My brother seemed
to have no intention of giving up the Villa de
Angelis. It was left complete with its luxurious
furniture, and with all his servants, under the care
of an Italian *maggior-duomo.* I felt that as John's
state of health forbade his entertaining any hope of
an immediate return thither, it would have been
much better to close entirely his Italian house. But
his great weakness made it impossible for him to
undertake the effort such a course would involve,
and even if my own ignorance of the Italian tongue
had not stood in the way, I was far too eager to get
my invalid back to Worth to feel inclined to import
any further delay, while I should myself adjust
matters which were after all comparatively trifling.
As Parnham was now ready to discharge his usual
duties of valet, and as my brother seemed quite
content that he should do so, Raffaelle was of course
to be left behind. The boy had quite won my heart
by his sweet manners, combined with his evident
affection to his master, and in making him understand that he was now to leave us, I offered him a
present of a few pounds as a token of my esteem.
He refused, however, to touch this money, and shed

tears when he learnt that he was to be left in Italy, and begged with many protestations of devotion that he might be allowed to accompany us to England. My heart was not proof against his entreaties, supported by so many signs of attachment, and it was agreed, therefore, that he should at least attend us as far as Worth Maltravers. John showed no surprise at the boy being with us; indeed I never thought it necessary to explain that I had originally purposed to leave him behind.

Our journey, though necessarily prolonged by the shortness of its stages, was safely accomplished. John bore it as well as I could have hoped, and though his body showed no signs of increased vigour, his mind, I think, improved in tone, at any rate for a time. From the evening on which he had shown me the terrible discovery in the Via del Giardino he seemed to have laid aside something of his care and depression. He now exhibited little trace of the moroseness and selfishness which had of late so marred his character; and though he naturally felt severely at times the fatigue of travel, yet we had no longer to dread any relapse into that state of lethargy or stupor which had so often baffled every effort to counteract it at Posilipo. Some feeling of superstitious aversion had prompted me to give orders that the Stradivarius violin should be left behind at Posilipo. But before parting my brother asked for it, and insisted that it should be brought with him, though I had never heard him play a note on it for many weeks. He took an interest in all the petty episodes of travel, and certainly appeared to derive more entertainment from the journey than was to have been anticipated in his feeble state of health.

To the incidents of the evening spent in the Via del Giardino he made no allusion of any kind, nor did I for my part wish to renew memories of so unpleasant a nature. His only reference occurred one Sunday evening as we were passing a small graveyard near Genoa. The scene apparently turned his thoughts to that subject, and he told me that he had taken measures before leaving Naples to ensure that the remains of Adrian Temple should be decently interred in the cemetery of Santa Bibiana.* His words set me thinking again, and unsatisfied curiosity prompted me strongly to inquire of him how he had convinced himself that the skeleton at the foot of the stairs was indeed that of Adrian Temple. But I restrained myself, partly from a reliance on his promise that he would one day explain the whole story to me, and partly being very reluctant to mar the enjoyment of the peaceful scenes through which we were passing, by the introduction of any subjects so jarring and painful as those to which I have alluded.

We reached London at last, and here we stopped a few days to make some necessary arrangements before going down to Worth Maltravers. I had urged upon John during the journey that immediately on his arrival in London he should obtain the best English medical advice as to his own health. Though he at first demurred, saying that nothing more was to be done, and that he was perfectly satisfied with the medicine given him by Dr. Baravelli, which he continued to take, yet by constant entreaty I prevailed upon him to accede to so reasonable a request. Dr. Frobisher, considered at that time the first living authority on diseases of the brain and nerves, saw him on the morning after our arrival. He was good enough to speak with me at some length after seeing my brother, and to give me many hints and recipes whereby I might be better enabled to nurse the invalid.

Sir John's condition, he said, was such as to excite serious anxiety. There was, indeed, no brain mischief of any kind to be discovered, but his lungs were in a state of advanced disease, and there were signs of grave heart affection.* Yet he did not bid me to despair, but said that with careful nursing life might certainly be prolonged, and even some measure of health in time restored. He asked me more than once if I knew of any trouble or worry that preyed upon Sir John's mind. Were there financial difficulties; had he been subjected to any mental shock; had he received any severe fright? To all this I could only reply in the negative. At the same time I told Dr. Frobisher as much of John's history as I considered pertinent to the question. He shook his head gravely, and recommended that Sir John should remain for the present in London, under his own constant supervision. To this course my brother would by no means consent. He was eager to proceed at once to his own house, saying that if necessary we could return again to London for Christmas. It was therefore agreed that we should go down to Worth Maltravers at the end of the week.

Parnham had already left us for Worth in order that he might have everything ready against his master's return, and when we arrived we found all in perfect order for our reception. A small morning-room next to the library, with a pleasant south aspect and opening on to the terrace, had been prepared for my brother's use, so that he might avoid the fatigue of mounting stairs, which Dr. Frobisher considered very prejudicial in his present condition. We had also purchased in London a chair fitted with wheels, which enabled him to be moved, or, if he were feeling equal to the exertion, to move himself, without difficulty, from room to room.

His health, I think, improved; very gradually, it is true, but still sufficiently to inspire me with hope that he might yet be spared to us. Of the state of his mind or thoughts I knew little, but I could see that he was at times a prey to nervous anxiety. This showed itself in the harassed look which his pale face often wore, and in his marked dislike to being left alone. He derived, I think, a certain pleasure from the quietude and monotony of his life at Worth, and perhaps also from the consciousness that he had about him loving and devoted hearts. I say hearts, for every servant at Worth was attached to him, remembering the great consideration and courtesy of his earlier years, and grieving to see his youthful and once vigorous frame reduced to so sad a strait. Books he never read himself, and even the charm of Raffaelle's reading seemed to have lost its power; though he never tired of hearing the boy sing, and liked to have him sit by his chair even when his eyes were shut and he was apparently asleep. His general health seemed to me to change but little either for better or worse. Dr. Frobisher had led me to expect some such a sequel. I had not concealed from him that I had at times entertained suspicions as to my brother's sanity; but he had assured me that they were totally unfounded, that Sir John's brain was as clear as his own. At the same time he confessed that he could not account for the exhausted vitality of his patient,—a condition which he would under ordinary circumstances have attributed to excessive study or severe trouble. He had urged upon me the pressing necessity for complete rest, and for much sleep. My brother never even incidentally referred to his wife, his child, or to Mrs. Temple, who constantly wrote to me from Royston, sending kind messages to John, and asking how he did. These messages I never dared to give him, fearing to agitate him, or retard his recovery by diverting his thoughts into channels which must necessarily be of a painful character. That he should never even mention her name, or that of Lady Maltravers, led me to wonder sometimes if one of those curious freaks of memory which occasionally accompany a severe illness had not entirely blotted out from his mind the recollection of his marriage and of his wife's death. He was unable to consider any affairs of business, and the management of the estate remained as it had done for the last two years in the hands of our excellent agent, Mr. Baker.

But one evening in the early part of December he sent Raffaelle about nine o'clock, saying he wished to speak to me. I went to his room, and without any warning he began at once, 'You never show me my boy now, Sophy; he must be grown a big child, and I should like to see him.' Much startled by so unexpected a remark, I replied that the child was at Royston under the care of Mrs. Temple, but that I knew that if it pleased him to see Edward she would be glad to bring him down to Worth. He seemed gratified with this idea, and begged me to ask her to do so, desiring that his respects should be at the same time conveyed to her. I almost ventured at that moment to recall his lost wife to his thoughts, by saying that his child resembled her strongly; for your likeness at that time, and even now, my dear Edward, to your poor mother was very marked. But my courage failed me, and his talk soon reverted to an earlier period, comparing the mildness of the month to that of the first winter which he spent at Eton. His thoughts, however, must, I fancy, have returned for a moment to the days when he first met your mother, for he suddenly asked, 'Where is Gaskell? Why does he never come to see me?' This brought quite a new idea to my mind. I fancied it might do my brother much good to have by him so sensible and true a friend as I knew Mr. Gaskell to be. The latter's address had fortunately not slipped from my memory, and I put all scruples aside and wrote by the next mail to him, setting forth my brother's sad condition, saying that I had heard John mention his name, and begging him on my own account to be so good as to help us if possible and come to us in this hour of trial. Though he was so far off as Westmoreland, Mr. Gaskell's generosity brought him at once to our aid, and within a week he was installed at Worth Maltravers, sleeping in the library, where we had arranged a bed at his own desire, so that he might be near his sick friend.

His presence was of the utmost assistance to us all. He treated John at once with the tenderness of a woman and the firmness of a clever and strong man. They sat constantly together in the mornings, and Mr. Gaskell told me John had not shown with him the same reluctance to talk freely of his married life as he had discovered with me. The tenor of his communications I cannot guess, nor did I ever ask; but I knew that Mr. Gaskell was much affected by them.

John even amused himself now at times by having Mr. Baker into his rooms of a morning, that the management of the estate might be discussed with his friend; and he also expressed his wish to see the family solicitor, as he desired to draw his will. Thinking that any diversion of this nature could not but be beneficial to him, we sent to Dorchester for our solicitor, Mr. Jeffreys, who together with his clerk spent three nights at Worth, and drew up a testament for my brother.

So time went on, and the year was drawing to a close.

It was Christmas Eve, and I had gone to bed shortly after twelve o'clock, having an hour earlier bid good night to John and Mr. Gaskell. The long habit of watching with, or being in charge of an invalid at night, had made my ears extraordinarily quick to apprehend even the slightest murmur. It must have been, I think, near three in the morning when I found myself awake and conscious of some unusual sound. It was low and far off, but I knew instantly what it was, and felt a choking sensation of fear and horror, as if an icy hand had gripped my throat, on recognising the air of the *Gagliarda*. It was being played on the violin, and a long way off, but I knew that tune too well to permit of my having any doubt on the subject.

Any trouble or fear becomes, as you will some day learn, my dear nephew, immensely intensified and exaggerated at night. It is so, I suppose, because our nerves are in an excited condition, and our brain not sufficiently awake to give a due account of our foolish imaginations. I have myself many times lain awake wrestling in thought with difficulties which in the hours of darkness seemed

131

insurmountable, but with the dawn resolved themselves into merely trivial inconveniences. So on this night, as I sat up in bed looking into the dark, with the sound of that melody in my ears, it seemed as if something too terrible for words had happened; as though the evil spirit, which we had hoped was exorcised, had returned with others sevenfold more wicked than himself, and taken up his abode again* with my lost brother. The memory of another night rushed to my mind when Constance had called me from my bed at Royston, and we had stolen together down the moonlit passages with the lilt of that wicked music vibrating on the still summer air. Poor Constance! She was in her grave now; yet *her* troubles at least were over, but here, as by some bitter irony, instead of carol or sweet symphony, it was the *Gagliarda* that woke me from my sleep on Christmas morning.

I flung my dressing-gown about me, and hurried through the corridor and down the stairs which led to the lower storey and my brother's room. As I opened my bedroom door the violin ceased suddenly in the middle of a bar. Its last sound was not a musical note, but rather a horrible scream, such as I pray I may never hear again. It was a sound such as a wounded beast might utter. There is a picture I have seen of Blake's, showing the soul of a strong wicked man leaving his body at death. The spirit is flying out through the window with awful staring eyes, aghast at the desolation into which it is going.* If in the agony of dissolution such a lost soul could utter a cry, it would, I think, sound like the wail which I heard from the violin that night.

Instantly all was in absolute stillness. The passages were silent and ghostly in the faint light of my candle; but as I reached the bottom of the stairs I heard the sound of other footsteps, and Mr. Gaskell met me. He was fully dressed, and had evidently not been to bed. He took me kindly by the hand and said, 'I feared you might be alarmed by the sound of music. John has been walking in his sleep; he had taken out his violin and was playing on it in a trance. Just as I reached him something in it gave way, and the discord caused by the slackened strings roused him at once. He is awake now and has returned to bed. Control your alarm for his sake and your own. It is better that he should not know you have been awakened.'

He pressed my hand and spoke a few more reassuring words, and I went back to my room still much agitated, and yet feeling half ashamed for having shown so much anxiety with so little reason.

That Christmas morning was one of the most beautiful that I ever remember. It seemed as though summer was so loath to leave our sunny Dorset coast that she came back on this day to bid us adieu before her final departure. I had risen early and had partaken of the Sacrament at our little church. Dr. Butler* had recently introduced this early service, and though any alteration of time-honoured customs in such matters might not otherwise have met with my approval, I was glad to avail myself of the privilege on this occasion, as I wished in any case to spend the later morning with my brother. The singular beauty of the early hours, and the tranquil-lising effect of the solemn service brought back serenity to my mind, and effectually banished from it all memories of the preceding night. Mr. Gaskell met me in the hall on my return, and after greeting me kindly with the established compliments of the day, inquired after my health, and hoped that the disturbance of my slumber on the previous night had not affected me injuriously. He had good news for me: John seemed decidedly better, was already dressed, and desired, as it was Christmas morning, that we would take our breakfast with him in his room.

To this, as you may imagine, I readily assented. Our breakfast party passed off with much content, and even with some quiet humour, John sitting in his easy-chair at the head of the table and wishing us the compliments of the season. I found laid in my place a letter from Mrs. Temple greeting us all (for she knew Mr. Gaskell was at Worth), and saying that she hoped to bring little Edward to us at the New Year. My brother seemed much pleased at the prospect of seeing his son, and though perhaps it was only imagination, I fancied he was particularly gratified that Mrs. Temple herself was to pay us a visit. She had not been to Worth since the death of Lady Maltravers.

Before we had finished breakfast the sun beat on the panes with an unusual strength and brightness. His rays cheered us all, and it was so warm that John first opened the windows, and then wheeled his chair on to the walk outside. Mr. Gaskell brought him a hat and mufflers, and we sat with him on the terrace basking in the sun. The sea was still and glassy as a mirror, and the Channel lay stretched before us like a floor of moving gold. A rose or two still hung against the house, and the sun's rays reflected from the red sandstone gave us a December morning more mild and genial than many June days that I have known in the north. We sat for some minutes without speaking, immersed in our own reflections and in the exquisite beauty of the scene.

The stillness was broken by the bells of the parish church ringing for the morning service. There were two of them, and their sound, familiar to us from childhood, seemed like the voices of old friends. John looked at me and said with a sigh, 'I should like to go to church. It is long since I was there. You and I have always been on Christmas mornings, Sophy, and Constance would have wished it had she been with us.'

His words, so unexpected and tender, filled my eyes with tears; not tears of grief, but of deep thankfulness to see my loved one turning once more to the old ways. It was the first time I had heard him speak of Constance, and that sweet name, with the infinite pathos of her death, and of the spectacle of my brother's weakness, so overcame me that I could not speak. I only pressed his hand and nodded. Mr. Gaskell, who had turned away for a minute, said he thought John would take no harm in attending the morning service provided the church were warm. On this point I could reassure him, having found it properly heated even in the early morning.

Mr. Gaskell was to push John's chair, and I ran off to put on my cloak, with my heart full of profound thankfulness for the signs of returning grace so mercifully vouchsafed to our dear sufferer on this happy day. I was ready dressed and had just entered the library when Mr. Gaskell stepped hurriedly through the window from the terrace. 'John has fainted!' he said. 'Run for some smelling salts and call Parnham!'

There was a scene of hurried alarm, giving place

ere long to terrified despair. Parnham mounted a
horse and set off at a wild gallop to Swanage to
fetch Dr. Bruton; but an hour before he returned
we knew the worst. My brother was beyond the aid
of the physician: his wrecked life had reached a
sudden term!

I have now, dear Edward, completed the brief
narrative of some of the facts attending the latter
years of your father's life. The motive which has
induced me to commit them to writing has been a
double one. I am anxious to give effect as far as may
be to the desire expressed most strongly to Mr.
Gaskell by your father, that you should be put in
possession of these facts on your coming of age.
And for my own part I think it better that you
should thus hear the plain truth from me, lest you
should be at the mercy of haphazard reports, which
might at any time reach you from ignorant or
interested sources. Some of the circumstances were
so remarkable that it is scarcely possible to suppose
that they were not known, and most probably frequently discussed, in so large an establishment as
that of Worth Maltravers. I even have reason to
believe that exaggerated and absurd stories were
current at the time of Sir John's death, and I should
be grieved to think that such foolish tales might by
any chance reach your ear without your having any
sure means of discovering where the truth lay. God
knows how grievous it has been to me to set down
on paper some of the facts that I have here narrated.
You as a dutiful son will reverence the name even
of a father whom you never knew; but you must
remember that his sister did more; she loved him
with a single-hearted devotion, and it still grieves

her to the quick to write anything which may seem to detract from his memory. Only, above all things, let us speak the truth. Much of what I have told you needs, I feel, further explanation, but this I cannot give, for I do not understand the circumstances. Mr. Gaskell, your guardian, will, I believe, add to this account a few notes of his own, which may tend to elucidate some points, as he is in possession of certain facts of which I am still ignorant.

# MR. GASKELL'S NOTE

◄◄◄◄◄◄ ◉ ►►►►►►

I HAVE read what Miss Maltravers has written, and have but little to add to it. I can give no explanation that will tally with all the facts or meet all the difficulties involved in her narrative. The most obvious solution of some points would be, of course, to suppose that Sir John Maltravers was insane. But to anyone who knew him as intimately as I did, such an hypothesis is untenable; nor, if admitted, would it explain some of the strangest incidents. Moreover, it was strongly negatived by Dr. Frobisher, from whose verdict in such matters there was at the time no appeal, by Dr. Dobie, and by Dr. Bruton, who had known Sir John from his infancy. It is possible that towards the close of his life he suffered occasionally from hallucination, though I could not positively affirm even so much; but this was only when his health had been completely undermined by causes which are very difficult to analyse.

When I first knew him at Oxford he was a strong man physically as well as mentally; open-hearted, and of a merry and genial temperament. At the same time he was, like most cultured persons—and especially musicians,—highly strung and excitable. But at a certain point in his career his very nature seemed to change; he became reserved, secretive, and saturnine. On this moral metamorphosis followed an equally startling physical change. His robust health began to fail him, and although there was no definite malady which doctors could combat, he went gradually from bad to worse until the end came.

The commencement of this extraordinary change coincided, I believe, almost exactly with his discovery of the Stradivarius violin; and whether this was, after all, a mere coincidence or something more it is not easy to say. Until a very short time before his death neither Miss Maltravers nor I had any idea how that instrument had come into his possession, or I think something might perhaps have been done to save him.

Though towards the end of his life he spoke freely to his sister of the finding of the violin, he only told her half the story, for he concealed from her entirely that there was anything else in the hidden cupboard at Oxford. But as a matter of fact, he had found there also two manuscript books containing an elaborate diary of some years of a man's life.* That man was Adrian Temple, and I believe that in the perusal of this diary must be sought the origin of John Maltravers' ruin. The manuscript was beautifully written in a clear but cramped eighteenth-century hand, and gave the idea of a man writing with deliberation, and wishing to transcribe his impressions with accuracy for further reference. The style was excellent, and the minute details given were often of high antiquarian interest; but the record throughout was marred by gross licence. Adrian Temple's life had undoubtedly so definite an influence on Sir John's that a brief outline of it, as gathered from his diaries, is necessary for the understanding of what followed.

Temple went up to Oxford in 1737. He was seventeen years old, without parents, brothers, or sisters; and he possessed the Royston estates in

Derbyshire, which were then, as now, a most valuable property. With the year 1738 his diaries begin, and though then little more than a boy, he had tasted every illicit pleasure that Oxford had to offer. His temptations were no doubt great; for besides being wealthy he was handsome, and had probably never known any proper control, as both his parents had died when he was still very young. But in spite of other failings, he was a brilliant scholar, and on taking his degree, was made at once a fellow of St. John's. He took up his abode in that College in a fine set of rooms looking on to the gardens, and from this period seems to have used Royston but little, living always either at Oxford or on the Continent. He formed at this time the acquaintance of one Jocelyn, whom he engaged as companion and amanuensis. Jocelyn was a man of talent, but of irregular life, and was no doubt an accomplice in many of Temple's excesses. In 1743 they both undertook the so-called 'grand tour,' and though it was not his first visit, it was then probably that Temple first felt the fascination of pagan Italy,—a fascination which increased with every year of his after-life.

On his return from foreign travel he found himself among the stirring events of 1745.* He was an ardent supporter of the Pretender, and made no attempt to conceal his views. Jacobite tendencies were indeed generally prevalent in the College at the time, and had this been the sum of his offending, it is probable that little notice would have been taken by the College authorities. But his notoriously wild life told against the young man, and certain dark suspicions were not easily passed over. After the *fiasco* of the Rebellion Dr. Holmes, then Presi-

dent of the College,* seems to have made a scape-
goat of Temple. He was deprived of his fellowship,
and though not formally expelled, such pressure
was put upon him as resulted in his leaving St.
John's and removing to Magdalen Hall. There his
great wealth evidently secured him consideration,
and he was given the best rooms in the Hall, that
very set*looking on to New College Lane which Sir
John Maltravers afterwards occupied.

In the first half of the eighteenth century the
romance of the middle ages, though dying, was not
dead, and the occult sciences still found followers
among the Oxford towers.* From his early years
Temple's mind seems to have been set strongly
towards mysticism of all kinds, and he and Jocelyn
were versed in the jargon of the alchemist and
astrologer, and practised according to the ancient
rules. It was his reputation as a necromancer, and
the stories current of illicit rites performed in the
garden-rooms at St. John's, that contributed largely
to his being dismissed from that College. He had
also become acquainted with Francis Dashwood,
the notorious Lord le Despencer, and many a
winter's night saw him riding through the misty
Thames meadows to the door of the sham Francis-
can abbey. In his diaries were more notices than
one of the 'Franciscans' and the nameless orgies of
Medmenham.*

He was devoted to music. It was a rare enough
accomplishment then, and a rarer thing still to find
a wealthy landowner performing on the violin. Yet
so he did, though he kept his passion very much to
himself, as fiddling was thought lightly of in those
days. His musical skill was altogether exceptional,
and he was the first possessor of the Stradivarius

violin which afterwards fell so unfortunately into Sir John's hands. This violin Temple bought in the autumn of 1738, on the occasion of a first visit to Italy. In that year*died the nonagenarian Antonius Stradivarius, the greatest violin-maker the world has ever seen. After Stradivarius's death the stock of fiddles in his shop was sold by auction.* Temple happened to be travelling in Cremona at the time with a tutor, and at the auction he bought that very instrument which we afterwards had cause to know so well. A note in his diary gave its cost at four louis, and said that a curious history attached to it. Though it was of his golden period, and probably the finest instrument he ever made, Stradivarius would never sell it, and it had hung for more than thirty years in his shop. It was said that from some whim as he lay dying he had given orders that it should be burnt; but if that were so, the instructions were neglected, and after his death it came under the hammer. Adrian Temple from the first recognised the great value of the instrument. His notes show that he only used it on certain special occasions, and it was no doubt for its better protection that he devised the hidden cupboard where Sir John eventually found it.

The later years of Temple's life were spent for the most part in Italy. On the Scoglio di Venere, near Naples, he built the Villa de Angelis, and there henceforth passed all except the hottest months of the year. Shortly after the completion of the villa Jocelyn left him suddenly, and became a Carthusian monk.* A caustic note in the diary hinted that even this foul parasite was shocked into the austerest form of religion by something he had seen going forward. At Naples Temple's dark life became still

142

darker. He dallied, it is true, with Neo-Platonism, and boasts that he, like Plotinus, had twice passed the circle of the *nous* and enjoyed the fruition of the deity;*but the ideals of even that easy doctrine grew in his evil life still more miserably debased. More than once in the manuscript he made mention by name of the *Gagliarda* of Graziani as having been played at pagan mysteries which these enthusiasts revived at Naples, and the air had evidently impressed itself deeply on his memory. The last entry in his diary is made on the 16th of December, 1752. He was then in Oxford for a few days, but shortly afterwards returned to Naples. The accident of his having just completed a second volume, induced him, no doubt, to leave it behind him in the secret cupboard. It is probable that he commenced a third, but if so it was never found.

In reading the manuscript I was struck with the author's clear and easy style, and found the interest of the narrative increase rather than diminish. At the same time its study was inexpressibly painful to me. Nothing could have supported me in my determination to thoroughly master it but the conviction that if I was to be of any real assistance to my poor friend Maltravers, I must know as far as possible every circumstance connected with his malady. As it was, I felt myself breathing an atmosphere of moral contagion during the perusal of the manuscript, and certain passages have since returned at times to haunt me in spite of all efforts to dislodge them from my memory. When I came to Worth at Miss Maltravers' urgent invitation, I found my friend Sir John terribly altered. It was not only that he was ill and physically weak, but he had

143

entirely lost the manner of youth, which, though indefinable, is yet so appreciable, and draws so sharp a distinction between the first period of life and middle age. But the most striking feature of his illness was the extraordinary pallor of his complexion, which made his face resemble a subtle counterfeit of white wax rather than that of a living man. He welcomed me undemonstratively, but with evident sincerity; and there was an entire absence of the constraint which often accompanies the meeting again of friends whose cordial relations have suffered interruption. From the time of my arrival at Worth until his death we were constantly together; indeed I was much struck by the almost childish dislike which he showed to be left alone even for a few moments. As night approached this feeling became intensified. Parnham slept always in his master's room; but if anything called the servant away even for a minute, he would send for Carotenuto or myself to be with him until his return. His nerves were weak; he started violently at any unexpected noise, and above all, he dreaded being in the dark. When night fell he had additional lamps brought into his room, and even when he composed himself to sleep, insisted on a strong light being kept by his bedside.

I had often read in books of people wearing a 'hunted' expression, and had laughed at the phrase as conventional and unmeaning. But when I came to Worth I knew its truth; for if any face ever wore a hunted—I had almost written a haunted—look, it was the white face of Sir John Maltravers. His air seemed that of a man who was constantly expecting the arrival of some evil tidings, and at times reminded me painfully of the guilty expectation of

144

a felon who knows that a warrant is issued for his arrest.

During my visit he spoke to me frequently about his past life, and instead of showing any reluctance to discuss the subject, seemed glad of the opportunity of disburdening his mind. I gathered from him that the reading of Adrian Temple's memoirs had made a deep impression on his mind, which was no doubt intensified by the vision which he thought he saw in his rooms at Oxford, and by the discovery of the portrait at Royston. Of those singular phenomena I have no explanation to offer.

The romantic element in his disposition rendered him peculiarly susceptible to the fascination of that mysticism which breathed through Temple's narrative. He told me that almost from the first time he read it he was filled with a longing to visit the places and to revive the strange life of which it spoke. This inclination he kept at first in check, but by degrees it gathered strength enough to master him.

There is no doubt in my mind that the music of the *Gagliarda* of Graziani helped materially in this process of mental degradation. It is curious that Michael Prætorius in the 'Syntagma musicum' should speak of the Galliard generally as an 'invention of the devil, full of shameful and licentious gestures and immodest movements,'*and the singular melody of the *Gagliarda* in the 'Areopagita' suite certainly exercised from the first a strange influence over me. I shall not do more than touch on the question here, because I see Miss Maltravers has spoken of it at length, and will only say, that though since the day of Sir John's death I have never heard a note of it, the air is still fresh in my mind, and has at times presented itself to me unexpectedly, and always with an unwholesome effect. This I have found happen generally in times of physical depression, and the same air no doubt exerted a similar influence on Sir John, which his impressionable nature rendered from the first more deleterious to him.

I say this advisedly, because I am sure that if some music is good for man and elevates him, other melodies are equally bad and enervating. An experience far wider than any we yet possess is necessary to enable us to say how far this influence is capable of extension. How far, that is, the mind may be directed on the one hand to ascetic abnegation by the systematic use of certain music, or on the other to illicit and dangerous pleasures by melodies of an opposite tendency. But this much is, I think, certain, that after a comparatively advanced standard of culture has once been attained, music is the readiest if not the only key which admits to the yet narrower circle of the highest imaginative thought.*

On the occasion for travel afforded him by his honeymoon, an impulse which he could not at the time explain, but which after-events have convinced me was the haunting suggestion of the *Gagliarda*, drove him to visit the scenes mentioned so often in Temple's diary. He had always been an excellent scholar, and a classic* of more than ordinary ability. Rome and Southern Italy filled him with a strange delight. His education enabled him to appreciate to the full what he saw; he peopled the stage with the figures of the original actors, and tried to assimilate his thought to theirs. He began

reading classical literature widely, no longer from
the scholarly but the literary standpoint. In Rome
he spent much time in the librarians'*shops, and
there met with copies of the numerous authors of
the later empire*and of those Alexandrine philosophers*which are rarely seen in England. In these he
found a new delight and fresh food for his mysticism.

Such study, if carried to any extent, is probably
dangerous to the English character, and certainly
was to a man of Maltravers' romantic sympathies.
This reading produced in time so real an effect
upon his mind that if he did not definitely abandon
Christianity, as I fear he did, he at least adulterated
it with other doctrines till it became to him Neo-
Platonism. That most seductive of philosophies,
which has enthralled so many minds from Proclus
and Julian to Augustine and the Renaissancists,*
found an easy convert in John Maltravers. Its passionate longing for the vague and undefined good,
its tolerance of æsthetic impressions,* the pleasant
superstitions of its dynamic pantheism,* all touched
responsive chords in his nature. His mind, he told
me, became filled with a measureless yearning for
the old culture*of pagan philosophy, and as the past
became clearer and more real, so the present grew
dimmer, and his thoughts were gradually weaned
entirely from all the natural objects of affection and
interest which should otherwise have occupied
them. To what a terrible extent this process went
on, Miss Maltravers' narrative shows. Soon after
reaching Naples he visited the Villa de Angelis,
which Temple had built on the ruins of a sea-
house of Pomponius.* The later building had in its
turn become dismantled and ruinous, and Sir John
found no difficulty in buying the site outright.

He afterwards rebuilt it on an elaborate scale, endeavouring to reproduce in its equipment the luxury of the later empire. I had occasion to visit the house more than once in my capacity of executor, and found it full of priceless works of art, which, though neither so difficult to procure at that time nor so costly as they would be now, were yet sufficiently valuable to have necessitated an unjustifiable outlay.

The situation of the building fostered his infatuation for the past. It lay between the Bay of Naples and the Bay of Baia,* and from its windows commanded the same exquisite views which had charmed* Cicero and Lucullus, Severus and the Antonines.* Hard by stood Baia,* the princely seaside resort of the empire. That most luxurious and wanton of all cities of antiquity survived the cataclysms of ages, and only lost its civic continuity and became the ruined village of to-day in the sack of the fifteenth century. But a continuity of wickedness is not so easily broken, and those who know the spot best say that it is still instinct with memories of a shameful past.*

For miles along that haunted coast the foot cannot be put down except on the ruins of some splendid villa, and over all there broods a spirit of corruption and debasement actually sensible* and oppressive. Of the dawns and sunsets, of the noonday sun tempered by the sea-breeze and the shade of scented groves, those who have been there know the charm, and to those who have not no words can describe it. But there are malefic vapours rising from the corpse of a past not altogether buried,* and most cultivated Englishmen who tarry there long feel their influence as did John Maltravers. Like so many *decepti deceptores**of the Neo-Platonic school, he did not practise the abnegation enjoined by the very cult he professed to follow. Though his nature was far too refined, I believe, ever to sink into the sensualism revealed in Temple's diaries, yet it was through the gratification of corporeal tastes that he endeavoured to achieve the divine *extasis*;* and there were constantly lavish and sumptuous entertainments at the villa, at which strange guests were present.

In such a nightmare of a life it was not to be expected that any mind would find repose, and Maltravers certainly found none. All those cares which usually occupy men's minds, all thoughts of wife, child, and home were, it is true, abandoned; but a wild unrest had hold of him, and never suffered him to be at ease. Though he never told me as much, yet I believe he was under the impression that the form which he had seen at Oxford and Royston had reappeared to him on more than one subsequent occasion. It must have been, I fancy, with a vague hope of 'laying' this spectre that he now set himself with eagerness to discover where or how Temple had died. He remembered that Royston tradition said he had succumbed at Naples in the plague of 1752, but an idea seized him that this was not the case; indeed I half suspect his fancy unconsciously pictured that evil man as still alive. The methods by which he eventually discovered the skeleton, or learnt the episodes which preceded Temple's death, I do not know. He promised to tell me some day at length, but a sudden death prevented his ever doing so. The facts as he narrated them, and as I have little doubt they actually occurred, were these: Adrian Temple, after Jocelyn's departure, had made a confidant of one Palamede Domacavalli, a scion of a splendid Parthenopean* family of that name. Palamede had a palace in the heart of Naples, and was Temple's equal in age and also in his great wealth. The two men became boon companions, associated in all kinds of wickedness and excess. At length Palamede married a beautiful girl named Olimpia Aldobrandini,* who was also of the noblest lineage; but the intimacy between him and Temple was not interrupted. About a year subsequent to this marriage dancing was going on after a splendid banquet in the great hall of the Palazzo Domacavalli. Adrian, who was a favoured guest, called to the musicians in the gallery to play the 'Areopagita' suite, and danced it with Olimpia, the wife of his host. The *Gagliarda* was reached but never finished, for near the end of the second movement Palamede from behind drove a stiletto into his friend's heart. He had found out that day that Adrian had not spared even Olimpia's honour.

I have endeavoured to condense into a connected story the facts learnt piecemeal from Sir John in conversation. To a certain extent they supplied, if not an explanation, at least an account of the change that had come over my friend. But only to a certain extent; there the explanation broke down and I was left baffled. I could imagine that a life of unwholesome surroundings and disordered studies might in time produce such a loss of mental tone as would lead in turn to moral *acolasia*,* sensual excess, and physical ruin. But in Sir John's case the cause was not adequate; he had, so far as I know, never wholly given the reins to sensuality, and the change was too abrupt and the breakdown of body and mind too complete to be accounted for by such events as those of which he had spoken.

I had, too, an uneasy feeling, which grew upon me the more I saw of him, that while he spoke freely enough on certain topics, and obviously meant to give a complete history of his past life, there was in reality something in the background which he always kept from my view. He was, it seemed, like a young man asked by an indulgent father to disclose his debts in order that they may be discharged, who, although he knows his parent's leniency, and that any debt not now disclosed will be afterwards but a weight upon his own neck, yet hesitates for very shame to tell the full amount, and keeps some items back. So poor Sir John kept something back from me his friend, whose only aim was to afford him consolation and relief, and whose compassion would have made me listen without rebuke to the narration of the blackest crimes. I cannot say how much this conviction grieved me. I would most willingly have given my all, my very life, to save my friend and Miss Maltravers' brother; but my efforts were paralysed by the feeling that I did not know what I had to combat, that some evil influence was at work on him which continually evaded my grasp. Once or twice it seemed as though he were within an ace of telling me all; once or twice, I believe, he had definitely made up his mind to do so; but then the mood changed, or more probably his courage failed him.

It was on one of these occasions that he asked me, somewhat suddenly, whether I thought that a man could by any conscious act committed in the flesh take away from himself all possibility of repentance and ultimate salvation.* Though, I trust, a sincere Christian, I am nothing of a theologian, and the question touching on a topic which had not

151

occurred to my mind since childhood, and which seemed to savour rather of medieval romance than of practical religion, took me for a moment aback. I hesitated for an instant, and then replied that the means of salvation offered man were undoubtedly so sufficient as to remove from one truly penitent the guilt of any crime however dark. My hesitation had been but momentary; but Sir John seemed to have noticed it, and sealed his lips to any confession, if he had indeed intended to make any, by changing the subject abruptly. This question naturally gave me food for serious reflection and anxiety. It was the first occasion on which he appeared to me to be undoubtedly suffering from definite hallucination, and I was aware that any illusions connected with religion are generally most difficult to remove. At the same time, anything of this sort was the more remarkable in Sir John's case, as he had, so far as I knew, for a considerable time entirely abandoned the Christian belief.

Unable to elicit any further information from him, and being thus thrown entirely upon my own resources, I determined that I would read through again the whole of Temple's diaries. The task was a very distasteful one, as I have already explained, but I hoped that a second reading might perhaps throw some light on the dark misgiving that was troubling Sir John. I read the manuscript again with the closest attention. Nothing, however, of any importance seemed to have escaped me on the former occasions, and I had reached nearly the end of the second volume when a comparatively slight matter arrested my attention. I have said that the pages were all carefully numbered, and the events of each day recorded separately; even where Temple had found nothing of moment to notice on a given day, he had still inserted the date with the word *nil* written against it. But as I sat one evening in the library at Worth after Sir John had gone to bed, and was finally glancing through the days of the months in Temple's diary to make sure that all were complete, I found one day was missing. It was towards the end of the second volume, and the day was the 23d of October in the year 1752. A glance at the numbering of the pages revealed the fact that three leaves had been entirely removed, and that the pages numbered 349 to 354 were not to be found. Again I ran through the diaries to see whether there were any leaves removed in other places, but found no other single page missing. All was complete except at this one place, the manuscript beautifully written, with scarcely an error or erasure throughout. A closer examination showed that these leaves had been cut out close to the back, and the cut edges of the paper appeared too fresh to admit of this being done a century ago. A very short reflection convinced me, in fact, that the excision was not likely to have been Temple's, and that it must have been made by Sir John.

My first intention was to ask him at once what the lost pages had contained, and why they had been cut out. The matter might be a mere triviality which he could explain in a moment. But on softly opening his bedroom door I found him sleeping, and Parnham (whom the strong light always burnt in the room rendered more wakeful) informed me that his master had been in a deep sleep for more than an hour. I knew how sorely his wasted energies needed such repose, and stepped back to

153

the library without awaking him. A few minutes before, I had been feeling sleepy at the conclusion of my task, but now all wish for sleep was suddenly banished and a painful wakefulness took its place. I was under a species of mental excitement which reminded me of my feelings some years before at Oxford on the first occasion of our ever playing the *Gagliarda* together, and an idea struck me with the force of intuition that in these three lost leaves lay the secret of my friend's ruin.

I turned to the context to see whether there was anything in the entries preceding or following the lacuna that would afford a clue to the missing passage. The record of the few days immediately preceding the 23d of October was short and contained nothing of any moment whatever. Adrian and Jocelyn were alone together at the Villa de Angelis. The entry on the 22d was very unimportant and apparently quite complete, ending at the bottom of page 348. Of the 23d there was, as I have said, no record at all, and the entry for the 24th began at the top of page 355. This last memorandum was also brief, and written when the author was annoyed by Jocelyn leaving him.

The defection of his companion had been apparently entirely unexpected. There was at least no previous hint of any such intention. Temple wrote that Jocelyn had left the Villa de Angelis that day and taken up his abode with the Carthusians of San Martino.* No reason for such an extraordinary change was given; but there was a hint that Jocelyn had professed himself shocked at something that had happened. The entry concluded with a few bitter remarks: '*So farewell to my holy anchoret,* *and if I cannot speed him with a leprosie as one*

*Elisha did his servant, yet at least he went out from my presence with a face white as snow."\**

I had read this sentence more than once before without its attracting other than a passing attention. The curious expression, that Jocelyn had gone out from his presence with a face white as snow, had hitherto seemed to me to mean nothing more than that the two men had parted in violent anger, and that Temple had abused or bullied his companion. But as I sat alone that night in the library the words seemed to assume an entirely new force, and a strange suspicion began to creep over me.

I have said that one of the most remarkable features of Sir John's illness was his deadly pallor. Though I had now spent some time at Worth, and had been daily struck by this lack of colour, I had never before remembered in this connection that a strange paleness had also been an attribute of Adrian Temple, and was indeed very clearly marked in the picture painted of him by Battoni. In Sir John's account, moreover, of the vision which he thought he had seen in his rooms at Oxford, he had always spoken of the white and waxen face of his spectral visitant. The family tradition of Royston said that Temple had lost his colour in some deadly magical experiment, and a conviction now flashed upon me that Jocelyn's face 'as white as snow' could refer only to this same unnatural pallor, and that he too had been smitten with it as with the mark of the beast.\*

In a drawer of my despatch-box, I kept by me all the letters which the late Lady Maltravers had written home during her ill-fated honeymoon. Miss Maltravers had placed them in my hands in order that I might be acquainted with every fact that could at all elucidate the progress of Sir John's malady. I remembered that in one of these letters* mention was made of a sharp attack of fever in Naples, and of her noticing in him for the first time this singular pallor. I found the letter again without difficulty and read it with a new light. Every line breathed of surprise and alarm. Lady Maltravers feared that her husband was very seriously ill. On the Wednesday, two days before she wrote, he had suffered all day from a strange restlessness, which had increased after they had retired in the evening. He could not sleep and had dressed again, saying he would walk a little in the night air to compose himself. He had not returned till near six in the morning, and then seemed so exhausted that he had since been confined to his bed. He was terribly pale, and the doctors feared he had been attacked by some strange fever.

The date of the letter was the 25th of October, fixing the night of the 23d as the time of Sir John's first attack. The coincidence of the date with that of the day missing in Temple's diary was significant, but it was not needed now to convince me that Sir John's ruin was due to something that occurred on that fatal night at Naples.

The question that Dr. Frobisher had asked Miss Maltravers when he was first called to see her brother in London returned to my memory with an overwhelming force. 'Had Sir John been subjected to any mental shock; had he received any severe fright?' I knew now that the question should have been answered in the affirmative, for I felt as certain as if Sir John had told me himself that he *had* received a violent shock, probably some terrible fright, on the night of the 23d of October. What the

156

nature of that shock could have been my imagination was powerless to conceive, only I knew that whatever Sir John had done or seen, Adrian Temple and Jocelyn had done or seen also a century before and at the same place. That horror which had blanched the face of all three men for life had perhaps fallen with a less overwhelming force on Temple's seasoned wickedness, but had driven the worthless Jocelyn to the cloister, and was driving Sir John to the grave.

These thoughts as they passed through my mind filled me with a vague alarm. The lateness of the hour, the stillness and the subdued light, made the library in which I sat seem so vast and lonely that I began to feel the same dread of being alone that I had observed so often in my friend. Though only a door separated me from his bedroom, and I could hear his deep and regular breathing, I felt as though I must go in and waken him or Parnham to keep me company and save me from my own reflections. By a strong effort I restrained myself, and sat down to think the matter over and endeavour to frame some hypothesis that might explain the mystery. But it was all to no purpose. I merely wearied myself without being able to arrive at even a plausible conjecture, except that it seemed as though the strange coincidence of date might point to some ghastly charm or incantation which could only be carried out on one certain night of the year.

It must have been near morning when, quite exhausted, I fell into an uneasy slumber in the armchair where I sat. My sleep, however brief, was peopled with a succession of fantastic visions, in which I continually saw Sir John, not ill and wasted as now, but vigorous and handsome as I had known

157

him at Oxford, standing beside a glowing brazier and reciting words I could not understand, while another man* with a sneering white face sat in a corner playing the air of the *Gagliarda* on a violin. Parnham woke me in my chair at seven o'clock; his master, he said, was still sleeping easily.

I had made up my mind that as soon as he awoke I would inquire of Sir John as to the pages missing from the diary; but though my expectation and excitement were at a high pitch, I was forced to restrain my curiosity, for Sir John's slumber continued late into the day. Dr. Bruton called in the morning, and said that this sleep was what the patient's condition most required, and was a distinctly favourable symptom; he was on no account to be disturbed. Sir John did not leave his bed, but continued dozing all day till the evening. When at last he shook off his drowsiness, the hour was already so late that, in spite of my anxiety, I hesitated to talk with him about the diaries, lest I should unduly excite him before the night.

As the evening advanced he became very uneasy, and rose more than once from his bed. This restlessness, following on the repose of the day, ought perhaps to have made me anxious, for I have since observed that when death is very near an apprehensive unrest often sets in both with men and animals. It seems as if they dreaded to resign themselves to sleep, lest as they slumber the last enemy should seize them unawares. They try to fling off the bedclothes, they sometimes must leave their beds and walk. So it was with poor John Maltravers on his last Christmas Eve. I had sat with him grieving for his disquiet until he seemed to grow more tranquil, and at length fell asleep. I was sleeping that night in his room instead of Parnham, and tired with sitting up through the previous night, I flung myself, dressed as I was, upon the bed. I had scarcely dozed off, I think, before the sound of his violin awoke me. I found he had risen from his bed, had taken his favourite instrument, and was playing in his sleep. The air was the *Gagliarda* of the 'Areopagita' suite, which I had not heard since we had played it last together at Oxford, and it brought back with it a crowd of far-off memories and infinite regrets. I cursed the sleepiness which had overcome me at my watchman's post, and allowed Sir John to play once more that melody which had always been fraught with such evil for him; and I was about to wake him gently when he was startled from sleep by a strange accident. As I walked towards him the violin seemed entirely to collapse in his hands, and, as a matter of fact, the belly then gave way and broke under the strain of the strings. As the strings slackened, the last note became an unearthly discord. If I were superstitious I should say that some evil spirit then went out of the violin, and broke in his parting throes the wooden tabernacle which had so long sheltered him. It was the last time the instrument was ever used, and that hideous chord was the last that Maltravers ever played.

I had feared that the shock of waking thus suddenly from sleep would have a very prejudicial effect upon the sleep-walker, but this seemed not to be the case. I persuaded him to go back at once to bed, and in a few minutes he fell asleep again. In the morning he seemed for the first time distinctly better; there was indeed something of his old self in his manner. It seemed as though the breaking of the violin had been an actual relief to

him; and I believe that on that Christmas morning
his better instincts woke, and that his old religious
training and the associations of his boyhood then
made their last appeal. I was pleased at such a
change, however temporary it might prove. He
wished to go to church, and I determined that again
I would subdue my curiosity and defer the questions I was burning to put till after our return from
the morning service. Miss Maltravers had gone in-
doors to make some preparation, Sir John was in
his wheel-chair on the terrace, and I was sitting by
him in the sun. For a few moments he appeared
immersed in silent thought, and then bent over
towards me till his head was close to mine, and said,
'Dear William, there is something I must tell you.
I feel I cannot even go to church till I have told you
all.' His manner shocked me beyond expression.
I knew that he was going to tell me the secret of
the lost pages, but instead of wishing any longer to
have my curiosity satisfied, I felt a horrible dread
of what he might say next. He took my hand in his
and held it tightly, as a man who was about to
undergo severe physical pain and sought the consolation of a friend's support. Then he went on—
'You will be shocked at what I am going to tell you;
but listen, and do not give me up. You must stand
by me and comfort me and help me to turn again.'
He paused for a moment and continued—'It was
one night in October, when Constance and I were
at Naples. I took that violin and went by myself to
the ruined villa on the Scoglio di Venere.' He had
been speaking with difficulty. His hand clutched
mine convulsively, but still I felt it trembling, and
I could see the moisture standing thick on his forehead. At this point the effort seemed too much for

him and he broke off. 'I cannot go on, I cannot tell you, but you can read it for yourself. In that diary which I gave you there are some pages missing.' The suspense was becoming intolerable to me, and I broke in, 'Yes, yes, I know; you cut them out. Tell me where they are.' He went on—'Yes, I cut them out lest they should possibly fall into anyone's hands unaware. But before you read them you must swear, as you hope for salvation, that you will never try to do what is written in them. Swear this to me now, or I never can let you see them.' My eagerness was too great to stop now to discuss trifles, and to humour him I swore as desired. He had been speaking with a continual increasing effort; he cast a hurried and fearful glance round as though he expected to see someone listening, and it was almost in a whisper that he went on, 'You will find them in—' His agitation had become most painful to watch, and as he spoke the last words a convulsion passed over his face, and speech failing him, he sank back on his pillow. A strange fear took hold of me. For a moment I thought there were others on the terrace beside myself, and turned round expecting to see Miss Maltravers returned; but we were still alone. I even fancied that just as Sir John spoke his last words I felt something brush swiftly by me. He put up his hands, beating the air with a most painful gesture, as though he were trying to keep off an antagonist who had gripped him by the throat, and made a final struggle to speak. But the spasm was too strong for him; a dreadful stillness followed, and he was gone.

There is little more to add; for Sir John's guilty secret perished with him. Though I was sure from his manner that the missing leaves were concealed somewhere at Worth, and though as executor I caused the most diligent search to be made, no trace of them was afterwards found; nor did any circumstance ever transpire to fling further light upon the matter. I must confess that I should have felt the discovery of these pages as a relief; for though I dreaded what I might have had to read, yet I was more anxious lest, being found at a later period and falling into other hands, they should cause a recrudescence of that plague which had blighted Sir John's life.

Of the nature of the events which took place on that night at Naples I can form no conjecture. But as certain physical sights have ere now proved so revolting as to unhinge the intellect, so I can imagine that the mind may in a state of extreme tension conjure up to itself some forms of moral evil so hideous as metaphysically to sear it: and this, I believe, happened in the case both of Adrian Temple and Sir John Maltravers.

It is difficult to imagine the accessories used to produce the mental excitation in which alone such a presentment of evil could become imaginable. Fancy and legend, which have combined to represent as possible appearances of the supernatural, agree also in considering them as more likely to occur at certain times and places than at others; and it is possible that the missing pages of the diary contained an account of the time, place, and other conditions chosen by Temple for some deadly experiment. Sir John most probably re-enacted the scene under precisely similar conditions, and the effect on his overwrought imagination was so vivid as to upset the balance of his mind. The time chosen was no doubt the night of the 23d of October, and

I cannot help thinking that the place was one of those evil-looking and ruinous sea-rooms which had so terrifying an effect on Miss Maltravers. Temple may have used on that night one of the medieval incantations, or possibly the more ancient invocation of the Isiac rite*with which a man of his knowledge and proclivities would certainly be familiar. The accessories of either are sufficiently hideous to weaken the mind by terror, and so prepare it for a belief in some frightful apparition. But whatever was done, I feel sure that the music of the *Gagliarda* formed part of the ceremonial.

Medieval philosophers and theologians held that evil is in its essence so horrible that the human mind, if it could realise it, must perish at its contemplation. Such realisation was by mercy ordinarily withheld, but its possibility was hinted in the legend of the *Visio malefica*. The *Visio Beatifica* was, as is well known, that vision of the Deity or realisation of the perfect Good which was to form the happiness of heaven, and the reward of the sanctified in the next world. Tradition says that this vision was accorded also to some specially elect spirits even in this life, as to Enoch, Elijah, Stephen, and Jerome.*But there was a converse to the Beatific Vision in the *Visio malefica*, or presentation of absolute Evil, which was to be the chief torture of the damned, and which, like the Beatific Vision, had been made visible in life to certain desperate men. It visited Esau, as was said, when he found no place for repentance, and Judas, whom it drove to suicide. Cain* saw it when he murdered his brother, and legend relates that in his case, and in that of others, it left a physical brand to be borne by the body to the grave. It was supposed that the Malefic Vision, besides being thus spontaneously presented to typically abandoned men, had actually been purposely called up by some few great adepts, and used by them to blast*their enemies. But to do so was considered equivalent to a conscious surrender to the powers of evil, as the vision once seen took away all hope of final salvation.

Adrian Temple would undoubtedly be cognisant of this legend, and the lost experiment may have been an attempt to call up the Malefic Vision. It is but a vague conjecture at the best, for the tree of the knowledge of Evil*bears many sorts of poisonous fruit, and no one can give full account of the extravagances of a wayward fancy.

Conjointly with Miss Sophia, Sir John appointed me his executor and guardian of his only son. Two months later we had lit a great fire in the library at Worth. In it, after the servants were gone to bed, we burnt the book containing the 'Areopagita' of Graziani, and the Stradivarius fiddle. The diaries of Temple I had already destroyed, and wish that I could as easily blot out their foul and debasing memories from my mind. I shall probably be blamed by those who would exalt art at the expense of everything else,* for burning a unique violin. This reproach I am content to bear. Though I am not unreasonably superstitious, and have no sympathy for that potential pantheism*to which Sir John Maltravers surrendered his intellect, yet I felt so great an aversion to this violin that I would neither suffer it to remain at Worth, nor pass into other hands. Miss Sophia was entirely at one with me on this point. It was the same feeling which restrains any except fools or braggarts from wishing to sleep in 'haunted' rooms, or to live in houses polluted with the memory of a revolting crime. No sane mind believes in foolish apparitions, but fancy may at times bewitch the best of us. So the Stradivarius was burnt. It was, after all, perhaps not so serious a matter, for, as I have said, the bass-bar had given way. There had always been a question whether it was strong enough to resist the strain of modern stringing. Experience showed at last that it was not. With the failure of the bass-bar the belly collapsed, and the wood broke across the grain in so extraordinary a manner as to put the fiddle beyond repair, except as a curiosity. Its loss, therefore, is not to be so much regretted. Sir Edward has been brought up to think more of a cricket-bat than of a violin-bow; but if he wishes at any time to buy a Stradivarius, the fortunes of Worth and Royston, nursed through two long minorities, will certainly justify his doing so.

Miss Sophia and I stood by and watched the holocaust. My heart misgave me for a moment when I saw the mellow red varnish blistering off the back, but I put my regret resolutely aside. As the bright flames jumped up and lapped it round, they flung a red glow on the scroll. It was wonderfully wrought, and differed, as I think Miss Maltravers has already said, from any known example of Stradivarius. As we watched it, the scroll took form, and we saw what we had never seen before, that it was cut so that the deep lines in a certain light showed as the profile of a man. It was a wizened little paganish face, with sharp-cut features and a bald head. As I looked at it I knew at once (and a cameo has since confirmed the fact) that it was a head of Porphyry. Thus the second label found in the violin was explained and Sir John's view confirmed, that Stradivarius had made the instrument

for some Neo-Platonist enthusiast who had dedicated it to his master Porphyrius.*

A year after Sir John's death I went with Miss
Maltravers to Worth church to see a plain slab of
slate which we had placed over her brother's grave.
We stood in bright sunlight in the Maltravers
chapel, with the monuments of that splendid family
about us. Among them were the altar-tomb of Sir
Esmoun, and the effigies of more than one Crusader.
As I looked on their knightly forms, with their heads
resting on their tilting helms, their faces set firm,
and their hands joined in prayer, I could not help
envying them that full and unwavering faith for
which they had fought and died. It seemed to stand
out in such sharp contrast with our latter-day sciolism* and half-believed creeds, and to be flung into
higher relief by the dark shadow of John Maltravers' ruined life. At our feet was the great brass
of one Sir Roger de Maltravers. I pointed out the
end of the inscription to my companion—'CVIVS
ANIMÆ, ATQVE ANIMABVS OMNIVM FIDELIVM DE-
FVNCTORVM, ATQVE NOSTRIS ANIMABVS QVVM EX
HAC LVCE TRANSIVERIMVS, PROPITIETVR DEVS.'*
Though no Catholic, I could not refuse to add a
sincere Amen. Miss Sophia, who is not ignorant of
Latin,* read the inscription after me. 'Ex hac luce,'
she said, as though speaking to herself, 'out of this
light; alas! alas! for some the light is darkness.'

# EXPLANATORY NOTES

*Notes preceded by an asterisk contain information which anticipates the denouement; readers may wish to consult these only after they have read the whole novel.*

The following abbreviations are used:

Grove  *The New Grove Dictionary of Music and Musicians*, ed.
      S. Sadie (1980).

Hart  G. Hart, *The Violin: Its Famous Makers and Their
      Imitators* (1884 edn.).

HBO  J. Meade Falkner, *Handbook for Travellers in Oxford-
      shire* (1894).

OED²  Oxford English Dictionary, 2nd edn. (1989).

DNB  *Dictionary of National Biography*

*Biblical references are to the Authorized Version; World's Classics edns. are used for Pater's The Renaissance, ed. A. Phillips (1986), and Marius the Epicurean, ed. I. Small (1986).*

* *Epigraph to the title*: the second half of the verse, 'But stripes and correction of wisdom are never out of time', should be borne in mind at the ultimate, inevitable moral reckoning, a notion found in all Falkner's novels.

*Title of letter: Student*: either an undergraduate (as Mr Gaskell is a 'student at' New College; p. 4) or a Fellow (then, as now, a Fellow of Christ Church was termed a Student; the capital letter is not decisive as 'Nephew' has one). At the time of the letter Sir Edward Maltravers was 23 born *c.* June–July 1844; pp. 91–2), and thus reached his 'coming of age' in 1865, two years before Sophia's letter.

3  *Maltravers . . . Worth*: Worth is in Dorset (pp. 32, 109), and Falkner has divided the name of the Dorset village of Worth Matravers, in the southern part of the Isle of Purbeck, 3 miles west of Swanage, for his surname and place-name; Worth was once held by the family of Mautravers or Maltravers. The surname is from French *mal* and *travers*, possibly meaning 'obstacle, trouble' or 'mishap, misfortune', an easily deducible and symbolically apt etymology which

may have commended the name to Falkner; for the suggestive significance of the surname *Carotenuto* see p. 110 n. The Christian name of Sophia ('wisdom'), a woman of sound sense, is likewise well-chosen, and the 'devoted consistency' (p. 15) of John Maltravers's wife Constance is aptly caught in her name. The Villa de Angelis, though referring presumably to a personal name, probably has a pointedly inappropriate play on 'angels'.

*Magdalen Hall*: part of the origins of Hertford College at which Falkner was an undergraduate, 1878–82. In 1822 Magdalen Hall, a dependency of Magdalen College, transferred from its Magdalen College site to that of Hertford College which had been dissolved in 1805; Magdalen Hall was in turn dissolved when Hertford was re-founded in 1874.

*Dr. Sarsdell*: the Principal at this time was actually Dr J. D. Macbride.

4 *D'Almaine*: Thomas D'Almaine (c.1784–1866) who became a partner in Goulding & Co., a London firm of music sellers, publishers, and instrument makers; by about 1834 Goulding's name was dropped, the firm becoming D'Almaine & Co.; the firm ceased trading with D'Almaine's death. (*Grove* s.v. *Goulding & Co.*).

5 *Graziani*: Bonifazio Graziani (1604/5–64) and Tomaso Graziani (c. 1550–1634) are of the right date (seventeenth century: p. 5) but their works, vocal and religious in nature, contain nothing like the piece described here; the composer is evidently fictitious.

6 * *l'Areopagita*: 'the Areopagite', a deliberately cryptic and arcane reference to Dionysius the Areopagite, so-called from his identification in the Middle Ages with the Dionysius Areopagita of Acts 17: 34, but in fact a late fifth-century neo-Platonic theologian who exerted enormous influence on mystical writings of the Middle Ages and Renaissance. As a neo-Platonist, he fits into a nexus of references connected with the music and the Stradivarius to such neo-Platonists as Porphyry (pp. 51, 165–6), Plotinus (p. 143), Proclus (p. 147), and others (pp. 143, 147, 148); his account of the soul's union with God by the rapture of divine love in the divine darkness is relevant to the later mention of the Beatific Vision (p. 163) and to the imagery of light and dark

EXPLANATORY NOTES

in Mr Gaskell's Note (see e.g. the last para., p. 166). For an excellent account of Dionysius see A. Louth, *The Origins of the Christian Mystical Tradition from Plato to Denys* (Oxford, 1981), pp. 159–78. For Pater's references to Dionysius and the neo-Platonists, see Introduction.

*Coranto*: 'a dance and instrumental form which flourished in Europe from the late sixteenth century to the mid-eighteenth, often as a movement of a suite' (*Grove* s.v. *Courante*).

*Sarabanda*: 'one of the most popular of Baroque instrumental dances and a standard movement, along with the allemande, courante and gigue, of the suite' (*Grove* s.v. *Sarabande*).

*Gagliarda*: 'a lively, triple-metre court dance of the sixteenth and early seventeenth centuries' (*Grove* s.v. *Galliard*).

7 *Minuetto*: 'a French dance in a moderate or slow triple metre, the most popular social dance in aristocratic society from the mid-seventeenth century to the late eighteenth. It appeared as a movement in some Baroque suites' (*Grove* s.v. *Minuet*).

8 *It was tolling . . . gates*: 'At 9.5 every evening this bell intimates to all the colleges the usual hour for closing their gates by 101 strokes, the number of students [undergraduates] which existed at Christ Church before the Act of 1854 for remodelling the University' (*HBO*, p. 17).

*Cesti . . . Buononcini*: more probably Antonio Cesti (1623–69). 'the most celebrated Italian musician of his generation' (*Grove*), though known rather for his operas and cantatas, than his nephew Remigio (*c.*1635–1710/17); *Buononcini*: probably either Giovanni Maria Bononcini (1642–78) or his eldest son Giovanni (1670–1747); the second son Antonio Maria (1677–1726) is possible: see *Grove* s.v. *Bononcini*.

*theory . . . basso continuo*: for the history and theoretical background of *continuo* playing, too long and complex to be summarized here, see *Grove* s.v. *Continuo*.

13 *Giga*: 'one of the most popular of Baroque instrumental dances and a standard movement, along with the allemande, courante and sarabande, of the suite' (*Grove* s.v. *Gigue*).

*Corelli*: Arcangelo Corelli (1653–1713), Italian composer and violinist.

13 *tripudistic*: not in *OED²*, exultantly and unrestrainedly rhythmical.

14 *fantastic . . . Renaissance*: such a style is extensively discussed in Pater's essay 'Joachim du Bellay' in his *The Renaissance* (1873); see Introduction.

*coved*: curved concavely.

\* *The shield . . . where*: the fictitious coat of arms of the fictitious Domacavalli family (p. 119); *or* is the heraldic term for gold. The design is reminiscent of the arms used by Giovanni Angelo Braschi as Pope Pius VI (1775–99); see D. L. Galbreath, *Papal Heraldry*, 2nd edn. by G. Briggs (London, 1972), p. 56, fig. 116; p. 103, fig. 190. Falkner may have seen the arms in a passage-way in St Peter's, Rome (a suggestion I owe to Dr Kenneth Warren). See Introduction for the significance of the lilies.

*set*: a technical term of dancing: 'To take up a position and perform a number of steps with one's face *to* one's partner or *to* the dancer on one's right or left' (*OED²*).

15 *Commemoration festivities*: in the nineteenth century the festivities in commemoration of the university's founders and benefactors were numerous, various, and lasted a week: concerts, sermons, a promenade of members of the university and their guests in the Broad Walk of Christ Church Meadow on 'Show Sunday', a procession of college boats on the Isis, a horticultural show in one of the larger college gardens, a university ball, college balls, a masonic ball (see p. 17 n.), a musical fête organized by the Apollo University Lodge of Masons in one of the larger college gardens and consisting of music provided by a military band and a glee club, the Encaenia ceremonies as today in the Sheldonian Theatre (but in the nineteenth century interrupted by rowdy undergraduate banter), and the conferring of non-honorary degrees (these details from the *Oxford Chronicle & Berks & Bucks Gazette*).

*Royston*: the only Royston in Derbyshire, a county Falkner may have visited in youth when his father had considered moving to the Midlands and the scene of Anthony Santal's home in Falkner's *A Midsummer Night's Marriage* (1896), is Roystone Grange, the site of a Bronze Age barrow, one mile north of Ballidon; the name could have suggested the idea of a grand house.

EXPLANATORY NOTES

16 *Friday . . . 1842*: in 1842, 18 June was a Saturday; Falkner
   did not attempt to reconstruct accurately this level of detail;
   cf. p. 81 n.

17 *grand ball . . . aprons*: a regular feature of the annual
   Commemoration festivities was the ball given by the Apollo
   University Lodge of Antient Free and Accepted Masons
   (still in existence), opened in 1819 as the Apollo Lodge but
   changing its name in the first year to the Apollo University
   Lodge. The ball generally took place in the Corn Exchange
   or Town Hall but in 1872 it was held at the Racquet Courts,
   Holywell; I have not found that it ever occurred at the
   Holywell Music Room (and it certainly did not during
   Falkner's period as an undergraduate). The current Secretary
   of the Lodge tells me that blue silk scarves are a 'poetic
   licence' and that small white aprons would indicate a new
   member of a month's, or at most two months', duration. I
   have not found Falkner's name in printed lists of members
   of the Apollo University Lodge.

   *to Didcot . . . mail for the west*: the mention of Didcot
   suggests that mail train, not mail coach, is meant. However,
   there is a slight anachronism in that there was no station
   there until the opening of the Didcot–Oxford line in June
   1844 (a line which Falkner correctly shows was not available
   in 1842) and which connected with the London–Bristol
   route completed in 1841. In 1842 the party, who were
   probably going to Bath, would have had to make a ten mile
   drive of about two hours by stage-coach to the station at
   Steventon, near Didcot.

   *aurum . . . satellites*: 'gold loves [*amat* in the following line]
   to make its way through the midst of sentinels'; Horace,
   *Carmen* III. xvi. 9.

19 *classic . . . schools*: an extraordinary error. The *schools*
   must refer to the Schools Quadrangle of the Bodleian
   Library, the schools being the old faculties once housed
   there; it has never been adorned with classical statues.
   Falkner must have in mind the statues of the Muses,
   designed by Sir James Thornhill, 1717, which surmount the
   Clarendon Building.

   *toast-and-water*: $OED^2$ records toast immersed in ale or
   water as a beverage between 1586 and 1888.

21 *war*: presumably the Crimean War, begun in 1854 and concluding in 1856.

26 *luxurious*: voluptuous.

27 *verses by Mr. Keble*: not by Keble but Newman; for bibliographical details, an accurate text of the full poem, and its significance in the novel see * Introduction.

29 *Westmoreland*: since 1974 absorbed into the south-western part of Cumbria.

30 *small cloud . . . man's hand*: 'there ariseth a little cloud out of the sea, like a man's hand' (I Kgs 18: 44). However, Falkner's cloud is the evil anti-type of the cloud reported to Elijah, which brings a welcome 'great rain' after famine. It is alluded to again in the following *fret* (squall) (p. 31) and in ch. 8's 'small cloud' (p. 52), thunderstorm (p. 54), and the advancing 'vague and shadowy' fear (p. 57).

*Encombe*: 2½ miles SSW of Corfe Castle, in a valley opening out to the sea.

31 *Smedmore*: 1 mile SE of Kimmeridge.

*glaucous*: a hue varying between dull or pale green and greyish blue; as this uncommon word is from Greek via Latin it appears a lapse of characterization to have it used by Sophia who knows neither classical language (pp. 17, 83, but cf. p. 166 n.).

32 *sordino*: mute.

35 *Payne & Foss*: in Pall Mall; founded by 'Honest Tom Payne' (1719–99), it ceased trading in 1850 (see A. N. L. Munby, *Phillipps Studies* nos. 3 (Cambridge, 1954), pp. 43–5, and 4 (Cambridge, 1956), pp. 1–3; I owe this reference to Mr Alan Bell, Librarian of Rhodes House, Oxford).

36 *sensibly heated*: heated by contact (conduction or convection) between one body and another (here the wall and the bookcase); see *OED*[2].

41 *The body . . . the scroll . . . free*: these two sentences contain a mosaic of phrases and information from George Hart, *The Violin: Its Famous Makers and Their Imitators* (London, 1875; 1884 edn.); in a number of cases the phrasing or information is so distinctive as to make it clear that Falkner used the book. George Hart himself appears in the novel as George Smart (see p. 45 n.), and his book on

the violin, though given a different title, is mentioned on pp. 45 and 48; *a light-red colour*: 'the Cremonese [varnish; Cremona was the city of Antonio Stradivari] is of various shades, the early instruments of the school being chiefly amber-coloured, afterwards deepening into a light red of charming appearance' (Hart, p. 70) '. . . light red, the quality of which is also very beautiful' (Hart, p. 179) '. . . a pale red, of great transparency' (Hart, p. 181); *a varnish . . . softness*: '[Neapolitan varnish lacks] the dainty softness of the Cremonese' (Hart, p. 70); *The neck . . . ordinary*: '[the "long Strad" received its title] not from increased length . . . but from the appearance of additional length, which its narrowness gives it, and which is particularly observable between the sound-holes [the two f-shaped holes on the top of the violin]' (Hart, p. 181); the 'long Strad' in fact belongs to the 1690s, the decade prior to the 'golden period' (see p. 46 n.) of *c.*1700–20, to which Maltravers's instrument belongs (p. 42), but this sort of slip is unimportant; *the scroll . . . free*: 'the scrolls [of the golden period] are of bold conception and finely executed' (Hart, p. 187). The scroll is the curved head at the end of the violin's neck, in which the tuning pegs are set.

*Pressenda*: Giovanni Francesco Pressenda (?1777–1854) of Turin; see Hart, pp. 150–3, and *Grove*.

*later . . . model*: Hart notes that the violins of 'his early period are chiefly of the Amatese [ref. the Amati family of violin makers; cf. p. 47 n.] character' (p. 153), but that otherwise they 'are chiefly of the model of Stradivari' (pp. 152–3).

42 *Antonius . . . 1704*: 'Antonio Stradivari of Cremona made [it], 1704'. The date is that of the famous Betts Strad (Hart, pp. 187, 445–8), bought by George Hart in 1878. On Stradivari (1644–1737) see Hart, pp. 165–205, and *Grove*.

45 *the late Mr. George Smart . . . dealer*: the name derives from George Hart (1839–91), of a family firm of violin makers and dealers, 'the late' to Falkner because of his death in 1891; however, his premises were in Wardour Street, London, and the Bond Street address given below (p. 45) is that of the yet greater family of violin makers and dealers, the Hill family, who moved from Wardour Street to 38 New Bond Street in 1888 and to 140 New Bond Street in 1895;

the Hills published specialized monographs on particular violins and makers (though that on Stradivari was not until 1902) but no general history; see *Grove* on both families.

46 *golden period*: 'what may be not inaptly named the golden period of his life, artistically considered (p. 185) . . . That which I have termed the golden period of Stradivari' (p. 186). W. H. Hill, A. F. Hill, and A. E. Hill, *Antonio Stradivari* . . . (London, 1902), p. 49, under the title 'The So-Called "Golden Period" ', attribute the original application of the term to Hart's use here, and it is now generally accepted.

*Dolphin*: made in 1714; 'regarded by the chief connoisseurs in Europe as a *chef-d'œuvre* of Stradivari . . . its beauty has excited the admiration of the Fiddle World. The splendour of the wood is unsurpassed in any Violin, ancient or modern, and it was named the "Dolphin" from the richness and variety of the tints it gives to the varnish' (Hart, pp. 189–90).

47 *Amati*: Nicolo Amati (1596–1684); for the variation in the tint of the varnish see Hart, pp. 179, 181, though the remarks do not relate to the golden period and Falkner over-simplifies the topic.

*breaking up*: this technical term is not in $OED^2$; Hart uses, without explanation, 'broken up' of varnish (p. 70).

*purfling*: a narrow inlay of wood in a trough cut just inside the outer edge of the back and belly (top) of the violin; it serves as protection and ornament.

48 *History . . . Violin*: see pp. 41 n., 45 n.

50 *late Mr. James Loding . . . Europe*: the name derives from that of a real collector: '. . . the collection . . . of the late Mr. James Goding, which was then the finest in Europe' (Hart, p. 340); Goding's collection once included twelve Stradivari, and was sold by auction in 1857 (Hart, p. 354).

51 *specimen . . . ninety-two*: 'In the possession of Mr. George H. M. Muntz, of Handsworth, is a Violin by Stradivari, dated 1736, and in the handwriting of its maker, the age given is ninety-two. Another Violin by Stradivari, made in the same year, and similarly labelled, is in the possession of the family of the late Mr. Fountain, of Narford Hall, Norfolk' (Hart, p. 170).

# EXPLANATORY NOTES

\* *Porphyrius philosophus*: 'Porphyry the philosopher'; AD 233–*c*.305. As a neo-Platonist, this is the second reference to this tradition (see *l'Areopagita*, p. 6 n.); he wrote a life of Plotinus (see p. 143 n.); for his association with the occult see p. 166 n.).

*"Peter" and "Paul"*: 'Veracini [Francesco Maria V., Italian composer and violinist, 1690–1768] . . . played . . . upon his Stainers [violins made by Jacob Stainer, Austrian violin maker, ?1617– 83], which he named "St. Peter" and "St. Paul" ' (Hart, p. 197).

52 *sound-post . . . bass-bar . . . modern stringing*: the sound post is a vertical post inside the violin between the top and the back; in addition to its function as support, its placing, here by Stradivari himself, is critical in producing the quality of sound. (See Hart, pp. 35–7, and *Grove* s.v. *Violin* and *Soundpost*); *bass-bar*: a strip of wood glued to the underside of the top (belly), used for supportive and acoustical reasons; its positioning is a matter of the greatest skill and delicacy (see Hart, pp. 34–5, and *Grove* s.v. *Violin* and *Bass-bar*); *modern stringing*: Hart indicates the importance of the material, strain, and pressure of the strings by devoting a whole section to the topic (pp. 41–53).

54 *polka . . . King Pippin*: a slight anachronism which Falkner, even if he had cared, probably did not have the knowledge to avoid. The date of the ball is 5 January 1843, but the polka, though introduced to Prague in 1837 and to Paris in 1840, was first performed in London on 11 April 1844 (*Grove* s.v. *Polka*). Mr Peter Ward Jones of the Bodleian Library, Oxford, has kindly informed me that the 'King Pippin' polka was composed by Charles Louis Napoléon d'Albert (1809–86).

59 *sensible*: registered by the senses.

*collect . . . Lent*: 'Almighty God, who seest that we have no power of ourselves to help ourselves; Keep us both outwardly in our bodies, and inwardly in our souls; that we may be defended from all adversities which may happen to the body, and from all evil thoughts which may assault and hurt the soul; through Jesus Christ our Lord. *Amen*.' (*Book of Common Prayer*).

60 *intelligence*: news.

60 *Holbein*: Hans Holbein the Younger, 1497–1543; Falkner probably had in mind one of the versions of the lost original of Holbein's Sir Thomas More and his family (he mentions a 'famous' one once at Burford Priory and now in the National Portrait Gallery in *HBO*, p. 201).

61 *counterfeit*: image, likeness.

63 *BATTONI . . . 1750*: 'Battoni painted [it], at Rome, 1750.' Pompeo Batoni (1708–87), was celebrated for his Grand Tour portraits, though this one is dated seven years after the sitter's (see p. 140); see A. M. Clark, *Pompeo Batoni: a Complete Catalogue of his Works with an Introductory Text*, ed. E. P. Bowron (Oxford, 1985). The picture of James Caulfield, Lord Charlemont, later 1st Earl of Charlemont (1728–99), 1753–5 (*Catalogue* no. 190), chosen for the cover of this World's Classics edn., is close in colouring to the painting described in the novel, and the nonchalant pose (with a view of the Colosseum in the background) has an intelligent, sensual, and arrogant expression appropriate to the novel's sitter. Falkner had presumably seen some Batoni portraits, but it is not claimed the ones mentioned in this edn. (see also p. 70 n.).

65 *Trappist monk*: 'a monk of the branch of the Cistercian order observing the reformed rule established in 1664 by De Rancé, abbot of La Trappe, in Normandy' (*OED*$^2$);the order is known for its stress on the virtue of silence.

*brand . . . burning*: cf. Amos 4: 11 ('ye [Israel] were as a firebrand plucked out of the burning') and Zech. 3: 2 ('is not this [Joshua] a brand plucked out of the fire?'); the image passed more widely into Christian writing (e.g. hymns: see *OED*$^2$).

66 *Tartini himself*: Giuseppe Tartini (1692–1770); 'Italian composer, violinist, teacher and theorist . . . he founded his "school" of violin instruction in either 1727 or 1728. Continued into his last years, it was to become a magnet for aspiring violinists from most of Europe' (*Grove*). For the story of Tartini's 'Devil's Trill' Violin Sonata in G minor, *c.*1714, related by Hart (pp. 411–13), knowledge of which adds a *frisson* to this passage, see Introduction.

68 *first . . . poems*: an error on Sophia's (and presumably Falkner's) part. The time is March 1843, and the volume

EXPLANATORY NOTES

'just published' must be the acknowledged *Poems. By
Alfred Tennyson* published in May 1842. The 'first volume'
must be the anonymous *Poems, by Two Brothers* [Alfred
and Charles, plus a few by Frederick] published in 1827.

70 *actual . . . identified*: one Batoni portrait does show real
music: John, Lord Brudenell, later Marquis of Monthermer,
1758, sits holding an oblong manuscript copy (cf. the novel,
pp. 5–6), open at a passage from the end of the last
movement, of Corelli's sixth violin sonata, Opus 5 (*Batoni
Catalogue*, p. 63 n., no. 202). I do not know if Falkner ever
saw this portrait which is at Boughton House, Geddington,
near Kettering, the Northants home of the Dukes of
Buccleuch and Queensberry. Neither the MSS inventories
at Boughton (1832, 1836) nor the printed *Catalogue* of its
pictures (1911) identifies the music.

*monument to Handel*: by Roubiliac, 1761.

73 *new bow of Tourte's make*: 'French family of bowmakers.
The most illustrious member . . . was François Tourte
[1747–1835], who is regarded as the "Stradivari of the
bow" ' (*Grove*).

75 *discovering*: revealing, showing.

79 *viva voce*: oral.

*division . . . line*: Falkner has his facts wrong. The First
Class was never divided; from 1809–25 the Second Class
was 'virtually subdivided into two by a line, above which
were placed the names of the more meritorious Candidates'
(what would now be called a 2:1); see *Oxford University
Calendar 1844*, p. 117. This divided Second Class was then
abolished between 1825 and 1985.

81 *Wednesday [23 October]*: the 23rd in 1843 was actually a
Monday; cf. p. 16 n.

84 *achievements*: shields with coats of arms upon them,
together with the supporters, helmet, etc. (granted in
memory of some achievement or feat).

85 *How easy . . . to raise*: untraced, but in content and metre
very like the evangelical poems and hymns composed for
children by Isaac Watts (1674–1748), and Ann (1782–
1866) and Jane (1783–1824) Taylor.

85 *a green coat*: this detail may have been suggested by one of

## EXPLANATORY NOTES

the charities of Sir George Fettiplace (d. 1743) of Swin-
brook, Oxon.: 'a distribution of green coats once a year'
(*HBO*, p. 194).

86 *Esmoun*: the Christian name was perhaps suggested by that
of Sir Esmoun de Malyns on one of the de Malyns brasses
(though not tombs) in the church at Chinnor, Oxon.; some
of the brasses in the church bear an inscription similar to
part of that given on p. 166 (see n.): see *HBO*, p. 141.

89 *convenient*: appropriate, proper (*OED*²).

*signs . . . period*: Constance was some 5 months or so
pregnant (Edward's birth seems to have been in June–July
(p. 91) ), a condition about which Mrs Temple has to
inform John in May (p. 90).

*Posilipo*: the firm of Armstrong Mitchell, of which Falkner
had become Secretary in 1888–9, had in the late 1880s set
up a plant for manufacturing guns and gunboats at Pozzuoli,
near Naples; George Rendel, who had left Armstrongs for
the Admiralty, had retired to a villa at Posilipo but still took
an active interest in the plant's operations, and senior
officers of the firm, who, from the knowledge of the area
shown later in the novel, must have included Falkner, made
regular visits to Pozzuoli, sometimes staying with Rendel;
see K. Warren, *Armstrongs of Elswick* (Basingstoke and
London, 1989), pp. 69–85.

90 *condescending*: gracious self-humbling, giving up an attitude
of aloofness, with none of today's pejorative connotations of
'patronizing'.

92 *Scarlatti . . . Bach . . . composers . . . less commonly
known*: probably Domenico Scarlatti (1685–1757); evidently
Johann Sebastian Bach (1685–1750). According to *Grove*
(xvi. 573–4), 'enthusiasm for the sonatas [of Domenico
Scarlatti] has never abated' in Great Britain, though his
father's reputation suffered a decline (xvi. 558). For the
Bach revival, see *Grove* (i. 883–6).

97 *we read . . . Jerusalem*: the portents before the final
destruction of the Temple at Jerusalem by Titus's legions in
AD 70 are described in Greek by Josephus, *The Jewish War*
vi. 299–300, and in Latin by Tacitus, *Historiae* v. 13; both
were available in translation.

178

99 *burden*: tune, melody; not a technical musical use of the word.

103 *classic*: (presumably) Italic; not a sense known to *OED*[2].

104 *posted*: travelled with relays of horses.

105 *black-vested priests . . . blue-coated soldiers*: priests wearing black vestments (soutane or cassock); soldiers at this time (1845) of the Kingdom of Naples and Sicily, ruled by the Bourbon absolutist Ferdinand II.

*post-boy*: postilion

*religious festival . . . Grotto*: La festa di Nostra Signora di Piedigrotta on 8 September; as it is only mid-August on p. 104 Falkner would seem to have placed the *festa* too early. *Notes on Naples and its Environs . . . by a Traveller* (London, [1838]) found this 'pious pageant' not, as Sophia did, shockingly pagan but merely 'a vain, and meaningless, and silly ceremony' (p. 164). Norman Douglas, *Siren Land* (London, 1911), observed, though without Sophia's evangelical horror, 'The madonnas of Naples . . . are all re-incarnations of antique shapes, of the Sirens, . . . and their cult to this day is pagan rather than Christian' (p. 10); see J. Pemble, *The Mediterranean Passion*, (Oxford, 1987) pp. 210–27.

107 *image and superscription*: echoes Luke 20: 24 (but with no thematic significance).

110 *Carotenuto*: the name means 'the one held dearly (or affectionately)'; * see Introduction for discussion of the nature of John Maltravers's friendship with him.

*past two years*: seemingly a slip in chronology. The time is August 1845 (p. 104); John first went to the Villa on his own in March 1844 (p. 89), and after a short stay back in England returned to Naples at the end of July (pp. 92, 99).

111 *moles*: jetties, breakwaters. Changes in sea-level are particu-larly common in the Naples area.

*tufa-rock*: a volcanic rock.

*these chambers*: the area has numerous caves and grottoes, and for a villa with 'excavations of a classic date' see the n. on Pollio's villa (p. 114). However, it is highly probable that Falkner also had in mind the famous Grotto of the Sibyl at the Lake of Avernus and the Sibyl's Cave in the hill of the

Acropolis (for descriptions see *Murray's Handbook for Travellers in Southern Italy*, Part I, 9th edn. (1890), pp. 169–70, 175). Some of their features have been thought to have been used by Virgil in his Cave of the Sibyl (*Aeneid* vi. 42 ff., 237 ff.), a passage certainly known to Falkner; see the edn. of *Aeneid* vi by R. G. Austin (Oxford, 1977), pp. 48–58, 108–9.

112 *Cells of Isis*: I have not come upon this name and it is probably Falkner's invention. Isis was a great Egyptian goddess who, *inter alia*, was regarded with her brother and husband Osiris as ruler of the Underworld. Her cult, a kind of mystery religion, spread to Rome in the second century BC. Pater, in *Marius the Epicurean (1885)*, had referred to 'her singular and in many ways beautiful ritual' (ch. xi, p. 105), and described the festival called *Isidis Navigium* (Ship of Isis) in exotic and attractive terms (ch. vi). However, others in the nineteenth century stressed a sinister side: *Notes on Naples*, referring to the Temple of Isis found at nearby Pompeii, says: 'the mystery of whose worship seems not even yet regarded without some sense of awe. Nor is this saying too much of the dark rites of the Egyptian Isis, with their dread veils, and uncouth signs, and dismal sacrifices, which appal the imagination to this hour' (p. 146); Edward Bulwer Lytton, *The Last Days of Pompeii* (1834, and frequently reprinted) shows in the character of the Egyptian Arbaces a gripping portrait of the evil, sensual, and corrupting follower of Isis. The 'Isiac rite' is referred to later (p. 163). Egyptian mythology was potent to a number of 19th-c. writers.

*Pompeii*: Roman town near Naples buried by pumice and ash from the eruption of Vesuvius on 24 August AD 79; it remained undiscovered and forgotten until 1748.

*drop-scene*: 'the painted curtain let down between the acts of a play to shut off the stage from the view of the audience' (*OED²*).

114 *grateful*: pleasing, welcome.

*epicure Pollio . . . "truce to care"*: Pausilypon was the name of the villa of Vedius Pollio and which he willed to Augustus in 15 BC; he was notorious for his luxurious and barbarous way of life (the villa's fishponds were fed with human flesh). For a description of its substructions in the sea and the excavation of the tufa cliffs for tunnels and canals to supply its fishponds and baths see *Murray's Handbook*, p. 88 (cf. the novel, p. 111). See also J. H. D'Arms, *Romans on the Bay of Naples* (Cambridge, Mass., 1970), pp. 229–30. Though the doctrine of the Greek philosopher Epicurus (341–271 BC) that pleasure is identical with the good had an austere stress on mental pleasure, it was in the corrupted sense of sensual pleasure-seeker that Pollio was an epicure. D. Viggiani, *I tempi di Posillipo: dalle ville romane ai 'casini di delizia'* (Naples, 1989), traces the history of villa-building in the area from Roman times to the twentieth century; its many illustrations include two (pp. 167, 177) of the Villa Rendel (cf. p. 89 n.).

*sans-souci*: (place where he had a) (lit. Fr.), 'care-free' state of mind.

117 *magazine*: store-room.

118 *fanning*: blowing on (cf. p. 14); looks like, but apparently is not, a technical term of heraldry.

119 *Domacavalli*: means 'a breaker-in of horses', but I see no symbolic significance in this.

120 *mould*: earth; on p. 121 *mould* = fungal growth.

124 *maggior-duomo*: house-steward.

126 *cemetery of Santa Bibiana*: not traced; probably fictitious.

127 *affection*: disease.

130 *discovered*: revealed, shown.

132 *evil spirit . . . abode again*: 'Then goeth he, and taketh with himself seven other spirits more wicked than himself, and they enter in [to a man] and dwell there: and the last state of that man is worse than the first' (Matt. 12: 45); in *The Nebuly Coat*, ch. 13, Falkner had echoed the previous verse's reference to the 'garnished house'.

*There is a picture . . . going*: Robert Blair (1699–1746), *The Grave, A Poem. Illustrated by Twelve Etchings Executed by Louis Schiavonetti, From the Original Inventions of William Blake* (London, 1808), facing p. 12 with the caption:

> Death of the Strong Wicked Man
> . . . . Heard you that groan?
> It was his last.

The text reads:

> What groan was that I heard? Deep groan indeed,
> With anguish heavy laden! let me trace it:
> From yonder bed it comes, where the strong man,
> By stronger arm belabour'd, gasps for breath
> Like a hard hunted beast;

Blair's 'hard hunted beast' is remembered in Sophia's 'wounded beast'. The picture is today readily accessible in G. E. Bentley, Jun., *Blake Records* (Oxford, 1969), Plate XXI. *The Grave*, 1st pub. in 1743, went through many edns. in the eighteenth and nineteenth centuries, often in conjunction with Gray's *Elegy*; Edmund Gosse (1849–1928), *Father and Son* (1907), ch. xi, describes the effect of Blair's 'melodious doleful images'.

133 *Dr. Butler*: Mr. Butler on pp. 85, 87; there is no knowing which Falkner intended, and so I have left the discrepancy.

139 *diary . . . life*: a version of a central Decadent motif, the 'fatal book' which poisons youth with its account of exotic and aesthetic pleasures. The most noted instance is Lord Henry Wotton's book in Wilde's *The Picture of Dorian Gray* (1890–1), chap. x ff.; see L. Dowling, *Language and Decadence in the Victorian Fin de Siècle* (Princeton, 1986), pp. 154–60, 169–74, 248.

140 *stirring events of 1745*: the attempt to regain the English throne for the Stuart line by the Young Pretender, Charles Edward Stuart, grandson of James II (hence 'Jacobite').

141 *Dr. Holmes . . . College*: William Holmes (1689–1748), President 1728–48; he was an exception to the College's Jacobite sympathies, the *DNB* observing: 'he was no doubt the first president who was loyal to the house of Hanover'.

*that very set*: poetic licence, for Magdalen Hall to which Adrian Temple removes was not on the Catte Street–New College Lane site of John Maltravers's day until 1822 (see p. 3 n.); furthermore, the block with the rooms looking on to New College Lane was erected only in 1820–2, and so did not exist in Adrian Temple's time. Falkner has suppressed fact in the interests of fiction. There is some evidence that for a year at least Falkner occupied a room with a similar location.

*occult sciences . . . Oxford towers*: though Boyle's *The*

*Sceptical Chymist* (1661) had ended alchemy's credibility for all but the credulous and fraudulent, 'in the seventeenth and early eighteenth centuries a vast amount of alchemical literature was published and eagerly read', though it was less practical and more metaphysical, and 'the Neoplatonists [cf. pp. 6, 51, 143, 147–9, 165–6], with their theory of the emanation of light from God and its descent into and animation of matter' were a significant element (F. Sherwood Taylor, *The Alchemists* (London, 1951), pp. 214, 217). Falkner may also have had in mind the notorious and sensational case of Dr James Price (1752–83) who, interestingly, had matriculated at Magdalen Hall in 1772, and claimed to be able to produce silver and gold by alchemy (see *DNB*).

*Francis Dashwood . . . Medmenham*: Sir Francis Dashwood, 2nd bt. and also Lord le Despencer (1708–81), of West Wycombe, Bucks., founded in the 1740s the Knights of St Francis of Wycombe (the Hell-Fire Club). He renovated and extended the ruins of the old Cistercian abbey at nearby Medmenham, together with the adjoining manor-house. Later the Knights of St Francis, also known as the Monks of Medmenham, were reputed to have met occasionally in the caves, originally made by chalk-quarrying 1748–54, at West Wycombe. The Knights, or Monks, it was said, were devoted to every kind of orgiastic licence and to the mockery of religion. See Sir Francis Dashwood (11th bt.), *The Dashwoods of West Wycombe* (London, 1987), pp. 26–51; *HBO*, pp. 136–7.

142 *In that year [1738]*: Stradivarius actually died in 1737.

*auction*: I have not found any reference to this.

*Carthusian monk*: on p. 65 Jocelyn was said to have become a Trappist monk, a branch of the Cistercian order (cf. p. 65 n. and p. 154 n.).

143 *Neo-Platonism . . . deity*: Plotinus, AD *c.* 205–70, the chief exponent of neo-Platonism. In his philosophy the universe is seen as a hierarchy of realities or principles (*hypostases*), in which the higher by a process of 'emanation' or overflowing generates the immediately lower; yet the lower seeks to return to the higher. At the top are three divine realities: the One or the Good, Intelligence or Mind (the *nous*), and

Soul; the next reality is Nature, the principle of life and growth, and below that is the lowest level, material things. Human beings contain within themselves a microcosm of Mind, Soul, Nature, and Matter; by moral and intellectual purification and discipline they can seek to rise to the level of Mind and even, by ecstasy (cf. 'the divine *extasis*', p. 149), to the One. Porphyry (see p. 51 n.) in his *Life* of Plotinus (ch. 23) says that while he knew him Plotinus four times achieved this rapturous union with the One 'in an unspeakable actuality' (Mr Gaskell's reference to 'twice' going beyond the *nous* to the One ('the fruition of the deity') is either a mis-remembering or a numbering of Temple's, not Plotinus', experiences). On Plotinus see Louth, *Origins*, p. 6 n., pp. 36–51. St Augustine was profoundly influenced in his mystical theology by Plotinus, and it is at first sight odd that Mr Gaskell should call his doctrine 'easy'. He probably, unfairly, has in mind later neo-Platonists, e.g. Iamblichus, Proclus (mentioned on p. 147), who used the rituals of magic and occult paganism to gain contact with supernatural powers, practices which could seem both 'easy', by contrast with moral and philosophical discipline, and unwholesome (cf. p. 163); see R. T. Wallis, *Neoplatonism* (London, 1972), Index s.v. the philosophers named above and s.v. 'Magic'; Temple had practised the 'occult sciences' of alchemy, astrology, and necromancy (p. 141).

145 *Michael Prætorius . . . movements*: Prætorius (*c*.1570–1621) was a German composer, theorist, and organist; the three short paragraphs on the Galliarda in vol. iii of his *Syntagma musicum* (1614–18) contain nothing corresponding to the alleged quoted translation, which is evidently Falkner's invention.

146 *music is the readiest . . . thought*: cf. above, p. 27; Pater, in *Marius the Epicurean* (1885) ch. ix, and 'Plato's Aesthetics' in *Plato and Platonism* (1893), had seen music in the sense of 'all those matters over which the Muses of Greek mythology preside' as the art in which to discuss the relation of the aesthetic and the moral: see Introduction.

*classic*: classical scholar.

147 *librarians*: booksellers; *OED*² records this sense once only, *ante* 1734.

## EXPLANATORY NOTES

*later empire*: later Roman Empire, beginning with the accession of Diocletian in AD 284.

*Alexandrine philosophers*: a grouping popular in the nineteenth century of neo-Platonists with Jewish and Christian thinkers resident in, or at some time associated with, Alexandria. Though the names of Philo, Clement, and Origen are reasonably well known, the works of e.g. Hermeias, his son Ammonius, Olympiodorus, Elias, *et al.* are indeed more obscure; see Wallis, *Neoplatonism*, p. 143 n., pp. 11–12, 138 ff.

*Proclus . . . Julian . . . Augustine . . . Renaissancists*: *Proclus*: AD 412–85; a neo-Platonist philosopher who spent most of his life at Athens; he influenced Dionysius the Areopagite (see p. 6 n.) who has been called the Christian Proclus; *Julian*: Roman emperor AD 360–3, called the Apostate because of his renunciation of Christianity; he was influenced by the neo-Platonist philosopher Maximus of Ephesus; *Augustine*: St Augustine AD 354–430; much influenced in his thinking by the neo-Platonist philosopher Plotinus (see p. 143 n.); *the Renaissancists* were Italian neo-Platonist philosophers of the Renaissance including, notably, Marsilio Ficino (1433–99), Giovanni Pico della Mirandola (1463–94) of whom Pater wrote an account in *The Renaissance* (1873; see Introduction), Francesco Patrizzi (1529–97), and Giordano Bruno (*c.* 1548–1600). In Renaissance neo-Platonism there was a powerful admixture of astrology and the occult, and a number of its tenets were condemned by the Church (Bruno going to the stake); see Wallis, *Neoplatonism*, p. 143 n., pp. 170–2. In *OED*² this passage provides the first quotation for *Renaissancist*, though its definition 'an advocate or student of a renaissance' is at best inadequate.

*aesthetic impressions*: both words are instances of the distinctive vocabulary which Pater gave to the Aesthetic Movement: see Introduction.

*pantheism*: the neo-Platonist had to resolve the dilemma of the One's immanence (pantheism) and its transcendence; for the Christian, whatever is said of God's immanence in creation, He must also be seen as transcendent. For Falkner's own alleged leanings towards pantheism see Introduction.

*the old culture*: the phrase is reminiscent of Pater's threefold reference to 'the old/er gods' which he said so fascinated Pico della Mirandola: see Introduction.

*sea-house of Pomponius*: 'sea-house' looks like an Anglicizing of the Latin *villa maritima*, a villa by the sea. Though a Q. Pomponius Maternus seems to have had a villa in the area (see D'Arms, *Romans*, p. 114 n., p. 223), this villa is probably fictitious.

148 *charmed*: the word (and cf. 'charm' in the next para.) is a favourite of Pater's (I have noted 'charm/charmed' 27 times in *The Renaissance*); its use twice on this page of an area which, though beautiful, is corrupting, is part of the novel's concluding critique of Paterian aestheticism.

*Cicero . . . the Antonines*: for their villas and connections with the area see D'Arms, *Romans*, p. 114 n.; *Cicero*: Marcus Tullius Cicero, 106–43 BC, Roman orator and statesman; *Lucullus*: Lucius Licinius Lucullus, *c.*114–57 BC; his sumptuous banquets have given the English words 'Lucullan' and 'Lucullian'; *Severus*: Alexander Severus, Roman emperor AD 222–35; *the Antonines*: the Age of the Antonines is the period AD 138–92, and is the reign of three emperors: Antoninus Pius, emperor AD 138–61, Marcus Aurelius, emperor AD 161–80, and Lucius Aelius Aurelius Commodus, emperor AD 180–92.

*Baia*: the resort and its villas were indeed notorious for every kind of luxury and vice; see D'Arms, *Romans*, p. 114 n.; it was sacked by the Saracens in the eighth century (Falkner says the fifteenth), and entirely abandoned because of malaria in 1500. Falkner's words are very reminiscent of an extensive and powerful denunciation of Baia, where 'the beauties of nature were tarnished by the foulness of vice', in J. C. Eustace, *A Tour Through Italy . . .* (London, 1813), i. 567–8; Eustace's guidebook (8 editions by 1841) influenced thousands of visitors, including J. M. W. Turner and his painting *The Bay of Baiae* (1823): see C. Powell, *Turner in the South: Rome, Naples, Florence* (New Haven and London, 1987), who quotes Eustace on Baia on p. 83.

*a continuity . . . shameful past*: Falkner had a similar response to some of the buildings of Sir Francis Dashwood (see p. 141 n.) at West Wycombe, though he was not apparently speaking of the neo-classical House and its templed grounds which were not then open to the public: 'The whole of the buildings have a strong savour of paganism about them, and seem instinct with the spirit of their wild builder, Francis Dashwood' (*HBO*, p. 137).

*sensible*: felt by the senses.

*malefic . . . buried*: the image is strikingly reminiscent of one used in Pater's account of Pico della Mirandola whose 'qualities are still active, and himself remains, as one alive in the grave' (*The Renaissance*, p. 32). The scene's atmosphere of mingled beauty, evil, and corruption is likewise Paterian in sensibility (though Mr Gaskell reacts with un-Paterian horror): of Leonardo da Vinci's painting of the dead Medusa Pater wrote of how 'the fascination of corruption penetrates in every touch its exquisitely finished beauty' (*Renaissance*, p. 68), and his portrait of Beatrice d'Este is 'full of the refinement of the dead' (p. 71); Milan was 'a life of brilliant sins and exquisite amusements' (p. 70). The 'malefic vapours' recall the novel's earlier 'malefic influence' (p. 91) and 'atmosphere of moral contagion' (p. 143) and will culminate in the *Visio malefica* (p. 163).

*decepti deceptores*: 'deceived deceivers'; the phrase is fairly common in Greek literature, but in Latin I know it only in Augustine, *Confessions* vii. 2 (of the Manichees).

149 *divine extasis*: the soul's union with the One (see p. 143 n.) in which the soul goes out of the body and itself.

150 *Parthenopean*: Neapolitan. Parthenope was one of the Sirens (female creatures who lured mariners to their death by their song); her body was washed ashore in the Bay of Naples and she was said to be buried at Neapolis. The classical allusion in the name emphasizes Falkner's theme of the persistence of the pagan past, and is also appropriate in the context of the *Gagliarda*'s destructive powers—the poem quoted by Mr Gaskell (p. 27) had spoken of 'The art of syren choirs'.

*Aldobrandini*: the surname of a real and celebrated Italian noble family, of Florence, three of whose members (though in the seventeenth century) bore the name Olimpia.

*acolasia*: lack of self-restraint, intemperance, 'sensual excess' in Falkner's translation; the word is used by Plato and Aristotle and is a well-established word in Greek philosophy.

151 *a man . . . salvation*: a number of Biblical passages speak of a sin which is unforgivable: (i) 'the blasphemy against the Holy Ghost' (Matt. 12: 31–2; cf. Mark 3: 28–9; Luke 12: 10); (ii) the 'sin unto death' (I. John 5: 16); cf. also Heb. 6: 4–8, and 10: 26–31. Commentators have interpreted these unforgivable sins variously, as a deliberate persistence in evil, denial of the Incarnation, apostasy. Mr Gaskell, however, regards the topic as more obscurely casuistical ('medieval romance') than its Biblical citation would suggest; the issue recurs on p. 164.

154 *Carthusians of San Martino*: at the Certosa di San Martino (Carthusian monastery of St Martin) on the Vomero hill overlooking the Bay of Naples; founded in the fourteenth century, since 1876 it has housed the Museo Nazionale di San Martino. For Falkner's oscillation over Jocelyn's order see pp. 65, 142 nn.

*anchoret*: an anchorite; Jocelyn is now with the Carthusians, an Order which was nearly eremetical in its life.

155 *a leprosie . . . white as snow*: Elisha's servant Gehazi attempted to deceive Elisha who had just cured Naaman of leprosy; Elisha then said to Gehazi: 'The leprosy therefore of Naaman shall cleave unto thee, and unto thy seed for ever. And he went out from his presence a leper as white as snow' (2 Kgs 5: 27).

*the mark of the beast*: in Rev. 13 there appears a beast with seven heads and ten horns 'and upon his heads the name of blasphemy'; at vv. 16–17 a second beast 'causeth all, both small and great, rich and poor, free and bond, to receive a mark in their right hand, or in their foreheads: And that no man might buy or sell, save he that had the mark, or the name of the [former] beast, or the number of his name'. In ch. 16 the first of seven angels pours out his vial of the wrath of God upon the earth: 'and there fell a noisome and grievous sore upon the men which had the mark of the beast, and upon them which worshipped his image'; in ch. 17 the Great Whore of Babylon sits upon the beast, and at 19: 20 the beast, his prophet, and those that worshipped his image are 'cast alive into a lake of fire burning with brimstone'.

156 *one of these letters*: see p. 81.

158 *another man*: presumably Adrian Temple.

163 *invocation of the Isiac rite*: the 'sea-rooms' which had terrified Sophia were called the Cells of Isis (see p. 112 n.). In ch. 10 of Porphyry's *Life* of Plotinus, which Falkner knew (see p. 143 n.), an Egyptian priest who wished to display his occult wisdom 'asked Plotinus to come and see a visible manifestation of his [Plotinus'] own companion spirit evoked' in the temple of Isis in Rome, though in the event it was a god and not a spirit which appeared. The occult terror of the occasion is more than hinted at in the account of the strangling of some birds; see E. R. Dodds, *The Greeks and the Irrational* (Berkeley and Los Angeles, 1956), pp. 283–311 on the relationship between occult magic and neo-Platonism. See below p. 166 n.

*Visio malefica*: the Vision of Supreme Evil; I have not come across the term.

*Enoch, Elijah, Stephen, and Jerome*: Gen. 5: 24 was taken to mean that Enoch received special divine revelations, and visionary works circulated under his name; for *The Book of Enoch* ('Ethiopian Enoch') see *The Apocryphal Old Testament*, ed. H. F. D. Sparks (Oxford, 1984), pp. 169–319; *Elijah*: no doubt arising out of 1 Kgs 19: 11–15 and especially 2 Kgs 2: 11, an *Apocalypse* was associated with Elijah by the early Church; for *The Apocalypse of Elijah* see Sparks, ibid., pp. 753–73; *Stephen*: for his vision see Acts of the Apostles 7: 55–6; *Jerome*: St Jerome AD c.347–420. His vision was not straightforwardly beatific: in Letter xxii. 30 he relates how he was 'ravished in spirit' before God's judgement seat; in the presence of a dazzling radiance he was admonished for being a Ciceronian, not a Christian, and ordered to be beaten.

*Esau . . . Judas . . . Cain*: after Esau had sold his birthright and been duped out of his father's blessing (Gen. 25: 29–34; 27: 1 ff.) 'he found no place of repentance, though he sought it carefully with tears' (Heb. 12: 17); *Judas*: for his suicide by hanging see Matt. 27: 5; *Cain*: 'And the Lord set a mark upon Cain, lest any finding him should kill him' (Gen. 4: 15). I have found no references to the Malefic Vision of any of these damned men.

164 *blast*: curse, destroy.

*tree . . . Evil*: 'the tree of knowledge of good and evil' (Gen. 2: 9).

*those who . . . exalt art . . . else*: cf. Pater on Botticelli, establishing 'the limits within which art, undisturbed by any moral ambition, does its most sincere and surest work' (*The Renaissance*, p. 36), and his argument for 'the love of art for its own sake' (ibid., p. 153); see Introduction.

*potential pantheism*: the indwelling of the intelligible (here evil) in the material (the violin).

166 *Porphyrius*: the association of neo-Platonism in its occult aspects with Porphyry (see p. 51 n.) probably derives from Augustine's attacks on him in Book X of *The City of God*; thus ch. 9 is headed: 'Concerning the forbidden arts in relation to the worship of demons, in which the Platonist Porphyry is experienced, approving of some and apparently disapproving of others'. Ch. 11 associates such sacrilegious rites (including the use of corpses) with Isis and Osiris (cf. p. 112 n., p. 163 n.).

*sciolism*: pretentious and superficial knowledge.

*CVIVS . . . DEVS* [Falkner has reproduced the inscriptional convention of representing *U* by *V*]: 'on whose soul, and on the souls of all the faithful departed, and on our souls when we shall have passed over from this life [*literally* light], may God have mercy'. Three of the brasses (including that of Reginald Malyns, Armiger (= Esquire), d. 1430, in the church at Chinnor, described by Falkner in *HBO* (see p. 86 n.), include the words 'cuius anime propicietur Deus'. The inscription is reminiscent of the final words of the *Inhumatio defuncti* (service for the burial of the dead) in the Sarum Missal (of which Falkner had an extensive collection both manuscript and printed): 'Anima eius et anime omnium fidelium defunctorum per misericordiam Dei requiescant in pace. Amen.'

*not ignorant of Latin*: this contradicts earlier statements (pp. 17, 83).

# THE WORLD'S CLASSICS

*A Select List*

JANE AUSTEN: Emma
*Edited by James Kinsley and David Lodge*

WILLIAM BECKFORD: Vathek
*Edited by Roger Lonsdale*

JOHN BUNYAN: The Pilgrim's Progress
*Edited by N. H. Keeble*

THOMAS CARLYLE: The French Revolution
*Edited by K. J. Fielding and David Sorensen*

GEOFFREY CHAUCER: The Canterbury Tales
*Translated by David Wright*

CHARLES DICKENS: Christmas Books
*Edited by Ruth Glancy*

BENJAMIN DISRAELI: Coningsby
*Edited by Sheila M. Smith*

MARIA EDGEWORTH: Castle Rackrent
*Edited by George Watson*

SUSAN FERRIER: Marriage
*Edited by Herbert Foltinek*

ELIZABETH GASKELL: Cousin Phillis and Other Tales
*Edited by Angus Easson*

THOMAS HARDY: A Pair of Blue Eyes
*Edited by Alan Manford*

HOMER: The Iliad
*Translated by Robert Fitzgerald*
*Introduction by G. S. Kirk*

HENRIK IBSEN: An Enemy of the People, The Wild Duck,
Rosmersholm
*Edited and Translated by James McFarlane*

HENRY JAMES: The Ambassadors
*Edited by Christopher Butler*

A complete list of Oxford Paperbacks, including The World's Classics, OPUS, Past Masters, Oxford Authors, Oxford Shakespeare, and Oxford Paperback Reference, is available in the UK from the Arts and Reference Publicity Department (RS), Oxford University Press, Walton Street, Oxford OX2 6DP.

In the USA, complete lists are available from the Paperbacks Marketing Manager, Oxford University Press, 200 Madison Avenue, New York, NY 10016.

Oxford Paperbacks are available from all good bookshops. In case of difficulty, customers in the UK can order direct from Oxford University Press Bookshop, Freepost, 116 High Street, Oxford, OX1 4BR, enclosing full payment. Please add 10 per cent of published price for postage and packing.